Also by Tom Turner

Charlie Crawford Mysteries

Palm Beach Nasty

Palm Beach Poison

Palm Beach Deadly

Palm Beach Bones

Palm Beach Pretenders

Palm Beach Predator

Palm Beach Broke

Palm Beach Bedlam

Palm Beach Blues

Palm Beach Taboo

Palm Beach Piranha

Nick Janzek Charleston Mysteries

Killing Time in Charleston

Charleston Buzz Kill

Charleston Noir

Savannah Sleuth Sisters Murder Mysteries

The Savannah Madam

Savannah Road Kill

Dying for a Cocktail

Broken House

Dead in the Water

PALM BEACH PERFIDIOUS

CHARLIE CRAWFORD PALM BEACH MYSTERIES BOOK 12

TOM TURNER

TRIBECA PRESS

JOIN TOM'S AUTHOR NEWSLETTER

Get the latest news on Tom's upcoming novels when you sign up for his free author newsletter at
tomturnerbooks.com/news

ACKNOWLEDGMENTS

I want to thank the following for their support, feedback, opinions, and—in several cases—just being incredibly loyal readers: George and Betsy Longstreth, Kathy Lombardo, Phoebe Dean, Maria Gerrity, Henry Hagan, Peter Farnum and John Gorsline.

ONE

The headline in the *Palm Beach Daily Reporter*, known locally as *The Glossy*, read: "Palm Beach Society Matron Brutally Murdered." Two observations: one, forty-three-year-old Antonia von Habsburg would have objected mightily to being referred to as a "matron"—society or otherwise—and, two, the phrase "Brutally Murdered" had to have been among the biggest understatements of any headline ever to appear in the august publication.

*****

You needed to have an exceedingly strong stomach to have been present at the crime scene on Dunbar Road where Antonia von Habsburg's body was found. Fact is, one relatively new crime-scene tech had already bolted from the room looking for a handy toilet to retch in. Charlie Crawford knew instantly that it was, by far, the most gruesome crime scene he had ever presided over. And he had been around some pretty grisly ones. Crawford had a theory, right off the bat, about what had inspired the horrifying murder of Antonia von Habsburg, and it was quickly confirmed by his partner, Mort Ott, when he arrived at the crime scene a little after Crawford.

Normally, Ott would get down in a crouch and studiously examine the body of a victim of foul play. He'd carefully study all the possible causes of the death and available clues before coming to any conclusions, but in this case, he took one long look at the victim from a standing position. There was no need to crouch, no need to hear the snap, crackle, and pop of Ott's football-injured knee as he lowered himself to the victim. No, this time, a standing observation from a few feet away was all he needed.

He glanced over at Crawford. *"Game of Thrones,* huh?"

"Yeah, Dominica thinks they used it in one of those *Fast & Furious* movies, too," Crawford said, looking over at Dominica McCarthy, crime-scene tech extraordinaire and his special friend.

Ten feet away, Dominica was down on all fours and clad in unflattering blue pants and a *Crime Scene* T-shirt. Wearing vinyl gloves, she had just picked up something with tweezers and placed it in an evidence bag. Hearing Crawford's comment, she nodded, but didn't look up. "I forget which episode. Pretty sure Vin Diesel wasn't in it, though," she said.

Ott glanced over at her. "Maybe *2 Fast, 2 Furious*, the second one?"

Dominica shrugged. "Coulda been," she said and went back to her tweezer work.

They were referring to rat tortures, in which a victim is tied up and immobilized on their back and a rat is placed in a metal bucket on the victim's chest or stomach. Then the bucket is heated up by way of a blowtorch or other source of heat. The rat, eager to escape the heat… well, you get the idea.

In this case, Antonia von Habsburg—naked—had a blue paisley necktie stuffed in her mouth. Right below her breasts and rib cage, the frenzied rat had punctured, invaded, and rendered her small and large intestines, pancreas, liver, and gallbladder inoperable.

Confirmation of the method used was a tipped-over aluminum bucket on the marble floor several feet away from the victim.

"Never seen anything like it," Ott said, shaking his head. "Movies don't do it justice."

Crawford nodded. "Not even close."

Crawford glanced over at Dominica who was now on the floor dusting the bucket for fingerprints.

"Anything there?" Crawford asked her.

"Nah," she said, looking up. "It was wiped clean."

"Question is," Ott said, "what happened to the rat?"

"Front door was left open," said Crawford. "He could be in the next county by now."

"So what do we know about her?" Ott asked, flicking his head in the direction of the victim.

"Not much," Crawford said. "Just that her name is Antonia von Habsburg, and her cleaning lady found her."

"She like royalty or something?" Ott asked.

"Oh, the name? I don't know," Crawford said. "I looked around a little. Saw a Poinciana Club book which lists all the members in her library, a letter from The Four Arts, and another one from the Norton Museum on her desk."

"Sounds like a bona fide member of the old guard, huh?"

Crawford pointed. "Except how many society women have a Harley-Davidson logo tattooed on their upper thigh."

"What?" This time Ott did get into his crouch for a closer look. "Ho-ly shit. Looks like she tried to have it removed."

"I agree, but the fact that it was there in the first place doesn't add up at all."

"Yeah," Ott said, "and the way she died is like something a Mexican drug cartel would come up with."

TWO

Beneath the glaring headline in the *Glossy*, the article began: "Antonia von Habsburg, 43, was discovered at her mansion on Dunbar Road this Monday morning, the victim of a sadistic murder, according to Palm Beach Police. Ms. Habsburg was thought to have been raised in the Austrian countryside, though no records have been found to confirm this. It appears further that she had been married once but it is not known whether she had children. It has been confirmed that Ms. Habsburg was a member of the Poinciana Club, the President's Circle of The Society of the Four Arts, and a board member of the Norton Museum, where she was known to be a generous donor and had an exhibition room named in her honor. Homicide Detective Mort Ott noted, 'It's too early to comment on the case,' but said the department would keep us informed as the investigation unfolds."

In truth, Ott never said he'd keep anyone informed of anything. And, fact was, the only ones he would keep informed would be his boss Chief Norm Rutledge and partner Charlie Crawford, who'd be up to speed on everything anyway. Thus far, the crime-scene techs—who Crawford and Ott agreed were as good as or better than any either had worked with in New York or Cleveland, their respective old stomping grounds—had come up with zilch. No fingerprints, no clothing fibers, no DNA whatsoever. Nothing but the found items relating to the victim herself.

So, at just past five thirty that afternoon, Crawford and Ott planned to hunker down in the palatial Mediterranean at the corner of Dunbar and North Ocean Boulevard for as long as it took to find something—anything—that would shed light on the life and death of Antonia von Habsburg. Ordinarily, they would have gotten permission to go through the house from next of kin, but no one had come forward or been found who claimed to be a mother, father, son, daughter, distant relative, or even a friend of the deceased. So instead, they got a court order to access and inspect the premises from a judge in West Palm with whom they'd had a friendly working relationship in the past.

Thus far, they had combed the ground floor of the von Habsburg mansion and had yet to come up with anything of value. They then decided that Ott would cover the upstairs while Crawford would look inside the substantial guesthouse located on the other side of the pool and tennis court.

A bedroom in the guesthouse turned out to be a gold mine. Von Habsburg had a large antique Victorian twin-pedestal desk under a portrait of an unsmiling couple dressed in costumes that Crawford guessed were from the nineteenth century. He further suspected they might be the victim's Austrian relatives... but then there was that Harley tattoo. That just didn't jibe at all.

The old desk had four drawers on either side and one in the top center. Crawford's instinct was to first start at the back of the bottom drawer on the right. Over the years, that's where he'd found people filed things that they least wanted others to see. Although in Palm Beach, many of its residents deposited their valuables and secret documents in wall safes—typically in large walk-in closets—or safe-deposit boxes at their banks. Crawford hit the jackpot at the back of the bottom drawer all right, but it was the one on the left, which led him to believe that von Habsburg might have been left-handed. Inside a green Pendaflex hanging file he found more mysteries than answers. First thing he came across was a birth certificate from the state of New Hampshire that said one Antoinette Huber had been born forty-eight years ago at the Elliot Community Hospital in Keene, the daughter of Tobias and Emilia Huber.

Something told him that Antoinette Huber was, in fact, Antonia von Habsburg, the victim of the rapacious rat, and that she had at some point morphed into the daughter of royalty, totally reinventing herself. Not to mention that (as people often do) she had shaved five years off her age.

Next thing he found was a marriage certificate. The bride was, once again, Antoinette Huber, and the groom a man named Larry Victor Wurfel.

Crawford had his phone out ready to dial when he heard a door open downstairs.

"Mort?"

"Yeah, where you at?"

"Bedroom upstairs, left at the top of the stairs."

Crawford heard Ott's thudding footsteps as he dialed his cell phone.

"Hello."

"Hey, Bettina, it's Charlie," he said to the Palm Beach Police Department receptionist, who always complained she never had enough to keep her active mind busy. She also got mad if you short-ened her name to Betty. "Do me a favor and run a background on a woman named Antoinette Huber. See if Antonia von Habsburg and Antoinette Huber are the same person. I'm ninety-five percent sure they are. And while you're at it, check out her husband or ex-husband, too,"—he read the name on the Certificate of Marriage—"Larry Victor Wurfel."

"On it," Bettina said, new purpose invigorating her at the end of a long workday. She loved to dig and always got back to him fast.

"What's up?" Ott asked, walking into the bedroom.

Crawford held up the birth certificate and Certificate of Mar-riage. "Surprise, surprise. Somebody else in Palm Beach who rein-vented themself."

"What a shocker. Our Antonia?"

Crawford cocked his head. "Is that a literary reference, Mort?"

"Only book I ever read at Cuyahoga Community College."

"I'm impressed," Crawford said. "So, it appears likely she started out life as Antoinette Huber in a small town in New Hamp-shire."

"So not a castle in Bavaria?"

Crawford shook his head and laughed. "Remember that time when you told me Andorra, between Spain and France, was an island in the Caribbean?"

"Kinda."

"Well, another geography correction: Bavaria is in Germany, not Austria."

Ott shrugged. "So shoot me."

"I got Bettina doin' a background on Antonia or Antoinette. Meantime, I was about to take a look at this,"—he held up a docu-ment—"her will."

"Shit, man, we allowed to look at that?" Ott asked. "Without permission?"

"Sure. Judge said everything in the house was fair game," he said, slipping the document out of a thick, open-ended envelope and reading, "'The Last Will and Testament of Antonia von Habsburg.' Wow, check out that coat of arms after her name."

Ott leaned closer. "A red lion with blue claws and a blue crown. Looks a little hokey to me."

"Yeah? What's the House of Ott coat of arms look like?"

Ott thought for a moment. "A pizza with a Budweiser can on either side," he said. "But I think we're looking for her beneficiaries, right?"

"Yeah, but we'll take whatever we can get at this point."

"Agreed," Ott said, as they hunched over the first page of the will.

"Ready?" Crawford asked as he finished page one, which was ninety percent boilerplate.

Ott nodded, and Crawford turned the page.

Nothing of any consequence on either page 2 or page 3. But on page 4…

"That's a church?" Ott said, dumbfounded.

He was referring to the "give and bequeath" line, which stated that virtually everything Antonia von Habsburg owned went to a church named The Five Wanderers of Gethsemane, located at 200 Crestwood Boulevard in Royal Palm Beach, Florida. Stocks, bonds, real estate, paintings, stamp collections, art, clothes, electronics, appliances, books, musical instruments—a list of more than thirty items were individually named and were part of the haul that The Five Wanderers of Gethsemane would receive when Antonia's estate was probated.

"Christ," Ott said. "She couldn't keep it simple and just give it to Bethesda?"

He was referring to the historic Episcopal church in Palm Beach, Bethesda-by-the-Sea, located only a few blocks from the von Habsburg estate.

"Question is, why the hell would she drive all the way out to East Jesus to go to church?" Crawford asked.

"East Jesus? You mean, in keeping with the religious theme?" Ott said, then added, "You know, I always thought 'give and bequeath' was kind of redundant. I mean, 'give' or 'bequeath' is enough, isn't it? No way you need both."

But Crawford was back to reading the will. "Well, that's it. The church is the only beneficiary," he said, looking up at Ott. "By the way, you find anything in the main house?"

"Found her computer and cell phone in the master," Ott said. "I'm guessing they might have a clue or two on 'em. Problem is, they're both off."

Crawford frowned. "Meaning we need passwords."

"Exactly."

"Damn."

Crawford's cell phone rang. He clicked on speakerphone so Ott could hear. "Hey, Bettina, whatcha got?"

"Well, first of all, as you suspected, Antonia von Habsburg and Antoinette Huber are one and the same. Born in some town in New Hampshire—"

"Yeah, that I know."

"Seems like she and her ex-husband, Larry Victor Wurfel, moved to Riviera Beach back in 2001. He has a sheet for a couple pretty minor things—"

"Like what?"

"Impersonating a police officer, falsifying documents, and—wait a second—criminal mischief, whatever that might be."

"How about her?"

"Clean as the proverbial whistle. Nothing. Not even a traffic ticket."

"So when they moved down here in 2001, was her name Huber or von Habsburg?"

"I was just getting to that," Bettina said. "She had it legally changed in 2002. That same year she set up an LLC called Distinguished Consorts, LLC."

Ott creased his brow and said, "What the hell is that?"

Bettina heard him. "Oh, you got Mort there," she said. "Hey, Mort."

"Hey, Bettina," Ott said. "A consort is like a... companion, right?"

"Yes," Bettina said. "Sort of a highfalutin word for it."

"What else you got?" Crawford asked.

"Jeez, Charlie, that's it. You only asked me to do this like ten minutes ago."

"Yeah, I know. Good job, by the way."

"Anything else?"

"Yes, see what you can find out about that business, Distinguished Consorts."

"Sounds like maybe a highbrow dating service," Ott said.

Crawford nodded. "That's what I was thinking," he said. "Okay, Bettina, thanks again. Let me know what else you find out." He started to hang up, then: "Oh wait, two more things. See if Larry Victor Wurfel and Antonia are still married. I'm guessing not. And also, try to get an address for him."

"You got it."

Crawford clicked off and glanced over at Ott.

"No way Larry Victor Wurfel or any man is living in the main house," Ott said. "No men's clothes or anything, place is immaculate. No sign of a guy messin' things up. One thing was odd, though."

"What was that?"

"With all her racks and racks of clothes and a shoe collection like Imelda Marcos, there was almost no jewelry."

Crawford nodded. "So, I'm guessing whoever did it must have filled up his pockets."

*****

Crawford and Ott went through the rest of the drawers in Antonia von Habsburg's antique desk but didn't find anything else that was helpful to the case. Getting access to her cell phone and computer was critical but impossible unless they got her passwords. But they had hit dead ends like this before and usually seemed to find a way around them.

Ott snapped his fingers. "Oh hey, I just remembered something. She's got a landline, 'cause I saw a cordless phone on a charger in the library. I was about to check it out but wanted to see what you'd come up with first."

Crawford nodded slowly. "So if we're lucky, there might be some messages on it. Calls from the last few days that Antonia never got a chance to hear."

"Yeah, let's go find out," Ott said.

They went down the stairs and exited the guesthouse, then passed the pool and tennis court.

"Why do I get the feeling she never used either of these much," Ott said, opening his hand to the pool and court.

"I don't know." Crawford said. "Why do you?"

"Well, maybe the pool a little. I'm not sure. I just don't get the sense she grew up in the world of tennis," Ott said, as they walked into the main house. "Too bad I didn't know Antonia when she was alive and single. I could have shown her a good time."

Crawford chuckled. "I can just see you on the golf course at the Poinciana with her. Or going to a black-tie opening at the Norton Museum."

Ott laughed. "Oh yeah, I'd fit right in," he said, leading Crawford into the library, where he pointed at the house phone.

The message indicator had the number *2* flashing.

"Might be in luck," Crawford said, "unless they're junk calls."

Three minutes later, they had retrieved the two messages.

The first one was indeed a junk call. It was a recording, actually, saying that the caller, a representative of Best Wheels Warranty Company, had discovered—God knows how—that "your automobile warranty has expired and with all the crazy drivers out there, don't you want to extend it? Call us," followed by a number, then *click.*

The next came from a woman with a problem. "Toni, that guy Warren was a real pig. Call me. That's the last I'm gonna see of that sick son of a bitch. You couldn't pay me another twenty to get anywhere near him." She left her cell number before hanging up.

Ott looked up at Crawford. "Well, well, isn't that interesting."

"Yeah, no kiddin'," Crawford said as his phone rang. He looked down at the number and said to Ott, "Bettina again," then to her, "Hey, what took you so long?"

"Ha-ha. So, first of all, splitsville for Larry Victor Wurfel and Antonia back in 2018."

"Splitsville? I like that. Very retro. What else?"

"Second of all, Larry Victor Wurfel bought a house in El Cid the same year. Address is 210 Sunset Road."

"Pretty snazzy address for a guy with a sheet," Ott said under his breath to Crawford.

"But nothing on Distinguished Consorts yet?" Crawford asked Bettina.

"Not yet. But I will."

Crawford nodded. "Thank you, Bettina. A stellar job as usual."

"You're welcome; anything else?"

"Not at the moment. Call it a day. But I'm sure I'll need you again tomorrow."

"Okay, well, bye, Charlie. Bye Mort."

"Bye Bettina," Crawford said.

"Bye Bettina," Ott said.

*****

At 8:15 that night, Crawford and Ott wrapped it up, knowing the next day would be a long and busy one.

"All right, Mort, who do you want?" Crawford asked before they split up. "The disgruntled woman who had a lousy time with 'that pig Warren' or Larry Victor Wurfel?"

"I'll take the disgruntled woman. Maybe I can un-disgruntle her."

"If anyone can, you can," Crawford said. "I'm just gonna show up unannounced at the Wurfel residence tomorrow. No telling what I'll find."

"Maybe he'll be impersonating a police officer again."

Crawford nodded. "Like you do every day, huh?"

THREE

Before going to drop in unannounced on Larry Victor Wurfel, Crawford told Ott he wanted to take an early trip out to Royal Palm Beach and check out the Five Wanderers of Gethsemane church on Crestwood Boulevard.

The difference between Palm Beach and Royal Palm Beach was the difference between the ultra-high-end shops on Worth Avenue and a lowly strip mall in Riviera Beach. That is to say, night and day. But the Five Wanderers of Gethsemane edifice was something else altogether. From more than a mile away, Crawford saw what appeared to be a church steeple. As he got closer, it vaguely resembled a rocket ship on a launch pad. It was clearly a church, but one of the most unusual and, well, unorthodox ones he had ever laid eyes on.

Off to one side of the church, he saw a man in jeans and a white T-shirt in a crouch, tending what looked to be a vegetable garden. The man, seeing Crawford approach, got to his feet and walked toward him.

Crawford slid out of the Crown Vic and waved at the man, who had dark hair, a tanned squarish face, and looked to be around thirty.

"Hi," Crawford said as he got close to the man, who had a few inches of height on him. "My name's Charlie Crawford, homicide detective with the Palm Beach Police Department."

The man nodded. "So this is about Antoinette? Her death?"

"Yes. Is that how you knew her? As Antoinette?"

"Yes, Antoinette Huber," he said. "I'm Frank Lincoln, the pastor here."

Crawford shook his hand. "Nice to meet you."

"You, too. What can I do for you, Detective?"

"Well, as you must already know, Antonia von Habsburg, whom you called by her maiden name, Antoinette Huber, left all her money to your church."

Lincoln smiled, looked up in the sky and pointed a finger. "Thank you, Mom."

It was only a mild surprise. "How'd you find out what happened to your... mother?"

"A neighbor, who I knew slightly, called and told me."

Crawford could actually see a resemblance between Lincoln and the tortured woman he'd examined the day before. "So she was your mother. But—"

"I know what you're thinking. She was only forty-three, how could... See, my mother was fifteen when she had me. They start 'em early up in New Hampshire."

"So I'm guessing that you *are* the church."

"Correct," Lincoln said. "I built the church. Live in the church. Grow vegetables for church members." He opened his hand to the patch of vegetables. "Yes, I am the church."

Crawford looked up at the structure. It looked to be at least ten stories high. "It's a beautiful building. Very unusual."

"Thank you, Detective. It's actually a copy of a church in Reykjavík, Iceland, of all places."

"Really? What's the name of that one?"

"The Church of Hallgrimur. The one there was designed to resemble the Icelandic landscape and remind people of the country's magnificent glaciers and mountains."

"So like, the total opposite of our local landscape."

"Yes, exactly. Very different. I studied in Iceland and became a regular member of that church there."

"So, if you don't mind me asking... the name, the Five Wanderers of Gethsemane, where does that come from?"

Lincoln laughed. "Well, tell you the truth, I just... made it up. I didn't want to call it something boring like the Church of Royal Palm or something, so it just came to me... in a moment of divine inspiration, you might say."

Crawford cocked his head. "So are there, or were there, Five Wanderers of Gethsemane in the bible or history or somewhere?"

"Not that I know of. It just struck me as kind of a catchy name."

"So was your mother a regular member of the church here?"

Lincoln shook his head. "Christmas and Easter. She'd come to the services, then we'd go to Dunkin' Donuts afterward. Chat a bit."

"Were you close, you and your mother?"

"Not particularly. She gave me up for adoption right after she had me, tracked me down later. But it wasn't as though we had a tearful reunion and lived happily ever after. Well, of course, *she* didn't…"

"I understand. But did she tell you that she was going to leave you everything she had?"

"Yes, she did."

"And, if you don't mind telling me, what did you say when she told you that?"

"Well, of course, the first thing I said was 'thank you.' But that was the second time I thanked her."

"And the first time…?"

He extended a hand toward the church. "When she put up a lot of the money for the church. She and a few rich parishioners paid the lion's share."

It wasn't particularly relevant to the case, but Crawford was curious. "So, I was wondering, what are the beliefs of the church?"

Lincoln shot Crawford a sneaky smile. "You thinking about joining, Detective?"

"I'm not much of a churchgoer. Plus, it's kind of a hike, all the way out here."

Lincoln laughed. "So we've got some tenets of Christian Science and some others of Scientology."

Crawford didn't feel it necessary to pursue this too far. Particularly since he knew next to nothing about those two except Tom Cruise and John Travolta were major benefactors of Scientology, and the Christian Scientists, as he recalled, didn't believe much in doctors.

"Mr. Lincoln, do you have any idea, any idea at all, who might have had a motive to kill your mother?"

Lincoln didn't have to think. "No idea whatsoever. You see, I knew very little about her life. I don't even know what she did. I mean, she was supposedly a headhunter for executives, at least that's what she told me, but I gather there was a lot more to it than that."

"Based on our preliminary investigation, there was," Crawford said. "Do you want to know what we've found out?"

"No, not really. I lead a pretty simple life, taking care of my garden,"—he pointed—"preaching to the members of my church. Why complicate it with what appears to be the very complicated life—and death—of my mother. A woman I saw twice a year. Do you know what I mean?"

"Yes, I totally understand," Crawford said, putting out his hand. "Well, I thank you for your time and would appreciate it if you call me if you have any further thoughts regarding your mother's death."

Lincoln nodded. "You're very welcome, but I wouldn't hold your breath."

FOUR

Mort Ott went to Antonia von Habsburg's house at eight that morning. He used the home's landline to dial the number of the nameless, disgruntled woman who had no time for "that pig Warren," figuring that she would be more prone to answer when she saw Antonia's number pop up on her phone. But it went to voicemail.

"Hello, this is DeeDee, leave a message and I'll get back to you ASAP."

"Hello, DeeDee, my name is Detective Ott. I'm investigating the murder of Antonia von Habsburg and would like to talk to you as soon as possible."

He left her his cell number and glanced back down at the answering machine. Based on past experience, Ott didn't expect DeeDee would be in too big of a rush to call him back.

He decided to go through Antonia's library and kitchen in the main house one more time, hoping he might dig up an address book.

He knew his best bet for finding phone numbers was on her iPhone and computer, so if he struck out on the address book and phone number list (and also didn't locate a written list of her passwords), he intended to see if the techs could get into the victim's iPhone and MacBook Air. If not, he'd have to try the state crime lab. He hoped it wouldn't come to that because it would eat up precious time.

*****

Crawford pulled up to the two-story colonial-style house at 210 Sunset Road and parked across the street. He got out of his Vic and walked across to the house. He opened the wrought-iron gate, which was set in a low stone wall. It was then that he saw an open garage and a man tinkering with a huge motorcycle.

The man, hearing the creak of the gate, turned and spotted Crawford.

"Who the hell are you?" he shouted, anything but welcoming.

Crawford walked over to the garage. "Mr. Wurfel?"

"Who wants to know?"

God, Crawford hated that question/answer.

He flashed his badge. "Name's Crawford. I'm a Palm Beach Police Department detective."

"Well, groovy for you," said Wurfel. "This obviously has to do with Antoinette."

Crawford nodded. "Antoinette Huber. Antonia von Habsburg. Take your pick."

"I'll take Antoinette Wurfel. A name she couldn't shit-can fast enough."

Clad in black jeans and a muscle shirt, Wurfel didn't look like he belonged in a high-cotton neighborhood like El Cid, where most people, Crawford had observed, were, if not the pink-and-green clubby types who couldn't quite afford Palm Beach, local white-collar lawyers, bankers, and doctors. Wurfel, who had a ruddy complexion, a reddish mustache that looked like it had a half-inch more hair on the right side than the left, and bright green eyes, appeared to be none of the above.

The man cocked his head to one side. "So what do you want to know, chief?"

"When did you last see your ex-wife?"

Wurfel worked his mouth into a sneer. "In other words, did I kill her?"

"I didn't ask you that."

"But that's where you were going." Wurfel shifted his gaze up to Crawford's eyes.

"When did you last see your ex-wife, Mr. Wurfel?"

"Last saw her a couple months ago. Last spoke to her maybe a week ago."

Crawford was beginning to sweat. It was eighty-eight degrees already. Wurfel had a chain of sweat beads clustered on his upper lip just below his mustache.

"You mind if we go inside?" Crawford asked, pointing to Wurfel's house.

"How 'bout the garage," Wurfel said. "I don't want you to see my pet rats in the house."

Crawford's eyes bored into Wurfel. "What's that supposed to mean?"

"You know, what happened to Antonia," Wurfel said. "That was one of the reasons Antoinette cut me loose. My lame jokes."

The thing that threw Crawford was that he had told everyone at the crime scene to keep quiet about the details of von Habsburg murder. In fact, he had stressed it more than once to all of them. But, he knew, leaks always seemed inevitable.

"All right, let's go into your garage," Crawford said, still amazed at the bad taste of Wurfel's rat joke.

Wurfel turned and walked back to the garage. Crawford followed him. The motorcycle Wurfel was working on was a Harley-Davidson. There were tools spread all over one bay. In the other bay sat an old yellow Jaguar.

Crawford walked up to the bike. "What is this?"

"A Fat Boy 114," Wurfel said. "It would leave your Vic out there in the dust."

"I believe it," Crawford said. "How much does one of these things go for nowadays?"

"Twenty grand for the basic. Tricked up… twenty-two, twenty-three."

"Jesus, really? You could get two shiny new Toyotas for that."

Wurfel patted the black leather seat. "But this is all-American, not some goddamn rice-burner."

Crawford crossed his arms and turned to Wurfel, who sat sideways on the Harley seat.

"Who do you think might have killed your ex-wife, Mr. Wurfel?" Crawford asked. "You obviously have given it some thought."

"Call me LV."

Crawford nodded. "Okay, LV, same question."

"I have no fucking clue," Wurfel said, "but, just in case you're curious, I was down in the Keys when it happened."

"How do you know when it happened?"

"Okay, put it this way, I just got back from the Keys, where I spent the entire last week."

"Doing what?"

"I was on a run with six other biker bros," Wurfel said, rubbing his bristly face with his hand.

"A run? Meaning—"

"Six guys on bikes down there to fish, have a few beers, chase women, you know…"

"You part of a gang or something?"

Wurfel laughed. "Nah, man, we just like to ride… hold up banks occasionally."

"There you go again with that sense of humor," Crawford said. "So how'd you find out about your ex-wife's murder?"

"Friend of hers called me. Woman who works for her actually."

"What's her name? Give me her number, too, please."

"Waverly. Waverly Bangs, I call her Bang-Bang," Wurfel said, reaching into his tight black jeans. "Hang on."

He pulled out a black Android and scrolled down. "Waverly, Waverly, Waverly… here we go."

Crawford had his iPhone out and typed in the number as Wurfel recited it.

He looked up at Wurfel. "You say this woman, Waverly, worked for Antonia. What exactly was it that Antonia did?"

Wurfel shook his head. "It's still hard for me to put her in the past tense… but Antoinette was a high-end matchmaker." *Theory confirmed.* "Ran a classy dating service."

"The dating service was very good to her," Crawford said.

"Oh, you mean, the house in Palm Beach."

"Yeah. What else?"

"Oh, a nice, big JP Morgan mutual fund."

"How much was that worth?"

"You think she'd tell *me?*"

"Who else worked for Antonia? Or was it just Waverly?"

Wurfel cocked his head. "Just Bang-Bang. Did a helluva job."

Crawford glanced out of the garage and across the street at a beige two-story Mediterranean. "This neighborhood, LV, not too shabby. You've done all right for yourself."

"That's 'cause it was my idea in the first place, the dating service. She just took it to another level, added a few wrinkles, then at some point decided she didn't need me anymore." He shook his head at the memory. "Kicked me to the curb. Booted me out as her partner… and husband."

"Really?"

"Yeah. By then she had a boyfriend… maybe two, on the QT."

"When you say, 'took it to another level, added a few wrinkles,' how so?"

"Well, for one thing, she'd advertise in high-class publications like the *Glossy* or those other society magazines."

"Society magazines?"

"Yeah, like there's one called *Palm Beach Society* and another one… shit, I forget, *Worth Avenue* or something. You know, pictures of fancy people all duded up, smiling their plastic smiles, posing in front of their Bentleys."

"So, advertise… what exactly would she advertise?"

"So for fifty thousand dollars, she would fix up men and women alike with—what was the phrase she came up with—oh yeah: 'Extraordinarily accomplished people of means who want the very best in companionship one imagines life can offer.' Some horseshit like that. Back when I was with her, we were averaging about twenty-five to thirty customers a year, so do the math: grossing 1.25 to 1.5 million with not much overhead. Just twenty-five grand or so on advertising. Plus, Waverly's salary, maybe 150 grand, total."

Crawford was still jolted by the initial figure. "Wait a minute, fifty grand? People paid that much?"

Wurfel nodded vigorously. "Yup. I mean we started much lower but as we classed it up, we made it really exclusive. People paid the fifty, no questions asked."

"That's incredible." Crawford had done the math. "So Antonia would pocket somewhere between like one million and 1.25 million a year?"

"Minus ten percent to me."

"So you'd get around a hundred every year?"

"Yeah, pretty lame considering I came up with the whole thing in the first place."

"Yes, but like you said, she came up with a bunch of profitable wrinkles."

"That she did. I'll give her that."

Crawford heard the rumble of what sounded like motorcycles off in the distance.

"Oh, here come the boys," said LV, walking out of the garage as five motorcycles, three from the Harley-Davidson family and two from the Indian family, rolled up LV's driveway, a sudden storm of noise echoing through the quiet neighborhood.

Crawford followed LV out of the garage. LV waved to the five bikers and turned back to Crawford. "We're off on another run. Up to Daytona to see a race. Just for the day."

"I need to ask you some more questions," Crawford said.

"Make it quick, bro. I gotta clean up and the hit the road."

Crawford thought for a second. "All right, tell you what, why don't you come by my station house tomorrow instead."

"Okay, you got it," LV said. "Maybe hit you up with a few more jokes too."

"I hope not."

Crawford saw a blond woman in baby blue golf shorts, a pink sleeveless top and cream-colored golf shoes run across the street in their direction. She was coming right at them and stopped in front of Crawford.

"I saw your car," she said. "Are you a policeman?"

"Ah, yes, ma'am, I am. Detective Crawford. Is there a problem?"

"A problem? Yes, there's a big problem. That ear-splitting noise. Those god-awful motorcycles. They're disrupting this neighborhood, and it's not the first time."

LV stepped forward. "Mrs. Truesdale, I'm LV; we met before. Me and my friends are about to leave. Sorry, I'll get them to turn off their bikes."

LV turned to the five riders and made a twisting sign to turn their engines off.

One by one, they did.

Mrs. Truesdale squinted at LV and put both hands on her hips. "'Bikes' you call them, I wish that's what they were. Then they wouldn't make all that racket."

LV looked at Crawford for help. Crawford smiled at Mrs. Truesdale. "'Bikes' is just a nickname for motorcycles, Mrs. Truesdale. Don't worry, they'll be gone in a few minutes."

Out of the corner of his eye, Crawford could see a couple with two fluffy poodles walking toward them at a brisk pace. They were most assuredly not coming to welcome the motorcyclists to the neighborhood.

Mrs. Truesdale turned to them as they approached and said to the man. "Don't worry, Harold, I've got things under control."

Harold gave Mrs. Truesdale a wink. "You always do, Lena. You always do."

Crawford turned to LV. "All right. So, my office at nine?"

"I'll be there," LV said, then with a smile. "You like donuts, Detective?"

"No, I'm good," Crawford said.

By then he'd have had his fill.

FIVE

After leaving the victim's mansion more or less empty-handed, Mort Ott knew that getting into Antonia von Habsburg's MacBook Air and iPhone were his best remaining shot at gleaning some solid clues about her murder, so he made that his top priority. So later that morning, Ott dropped by crime-scene tech Dominica McCarthy's cubicle, only to find she wasn't in. Ott left her a note, along with the vic's laptop and phone:

Dominica,
How 'bout being a hero and cracking von Habsburg for us? Just do your magic and figure out how to open one or both of these things.
Mort

He got a call back an hour later from Dominica. "You would have to give me Apple products."

"What do you mean?"

"They're the toughest ones to crack into without a password."

"Is there a 'but' here?"

"You know me too well," Dominica said. "*But...* I did manage to get into the iPhone. Lots of names in her Contacts."

"You're the best. How'd you do it?"

"Come on, Mort. A magician never reveals her secrets. I'm still working on the computer."

"I'll be right down."

Three minutes later he was at her cubicle.

She looked up and he bumped fists with her. "Thank God for cops like you."

"Thank you, Mort. But I'm not sure I've ever been called a cop before."

"Hey, we're both cops. I'm the detective variety and you're the crime-scene evidence tech variety."

"There you go," she said, handing him the iPhone. "So get your clues out of this and put someone in the slammer by the end of the day."

"Wish I could… but that might be pushing it a little."

*****

He called Crawford immediately to tell him about the phone.

"Girl's good," Crawford said.

"You would know."

Crawford didn't dignify that, but twenty minutes later was in Ott's office.

"So whaddaya got so far?" he asked.

"I got a list of names like you wouldn't believe."

"Like who?"

"Well, you remember that list of billionaires the *Glossy* published a couple months back?" Ott asked.

"Yeah."

"Okay, so far I got four guys from that list and, surprise, surprise, one woman. And guess what, three of the men and the one woman are married."

"Why am I not surprised?"

"Yeah, and I've also got two aging rock-and-roll legends, a big-time actor now in his seventies, a bestselling author, and I'm only up to the Ns."

"Wow, you hit the jackpot."

"Dominica hit it for us. I'm just reading names and numbers," he said. "So what about Larry Victor Wurfel?"

"My biker buddy? We're on friendly terms now. Even asked me to call him LV," Crawford said. "He also confirmed what we already suspected. That Antonia ran a dating service, an ultra-high-end one. Cost fifty grand to play. But I got a feeling there's a lot more to it than a simple dating service. He's coming in here tomorrow morning so we can both question him. He also gave me the name and number of a woman who worked for Antonia who I'm about to call."

"You're shittin' me. The thing cost fifty *grand*?"

"Yeah, but that's not a big shocker based on the list of players you found."

"So what are we gonna do about that list?"

Crawford thought for a moment. "Before we do anything or question any of 'em, let's start with the woman who worked for Antonia. Try to get a handle on the ins and outs of the whole thing"—Crawford realized what he had said—"so to speak. Save the fat cats for last. Once we've got a better handle on the operation."

"Makes sense. I called that woman DeeDee but she didn't pick up—surprise, surprise. Who's the woman you're calling?"

"Name's Waverly Bangs."

Ott laughed. "Waverly Bangs. I love it. You s'pose that's actually the name on her birth certificate?"

"Somehow I'm thinking that might be an alias."

"Somehow I think you're right. Sounds like the name of one of James Bond's hussies."

"All right, I'm gonna go back to my office and call her now."

"Waverly?"

Crawford nodded.

"Want a little privacy for your call, do ya?"

"Jesus, Mort. You never quit."

*****

"Ms. Bangs?"

"Yes, who's this?"

"My name is Detective Crawford, Palm Beach Police Department."

Click.

This wasn't the first hang-up Crawford had ever had. In fact, over the last eighteen years, he had probably been hung up on between fifty and a hundred times. Maybe more.

So he did what he always did. Called back.

Second go-round, he always got either an answering machine or endless rings.

This was an answering machine.

"This is Wave. You know what to do."

"Ms. Bangs, it's Detective Crawford again. It's very important I speak with you. So call back as soon as possible, or come to the Palm Beach Police Department at 345 South County Road in Palm Beach. It's not a good idea to ignore this message. You could get into a lot of trouble if you do."

That was his standard message. If someone was innocent or had nothing to hide, it usually was enough to get them to respond pretty fast. In his experience, hang-ups were most often caused by panic reflexes at hearing the words "Palm Beach Police," not by being guilty of a crime. It was not every day you got a call from a detective, and most people probably went through their entire lives never getting one. Those who had probably didn't consider themselves among the fortunate.

Twenty minutes later, Crawford got a call on his cell. It was Waverly Bangs.

"Detective Crawford?"

"Yes, Ms. Bangs."

"Sorry, I had another call on call waiting and disconnected you by accident." *Yeah, sure, likely story.* "Anyway, here I am."

"Where exactly are you, Ms. Bangs? I'd like to come talk to you face-to-face."

"About Antonia, right?"

"Right."

"I'm at 2600 North Flagler in West Palm, the Northwood area."

"Okay, I'm going to leave right now. Be there in ten minutes."

She sighed like she wasn't thrilled with the idea. "Okay, I'll tell the doorman to expect you."

"See you shortly," Crawford said and clicked off.

*****

Fifteen minutes later, Crawford was in the living room of Waverly Bangs's apartment overlooking the Intracoastal and Palm Beach off in the distance.

"Beautiful view," he said.

"I bought it for the view—" she began, but was interrupted by the sudden noise of an electric drill and a power saw. "Oh my God, here they go again. I call this building 'The Noise Palace.' Friend of mine here calls it 'The Jackhammer Arms.'"

"It *is* kind of loud," Crawford said.

"What?"

He raised his voice. "I said, it *is* kind of loud."

"No kidding," she said. "I complain, nobody listens."

"So, Ms. Bangs, Larry Victor Wurfel gave me your name and number, said you worked for Antonia von Habsburg."

Bangs nodded. "Such a terrible thing, what happened to her. I mean how could anybody…" Her voice trailed off as the pounding of a hammer joined the chorus of electric drills and saws. "Sorry about that," she shouted. "Friend I mentioned calls that racket the 'Portofino Philharmonic'… sorry, where were we?"

Crawford raised his voice. "Tell me about the business. All I know is that it was a very high-end dating service. And while you're at it, I'd like to hear any thoughts you might have on who might have killed Ms. von Habsburg."

Waverly Bangs glanced away from Crawford and started tapping her fingers on the side of her chair. She was a large woman with bleached blond hair and striking, emerald eyes. She wore sweat pants and a loose-fitting white T-shirt with a swoosh on it.

"We charged a lot because we had the best clientele in the world. I mean that literally. Antonia was the most discriminating woman you could ever meet. She interviewed candidates at least three times, sometimes more. I mean, just vetted them to death. Only about twenty percent of people who applied and who she interviewed actually made the cut. It was like getting into Harvard or something."

"And I know she charged a small fortune," Crawford said.

"Yeah, fifty thousand up to seventy-five for the really, really wealthy ones."

Crawford shook his head. "Seventy-five thousand? I find that just incredible," he said. "For how many names and numbers?"

"Ten." Waverly said. "But they were the absolute crème de la crème."

"You're talking about women now?"

"Yes, of course."

"Because you also catered to women. Correct?"

"Yes, but very few of them."

Crawford leaned toward her. "Define what you mean by that, please? Crème de la crème?"

"What don't you understand? The most beautiful women around."

"Yeah, but also what they were like, their characteristics?" Crawford said. "I already made the assumption they were beautiful."

"That's for sure," she said, her fingers back to tapping. "Well, okay, so… intelligent, classy, funny, well-bred, articulate, possessing good manners…"

"And the men? The clients."

"Wealthy."

"So that was it? They just had to be rich?"

"I said wealthy. There's a difference."

"There is?"

"Sure. Rich is more a nouveau thing; wealthy is more… old money."

Crawford shrugged. "Who knew? So are you saying that she rejected nouveau riche men?"

Waverly thought a second, tugging at a blond forelock. "Ah, no, she just preferred old-money guys. Told me they were better behaved."

"Behaved?"

"Yeah, you know."

Not really, but he could guess.

"So the men just had to be wealthy or rich, and hopefully well-behaved… but weren't always."

She laughed and nodded.

"Back to my second question, who do you think might have killed her?"

A double shoulder shrug. "I suppose it wouldn't hurt to speculate a little."

"Please do."

"Well, I'd look into her boyfriend for one. Though, truth is, she had more than one."

"What's his name and why do you mention him?"

"Jimmy Marston's his name, and because he found out she was messing around with one of the clients. The two had a pretty hot and heavy thing going for a while."

"What's the client's name, and how would I find Jimmy Marston?"

"No clue about the client, she didn't tell me everything. And Jimmy Marston works at one of those fancy trust companies on Royal Palm Way. Starts with a B, I think."

"Bessemer Trust?"

"No."

It was time for Crawford to thrum his fingers on his chair. "Oh, I know, Brown Brothers Harriman, maybe?"

"Yeah, yeah, that's it."

"Okay, so who else? On the list of potential killers of Antonia?"

Waverly cocked her head and put a finger up to her lip. "Well, there was this English guy she went out with for a while. I think he was after her for her money. You know those Brits, never have any money, always looking for the gravy train."

"I'll take your word for it. But what was his name?"

"I can't remember now. One of those Brit names. You know like Oliver, Nigel, Alfie or… Cuthbert."

Crawford laughed.

"What?"

"I just don't remember running across a lot of Cuthberts, British or otherwise."

Waverly shrugged again. "Sorry, I just don't remember the name."

"What do you think about LV Wurfel?"

"As Antonia's killer? Nah, no way. Why do you say him?"

"Well, because he used to own fifty percent of the business. But Antonia was only giving him ten per cent of the money she made."

"Well, he wasn't involved in the business anymore."

"I know, but that wasn't his choice, was it?"

Waverly nodded. "Well, that's true."

"Clearly, Antonia controlled the purse strings."

"She absolutely did. There's no doubt about that."

"Okay, Jimmy Marston and this Brit. Do me a favor, when you remember his name, please get back to me."

"I will, but what if I can't remember it?"

"Who else might know his name?"

"I really don't know. I just met him once."

"Anybody else on your list?"

She gave him a faux-angry sigh. "Isn't that enough? That's two more suspects than you had when you got here."

SIX

Royal Palm Way was on the way back to the station on South County Road so Crawford stopped in at Brown Brothers Harriman, hoping he'd catch Jimmy Marston there. He was in luck. He gave the receptionist the smile he used when he wanted something. She gave him back what appeared to be an accommodating smile and asked him his name and who he'd like to see.

"Charlie Crawford to see Mr. Marston, please," he said, figuring he'd leave out "Detective" this time and hope Marston would be curious enough to want to know who Charlie Crawford was and exactly what he wanted. Maybe his next million-dollar client.

A man in a crisp grey pinstripe suit walked up to the receptionist desk. Crawford was surprised. He thought everyone dressed casually these days. Marston had a bulbous nose, greying hair, and about the straightest part Crawford had ever seen. Not one stray hair to the left or right of the dividing line.

"Charlie Crawford?"

"Yes, hello, Mr. Marston," he said and lowered his voice. "I'm a detective with the Palm Beach Police Department investigating the murder of Antonia von Habsburg and I'd like to ask you a few questions."

Marston's face flushed a bright matador red. "Come on back to my office."

He started fast-walking out of the reception area like he wanted to ditch Crawford. But Crawford kept up as Marston turned into an office at the end of a corridor that had tinted glass walls on either side of the door and a view of a stand of sabal palms through the back window. Marston, who looked to be fifty, had a large framed photo of a blond-bouffanted woman and two teenage boys decked out in blue blazers—nobody smiling—placed prominently on his desk.

Just for confirmation, Crawford glanced at Marston's ring finger and saw a standard-size gold wedding band.

"Have a seat," Marston said, as all-business as one could get, dropping into his chair and straightening the crease on his pant leg until it was back to being knife-like.

Crawford hesitated, then sat down opposite him.

Marston dived right in. "Detective, what happened to poor Antonia was the most detestable, villainous, act I've ever heard of. I mean, the savagery, the, the… brutality, the inhumanity, the—"

"I agree with you Mr. Marston, it was really bad."

Marston was shaking his head now. "I mean, Jesus God, just horrible—" then he seemed to change the channel and turn down the volume. "I have a place of respect in this community, Detective, and need to know that what we're going to discuss is between you and me. Otherwise, I'm going to have to bring a lawyer into the picture."

Crawford held up his hands. "There's no need for that, Mr. Marston. But, of course, that's your prerogative to do at any time. Just so you know, detectives, or for that matter, anyone in law enforcement, don't last long if they've got loose lips. And I've been doing this for quite a while now."

Marston gave him a prim nod. "So what do you want to know?"

"Well, of course, what I really want to know is who killed Antonia von Habsburg, but for the moment I'll settle for knowing about your relationship with her."

Marston leaned back in his black leather chair and put his hands behind his head. "I had no relationship with Antonia, except as her investment advisor."

Crawford nodded his head slowly. "O-kay," he said. "I heard things a little differently."

"You heard that I was having a torrid romance with her, is that it?"

"The word *torrid* didn't come up, but yeah, that was the gist of it."

"Well, you can tell Waverly that was not the case. That was never the case. We went out for dinner a couple times, had drinks, but I do that with lots of my clients."

"I understand," Crawford said. "I wonder why… the person I heard it from was pretty convinced you and Antonia… had a thing."

"Don't play games. I know that *person* was Waverly. She's a known busybody who jumps to conclusions without having any grasp of the facts. How long have you been a detective here, Charlie?"

"A little less than five years."

"And how long did it take you to realize gossip is more common here than a sunny day?"

Crawford nodded. "Not long. So there's no truth to that?"

"Me and Antonia? That I was her boyfriend? I already told you. Absolutely no truth to it whatsoever."

"How was she as a client?"

"What do you mean?"

"I mean, did she come in all the time, or, you know, call a lot, or was she more passive?"

"She was the ideal client. A conservative, prudent investor who let me do what I do."

Crawford glanced out Marston's window. "Well, I guess that's good enough for me,"—*standard question time*—"but I'd be remiss if I didn't ask you who you think might have killed her."

Marston released his hands from his head and leaned forward. "Do you know the name Luther King?"

"No. Can't say I do."

"Well, Luther *really was* her boyfriend. I don't know whether they were going out at the time Antonia was killed, but I believe they were."

"So, tell me more about him."

"Luther sold his auto parts company, up in Michigan I think it was, about five years ago for $800 million and moved down here. Ditched his wife and started skirt-chasing like it was his new business. He's notorious for going out every single night of the week. I mean, literally, every single one."

"You mean, out for dinner or what?"

"Yeah dinner, then he makes the rounds of other restaurants and gin mills. Lola, HMF, Buccan, La Goulue, Cucina, Meat Market, Henry's… you name it."

"So clearly the man gets around."

"I'll say. Climbs into his limo and hops from place to place is what I hear. Checks out the bars for hot prospects. Sometimes has a drink, sometimes not. Sometimes hauls a woman out of one or the other, sometimes not. When he gets a woman in the car, I hear, he shakes out a couple lines of cocaine, if they're so inclined. Never touches the stuff himself."

"How do you know all this, Mr. Marston?"

"Because Antonia told me. We didn't just talk stocks and bonds all the time. She told me that was how she first met King. At the bar at Buccan. Picked her up and started launching into how he was really pissed that he hadn't made the billionaires list in the *Glossy*. You know what I'm talking about?"

"Sure, I've seen it."

"Forty-three at last count," Marston said, shaking his head. "So, Antonia told me Luther actually went to the *Glossy* publisher and demanded to know why he wasn't on the list. And the publisher told him, 'Because you're only worth $950 million, Mr. King. We do extensive research on this.' And Luther pitches a fit and says, 'For Chrissake, can't you just round it up a little?'"

Crawford laughed, but this detour wasn't getting him any closer to how Luther King might be his killer—what the man's motive might have been.

"Okay, so why would King want to kill Antonia?"

Marston put up his hands. "That's your job to find out, Detective. But I think because she hurt his reputation as Palm Beach's leading ladies' man... maybe. Because she was kind of a serial cheater... maybe."

"So, you mean, people would think he wasn't much of a ladies' man if his leading lady was... well, stepping out on him?"

Marston nodded. "Very well put, Detective."

"Seems a little thin to me, Mr. Marston," Crawford said, though Luther King certainly sounded like an interesting enough character to put on top of his interview list.

SEVEN

Meanwhile, Ott had just about run out of patience with the "disgruntled woman," aka DeeDee. He had now called her four times and had gotten no call back, nor had she stopped by the station as he had first requested, then demanded, she do.

So Ott dialed again intending to ratchet up even more of the Ott-ese bluster and hyperbole. "DeeDee, this is Detective Ott calling you for about the fourteenth time. I just want you to know that a warrant for your arrest will be issued unless you either return this call or come into police headquarters at 345 South County Road in Palm Beach"—he glanced at his watch—"in the next three hours. It is now one thirty, you have until four thirty."

He clicked off. There would, of course, be no warrant for her arrest because there was no conceivable charge. You couldn't throw someone in the can for not calling you back. But he had used the threat in the past and it never failed. At this point, he only wished he had issued it sooner.

And, sure enough, within fifteen minutes, his cell phone rang. The caller read: DeeDee Dunwoody.

"Where you been hidin', DeeDee?"

"Oh, Detective Ott, I am so, so sorry. I misplaced my cell phone and just found it a few minutes ago. But anyway, here I am, how can I be of help?"

The old misplaced phone story, thought Ott. Heard it a few hundred times before. "How far are you from my station, Ms. Dunwoody?"

"Not far. Maybe fifteen minutes away."

"Okay, great, see you in fifteen minutes," he said, wanting to add, *that is, if you don't lose your car.*

*****

She was there in less than fifteen minutes.

He met her out in the reception area. She was a drop-dead knock-out. Tall, generously endowed, and not shy about displaying her attributes in a cleavage-enhancing yellow sundress. With her skin tanned to a deep mahogany brown, DeeDee Dunwoody was a stunner.

Ott forgave her for not returning his calls before she finished making the apology again. "That's all right, Ms. Dunwoody. As I'm sure you can appreciate, my partner and I are eager to solve Ms. von Habsburg's murder as soon as possible and, thus far, have limited information. I'm hoping you can change that."

"Maybe I can. I hope so anyway," DeeDee said. "Jeez, I went by Antonia's house and couldn't believe all those reporters and news people there. Trucks and vans up and down the street. Plus, some outside of here."

"I know," Ott said, "and sometimes they can get in the way."

"I bet."

Ott put out his hand. "Okay, let's have a seat over there," he said, pointing to two chairs near the west window of the reception area.

She sat down, and Ott did too. He tried not to stare at how her sundress rode up over her knees to her lower thighs, but it was difficult not to.

"So, Ms. Dunwoody—"

"Please, DeeDee," she said. "Dunwoody's such a dumb name."

He had run across a lot of people with dumb names over the years, but no one yet who actually said their name was a dumb name. Come to think of it, Ott was kind of a dumb name, too. Short and dumb.

"So, I'm just going to take some notes on my phone, if that's all right with you."

"Sure that's fine," she said with a shrug. "Whatever you like."

"I don't quite understand something," Ott said.

"What's that?"

"The relationship between you and Antonia von Habsburg. Can you explain it?"

No hesitation. "Not much to explain: Antonia and I were friends, that's all."

"But you said on her message machine, words to the effect that, a man named Warren was a 'real pig' and that, after your date with him, 'that was the last time you were going to see…' I believe your exact words were 'that sick son of a bitch.'"

DeeDee frowned. "I said that? That doesn't sound like me."

"It's pretty much verbatim."

She laughed. "Well, I guess I better mind my tongue in the future."

"Was this date you had… with Warren, was this something that Antonia set up, I mean, through her company, Distinguished Consorts?"

"Yes, it sure was. Why? What did you think?"

"So you paid her fifty thousand dollars for introducing you to that… to Warren. Plus, nine other men?"

"No, I got what I guess you'd call the 'friends and family discount.'"

"How much did it cost you?"

"Just five thousand dollars."

Ott's brow furrowed. It was his skeptical default expression. "I want to be careful how I say this, but you don't strike me as the type of woman who needs a dating service."

"Well, Distinguished Consorts is not just a dating service. It provides only the best… companions."

"Except for Warren, of course."

DeeDee shot him a nervous smile and sighed. "Well, I guess every once in a while one slips through the cracks."

"I guess so. You also said on the phone message, 'You couldn't pay me another twenty to get within a mile of him.' What was that a reference to?"

For the first time, she averted her eyes. "Oh, you know, that was just kind of a figure of, ah, speech."

Uh-huh, Ott thought. "I'm not sure I understand. So when you said 'twenty,' what was that specifically referring to?"

"Oh God, I don't know, twenty million, twenty billion, twenty cents. Just sort of a throwaway line. Meaning I wouldn't touch the guy with a ten-foot pole."

There was more to this, but Ott thought it best to circle back to it.

He smiled. "I'm still stuck on thinking you're about the last woman in the world—let alone Palm Beach—who'd ever need to get, ah, fixed up."

"That's very nice of you to say, Detective, but it gets very old going to bars and dealing with men and their, um, pathetic lines, not to mention, actions."

"I'm sure, but a woman like you—" He was starting to get somewhat smitten now. "I'm sure you meet people at work or... What do you do, by the way?"

"For work, you mean?"

"Yes."

"Let's just say I'm in between opportunities at the moment."

"What did you used to do?"

"Well, depends how far back you go. Once upon a time I was a model in New York. After that I was a stylist on commercial shoots. You know, the hair and make-up girl. Then I did some waitressing up there,"—Ott could see this wasn't going in the right direction—"then I decided to move down here and got a real estate license. Problem is that if you don't know a lot of people, it's tough to get listings or find people looking to buy. Know what I mean?"

Ott nodded.

"So that kind of petered out," DeeDee said with a shrug. "I still have my license at Corcoran but no listings or anything."

So, the obvious question was: *but you had five thousand dollars to give Antonia von Habsburg to find you a man.* Which, for the moment, he refrained from asking.

Instead, he asked. "So how did you meet Antonia?"

DeeDee didn't hesitate. "Same hairdresser. We got talking when we were waiting. She was so nice. She asked me over to her house for a glass of wine."

"Her house on Dunbar?"

"Uh-huh. I'd never been to a place like that before."

"I know what you mean. It's a pretty incredible house," Ott said. "Was anybody else there?"

"Ah, let's see... two men and Antonia."

"Do you remember the men's names?"

"One's name was Bob Jones. I remember that because there was a Bob Jones in my high school class. The other one... was named Courtie."

"And they were friends of Antonia's."

"Well sure, I guess. I mean, why would they be there if they weren't her friends?"

"Tell me about the one, Bob Jones?"

"Okay. He was quite a bit older, but a very handsome man."

"How old?"

"Um. I'd say around sixty-five. Full head of white hair, good tan, looked like he was in really good shape. I remembered he said he lived down in Gulfstream. Not that it was any of my business, but I think he was married."

Ott typed that into his phone and looked up. "You saw a ring or what?"

"Just the opposite: I saw very white skin where a ring would normally be."

"The old hide-the-ring trick, huh?" Ott said. "And the other man, Courtie?"

"Tall. Handsome, too. Pretty sure he was married. Had a funny laugh. One of those rat-a-tat-tat laughs. Ha-ha-ha-ha-ha-ha. I thought at the time that he and Antonia might have had something going. Except she told me later she was going out with someone else."

"Jimmy Marston?"

"Um, maybe that was it."

"So what you're saying, seems to me, is that Antonia would sometimes go out with married men?"

DeeDee looked offended. "I never said that."

"Well yeah, you said Antonia 'might have had something going with,' ah, Courtie, who you speculate was married."

"What I meant was… just kind of flirting."

"I see," Ott said. "So, Courtie… did he live in Palm Beach?"

"Yes, he said something about the 'estate section.' He mentioned he was thinking about selling his house there and moving into a smaller place. Matter of fact, he said, '*We're* thinking of selling it', I remember. Downsizing is what he called it."

Ott looked up from his iPhone. "So he definitely *was* married?"

"So it seemed at the time," DeeDee said.

"How long ago was this?"

"Ah, eight to ten months ago, I'd say."

"So you just had a few glasses of wine at Antonia's, then what?"

"Then I left."

Ott nodded thoughtfully. "So let me ask you this… have you seen or heard from either Bob Jones or Courtie since then?"

"Yup, just so happened Bob called the next day."

Ott was not the least bit surprised.

"You had given him your number?"

"Oh, no. I don't know how he got it. Maybe Antonia."

Maybe? "Okay, so what did he say?"

"Asked me out for dinner at some place in Boca."

"And?"

"I said, 'Bob, you seemed like a very nice guy, but I don't go out with married men.'"

"And what did he say?"

"He seemed kind of surprised but said, 'Okay, well, if you ever change your mind, I'll text you my number.'"

"And he did?"

She nodded.

Ott looked up. "So, do you still have it?"

"I s'pose. Somewhere in my phone."

"Could you give it to me, please?"

"Sure, hang on a minute," she said and reached into her rose-colored leather handbag.

"But did he ever call again? Or have you seen him since?"

DeeDee shook her head as she scrolled through her phone. "No, that's the last I heard from him. Here you go—" and she gave him the number.

"Thanks. And what about Courtie?"

"He called, too."

Popular girl.

"And what happened?"

"Well, that was a little different. See, he told me he had just gotten divorced and so I figured a drink or two wouldn't hurt."

"But he had just said before, '*we* were thinking of selling' the house in the estate section? I mean, that sure sounds like he was referring to a wife."

"I know. I asked him about that and he said he meant his sister. Told me they had inherited the house from their mother."

Ott cocked his head and thought for a moment. "Okay... so did you and Courtie go out? And by that point you must have known his last name?"

"Yes, sorry, it's Courtie Hiller, and he took me for a nice dinner up in Jupiter at a place he raved about. When we got there, and it was only okay, I figured it was a place where he knew he wouldn't run across anyone he knew. So, I was back to thinking he was definitely married."

"You mean, so it was like Bob Jones wanting to take you to a place in Boca, presumably so nobody from Gulfstream would see you with him?"

DeeDee nodded and smiled brightly. "You catch on quick, Detective. Guess that's why you're a detective."

"Thanks. I try," Ott said. "So, if you don't mind me asking, where'd it go with Courtie?"

"Well, actually Detective, I do kind of mind. With all due respect, I don't think it's your job to ask women about their love lives. Besides, I'm not a girl who kisses and tells."

"Okay, fair enough." He was beginning to really like this woman. Spunky. Funny. Not to mention the obvious ten-out-of-ten looks. "But I'm still back to you paying five thousand dollars to your friend Antonia to fix you up with men, when it sounds like she was fixing you up already. For free."

"Well, first of all, I ended up inheriting some money from my great-aunt. Some of it went to Antonia. And, let's just say, it ended kind of abruptly with Courtie. I'm not going into details about that. Then came a long dry spell when I wasn't working and I wasn't dating. The thought occurred to me that even though I'm not a girl out to snag a rich man, there are a lot of rich men in Palm Beach, and some are single, and maybe some are nice. And, from what she told me, Antonia had a big ol' Rolodex of 'em."

Ott, nodding slowly and thoughtfully, was thinking, *Yes, some of them are rich, single and nice, and some of them are rich, married and not-so-nice, but every damn one of them would love to get a woman like DeeDee in the sack with them.*

EIGHT

Ott was in Crawford's office, the two comparing notes. Ott had just told Crawford about his conversation with DeeDee Dunwoody.

"So what's your take on the whole thing?" Crawford asked.

"I have a bunch of takes," Ott said. "One, we're going to have an ever-expanding cast of suspects. I mean, Antonia clearly knew a lot of men. In some cases, biblically, in some cases as guys who gave her 50K to hook 'em up, and in one case an ex-husband who saw his piece of the pie get very small. I mean—"

"Biblically, huh? Like Luther King, the limo man, and maybe Jimmy Marston, her money man—"

"—and who knows about these guys Courtie Hiller and Bob Jones. I mean look at her contacts. The woman got around."

"That's for sure," Crawford said. "So what's your take on DeeDee?"

Ott leaned back in his chair facing Crawford and put a hand on his forehead. He had spent a lot of time thinking about her since their conversation in the reception area. Too much, maybe.

"Well, that's a damn good question. Here's what I think: I think she might have been telling me seventy-five percent of the truth. 'Cause some of it just doesn't add up."

"You mean, like what the 'twenty' reference was all about and how she came up with five thousand bucks to give to Antonia to meet men. 'Cause I'm not sure I'm buyin' the great-aunt thing. Are you?"

Ott nodded. "Yeah, I don't know," he said. "And, again, why would she have to? I mean, trust me, that's a woman who'd have no problem meeting men, even though she's not working and has no interest in hanging out in bars. There're a million other ways: spend the day on Worth Avenue going to galleries, or shopping, or going to the beach. She'd have guys flocking to her."

"But aren't we talking about everything but the most obvious thing?"

Ott knew exactly where Crawford was going. "That guys were paying her to have sex, you mean?"

Crawford nodded.

"Like that Courtie dude," Ott said. "And maybe Bob Jones, even though she said she never saw him again after drinks at Antonia's."

"Exactly. That could be part of the twenty-five percent that wasn't true."

"So you're thinking we have a possible prostitution angle here?"

Crawford shrugged. "Seems like we both thought about it at different times."

Ott was silent for a few moments, looking down at his shoe tops. "I gotta tell you something, Charlie."

"Okay, tell me."

More silence. Then, "I've been thinking about asking her out," he said. "You know, to get more info out of her."

Crawford laughed. "Oh, is that it? To get more info?"

Ott nodded with a straight face.

"Come on, Mort. It's Charlie you're talking to."

"Okay, well then, if it goes somewhere that would be good, too."

"But you're mainly in it to push the case along, right?" Crawford said, with a wide smile, "To see justice prevail, is that it?"

Finally, Ott couldn't maintain the straight face any longer and burst out laughing. "Okay, okay… busted. You're a tough interrogator."

Crawford reached across his desk and patted Ott's arm. "Learned it all from you, old buddy."

NINE

"Thanks, finally the recognition I deserve," Ott said. His straight face was back.

"You know damn well you like this woman."

Ott threw up his hands. "Well, maybe a little, but if she's..."

Crawford filled in the blank. "Taking money for sex?"

"Yeah, for starters, it's illegal, and two, I'm not real keen on dating a... prostitute. But, I mean, gotta say, she seems like one *hell* of a classy babe to me."

"So what are you waiting for? Go for it."

Ott smiled and shook his head. "I can't believe you, the straightest guy in the world."

"Hey, man, sometimes you gotta just follow your heart."

"Christ, you sound like a goddamn romance novel."

"Plus, maybe you *will* get some insight into who killed Antonia."

Ott did an exaggerated nod. "Aha, there it is. That's your real motivation. That's why you're giving me the green light."

"What are you talking about? As if you need a green light from me. As you'll recall, I'm the same guy who went out with a woman who's doing time up in a North Carolina jail right now."

He was referring to Lil Fonseca, a former art gallery owner and Crawford's first girlfriend when he moved down to Florida. She had been the ringleader in an art swindle that took place right under Crawford's nose.

"I don't know," Ott said. "She's the first woman who got me fired up in a long time. Definitely because she's good-looking, but I also dug her personality. She's got, I dunno, pizazz... Shit, listen to me, I sound like a dopey teenager."

"Hey, man, you're allowed. You've been on the sidelines for a while. I always told you I thought you were too damn discriminating."

"Yeah, easy for you to say, you got your pick of Dominica or Rose or God knows who else."

"Don't be so sure," Crawford said. "Hey, I just have one question: is 'fired up' like a medical term or something?"

"Fuck off."

Crawford laughed. "Okay, back to work. I'm thinking we split up interviews with Courtie Hiller, Bob Jones, Luther King, plus I got LV Wurfel again tomorrow morning. So how 'bout you take Hiller and Jones, I take the other two."

"Okay, Jones and Hiller should be easy enough to track down."

"If you can find time between dates with DeeDee."

"Gimme a break," Ott said. "I doubt she'll even say yes."

"Don't gimme that, Mort. I've seen how women respond to that laidback Midwestern charm of yours."

Ott leaned across Crawford's desk and put up a hand for a fist bump. "Put me in, Coach. I'm ready to play."

*****

Ott called Bob Jones and explained who he was and why he was calling: that he knew Jones was an acquaintance of Antonia von Habsburg, who, as Jones undoubtedly knew, had been murdered three days before. As Ott fully expected, Jones claimed he barely knew the woman, so Ott countered by saying, "You knew her well enough to have had drinks at her house eight or ten months back."

That put an end to Jones's denials, and Ott suggested he come down to Gulfstream for a visit. The panic in Jones's voice registered right away as he responded to the suggestion. He said he planned to be up in Palm Beach later that day and would be happy to, as he said, "do my civic duty" and drop by the Palm Beach Police station.

At three o'clock sharp he showed up, and Ott introduced himself at the reception desk and led him back to his cubicle. The man was handsome and tall, but looked kind of vacuous to Ott. Maybe he thought that because somehow, he saw Jones as a potential rival.

"Appreciate you… doing your civic duty and coming in," Ott said, trying to go light on the sarcasm.

"I'm happy to help in any way I can, but as I told you, I barely knew Antonia von Habsburg."

"Yes, and as I said to you, you knew her well enough to have been invited to her house to have drinks," Ott said.

"How do you even know about that?" Jones asked,

"Just part of our investigation," Ott said obliquely. "So, just how did you know Ms. von Habsburg?"

"Well, see, Ms. von Habsburg was interested in joining a country club up in New York that I'm president of, so through a mutual friend, I volunteered to meet with her and discuss her joining."

"Okay, and where exactly is this club?"

"East Hampton. Long Island."

"As in… *the Hamptons*?"

"The very same," Jones said and a bright smile lit up his bronzed, chiseled face. "I'm surprised you've heard of the Hamptons."

"Yeah, well… So that was it, you were interviewing her to join your little club up there?"

"Pretty much."

"Who else was there at Ms. von Habsburg's house?"

"A friend of mine. Name's Courtie Hiller."

"That was it?"

Jones nodded.

"You sure?"

"Yeah, I'm sure."

Ott's eyes bored into his. "You either have a terrible memory, Mr. Jones, or you're lying through your teeth," he said. "I sure hope it's not the latter, because I so wanted to believe you came here to do your civic duty."

Jones did his best to look outraged at Ott's accusation. "This was a while ago, Detective, and I don't have a perfect memory."

"Think hard, Mr. Jones."

Jones nodded just once. "Maybe there was another woman there."

"Maybe?"

"There definitely was another woman there."

"And what was her name?"

"Oh God, I have no clue. It was almost a year ago and I had a few drinks—"

"And don't have a perfect memory."

"Right."

"Mr. Jones, this is a question you don't have to have a great memory to remember. Did you have sex with that other woman who was there?"

Jones's whole body seemed to contort. "Are you kidding? That was the first and last I saw of her. Besides I'm a—"

"Happily married man?"

"Damn right," Jones said, with what looked to Ott like another bad impression of deep indignation.

"What more can you tell me about Antonia von Habsburg?"

"I don't know much of anything. I told you, I was just doing a friend a favor and interviewing her for my club. Which is exactly what I did."

"Well, now that seems a little peculiar to me," Ott said. "Because if you're president of this club in the *Hamptons* and you interviewed her to become a member, you'd presumably find out a fair amount about her. I mean, that was the whole purpose... right?"

"Well, yes, but...."

"But what?"

"Well. I kind of got the impression that she might be holding back. Not giving me the full picture."

"Okay, so tell me what you *did* find out about her."

"She grew up somewhere up north. Went to college up there."

"Do you remember which one?"

"I don't think she said."

"Okay, then what?"

"She moved down here about fifteen, twenty years ago and started a business. A headhunter business, you know, where they get jobs for people. I got the impression that these were pretty big jobs. Like bank executives, lawyers, financial and insurance positions, stuff like that. She was married when she came down, but got divorced a while back."

"What was the name of her company?" Ott asked. "Do you remember?"

"She never said."

"And you never asked?"

Jones shook his head. "I was beginning to get the sense she wasn't right for our club."

"Why not?"

"Well, don't take this the wrong way, but she just wasn't really the same class as the rest of our membership."

"What made you decide that?"

Jones pulled at his earlobe and squinted. "Well, for one thing she had this accent."

"She grew up in New Hampshire."

"Maybe that was it. Kind of a hick accent."

Ott laughed. "Really? Don't know if I've ever heard a 'hick accent' before."

But Jones was on a roll. "Then there was the whole von Habsburg thing. I mean, where'd that come from? European royalty was the last thing that woman was."

"That woman?"

"Antonia."

"Yes, I knew who you were talking about. So, you didn't let her into your club."

"Correct, but here's the amazing thing. A few months later I heard she got into the Poinciana."

Ott feigned surprise. There was not a higher social mountain to climb than the Poinciana Club. "No kidding, with that hick accent and everything."

Jones missed Ott's sarcasm. "Yeah, she must have had some pull, 'cause even I'd have a hard time getting in there."

"Wow, even you," Ott said, tongue even deeper in his cheek. "How do you think she was able to swing it?"

"I don't know, but I could hazard a guess."

"Please do."

"Well—" Jones suddenly glanced away. "No, I better not."

"Come on, I need your help here."

"Well, "—his eyes slowly circled back to Ott's—"the president of the Poinciana kind of has a reputation. Let's just say, he has an eye for the single ladies. One of the men on the membership committee does, too. But, you know, that's just a rumor. I have no idea, no first-hand knowledge whether it's true or not."

"Keep going."

"Well, that's really it."

"I'd appreciate all the details you can give me." It seemed Jones could go either way: clam up or open up. "Everything you know, please."

"All right, well supposedly—this is from a guy I play golf with, who's also a member of the Poinciana—the president has a beach cottage on the other side of North Ocean from his house,"—Jones thrummed the arm of his chair—"so they have these Friday night dances at the Poinciana in season, where the president goes around on the QT and tells a bunch of the single woman he's having an after-party at his cottage. So, he and a couple of male friends and a bevy of single women show up and apparently, it gets pretty wild."

"What do you mean?" Ott could only imagine. "Like spin the bottle or something?"

Jones laughed. "Almost. Apparently, they play these strip games."

"Strip games?" Ott was... flabbergasted was the best word for it.

"Well, like Charades, for example. Where you have to take off something if they don't get what you're trying to act out. Or naked Twister."

Ott couldn't hold back. "We're talking about grown men and women here?"

Jones nodded eagerly. "Yeah, from the highest level of society."

"Wow? What else."

"Well, let's see, I heard about another one they made up called, 'Find the Tattoo,'" Jones said. "I don't quite know how it works, but supposedly two of these young women had little tattoos on their... well, private areas. And the idea was to, ah, try to find them."

"Okay," Ott said, fighting off a full-throated guffaw. He couldn't wait to tell Crawford how the rich whiled away their late-night hours. "What else?"

"Isn't that enough?"

"Is this pretty common? At clubs in general, I mean?"

"Well, definitely not down in Gulfstream. People are pretty straitlaced at my club. Just, you know, the usual."

"No, what's the usual?"

"Well, you know, some guys have a little side action. Some women, too. They have...boy toys."

Ott put a hand to his chin, looking thoughtful. "I've heard that expression. How would you define a 'boy toy'?"

Jones cupped his own chin, unconsciously mirroring Ott. "Well, I'd say a boy toy is like some good-looking kid who's an assistant tennis pro at one of the clubs. Or an assistant golf pro."

"They have to be assistants?"

"No, no... just young guys that rich women run across in the course of their typical day."

"Gotcha, so not like a bagger at Publix, or a pool cleaner."

Jones burst out laughing. "Oh God no, way too déclassé."

"What's that mean?"

"You know… lowly, humble."

"Gotcha," Ott said. He really had to get to Crawford fast. Tell him what really went on behind the twenty-foot hedges. "Okay, Mr. Jones. I thank you for all your time. It's been a real education."

"You're welcome. I hope some of it was useful."

Useful, Ott wasn't so sure. But lurid and riveting? For damn sure.

TEN

It was eight the next morning, and Crawford was in his office with the usual Dunkin' Donuts breakfast spread laid out in front of him. Chief Norm Rutledge had just called and told him that he and the mayor, Mal Chace, wanted to meet with him and Ott at nine that morning. *Can't make it, got a conflict* wouldn't cut it, so he said, "See you then." Then he called LV Wurfel, pretty sure he woke him up, and rescheduled with him for later in the day.

A few minutes later, Ott walked in and recounted his Bob Jones interview from late yesterday in very specific detail.

"Jesus, Mort," said Crawford after hearing it through to the end. "So that's what the other half does for kicks on a Friday night?"

"Half?" said Ott. "Try upper one half of one percent."

Crawford nodded. "So bottom-line it, will ya?"

"Okay, bottom line: Bob Jones is a hell of a chronicler of Poinciana escapades, but no way in hell is he our guy," Ott said. "I mean, when you look at how brutally Antonia was murdered, you realize there're probably very few people out there capable of something so vicious and sadistic. I mean really, think about it, this was no everyday murder. Whoever did it: a) had a strong stomach and zero conscience; and b) had a colossal grudge against von Habsburg. So, when you look at it like that, it kinda eliminates some suspects from serious consideration. Jones definitely for one."

Crawford nodded, realizing that Ott had totally nailed it.

"You speak to Luther King?" Ott asked.

"Yeah, I went to his place on Middle Road. We had a nice chat."

"Let's hear about it."

"Well, so I barely had a chance to sit down in his gaudy living room when he tells me about his neighbors named Morris Leitner and Jennie Tarbell on either side of him."

Ott shrugged. "Can't say I know either one of those names."

"Yeah, neither did I, but he proceeds to say that they're both billionaires. One's a dot-com guy and the other one... invented some kind of special girdle or something."

Ott snapped his fingers. "Oh, you mean, Spanx. I heard she had a place down here."

"Spanx? What the hell—"

"Oh, man, they're the best. Make chubby babes thin. Course when they get naked—"

"Okay, okay, TMI. I don't need any more specifics," Crawford said. "So, bottom line on Luther King is... I don't really have a bottom line. He's not the most forthcoming guy I've ever met, that's for damn sure. He told me at first how Antonia was the love of his life, then later how she was screwing every man on the island of Palm Beach and half of West Palm, too."

"That's a lot of screwing."

"Yeah, no shit. So, it seems like his only motive would be jealousy."

Ott slouched down and put his feet on the chair next to him. "Which we both know has gotten plenty of people killed over the years."

"Yeah, true, but like you went into before, he didn't strike me as the vicious, sadistic type, but I did get the sense he might be holding back something. I just don't know what."

"Were he and Antonia still going out at the time of her death?"

"Yeah, he said they were. He also said he was looking around for a woman to have a more stable relationship with. Guess Antonia was not that gal," Crawford said. "He also asked me if it was really true how she died. The rat. By now, I figured, it's out. Everyone knows, so I told him it was. He said something that made me think he just couldn't possibly be our guy. Like, 'How could anybody dream up something so horrible as that, let alone carry it out?' He said it in such a way that I believed there was no way in hell he had anything to do with it."

"And you've got one of the best bullshit detectors around."

Crawford nodded. "It's pretty reliable."

"But as we both know, you can hire people to do just about anything for you," Ott said. "All you have to do is pay 'em enough."

*****

Five minutes later, Crawford heard the unmistakable, plodding footsteps of Chief Norm Rutledge, which somehow always reminded Crawford of the shambling Lurch character from the old TV show, *The Addams Family*.

But this time was different because Mal Chace plodded along behind him. It was a grim-looking two-fer: first Rutledge, then an even grimmer Mal Chace.

Rutledge eyed Ott, who had just taken his feet off of the second chair facing Crawford. "Can you get us another one, Ott?"

"Sure, Norm, anything for you," Ott said. "Hello, Mr. Mayor."

"Mort," said Chace, then to Crawford, "Charlie."

Crawford nodded. "Mr. Mayor."

Mal Chace sat in the chair previously occupied by Ott's feet as Rutledge sat in Ott's chair and Ott disappeared to fetch another one.

"So, I'll get right to it," Chace said, as Ott carried in an extra chair and plopped down into it. "We've had conversations like this before, but we've never had a homicide like this before. Not even close."

"Yeah, I know," Crawford said.

"The press," Chace went on, "from all over the world, it seems, have been having a field day with the damn thing."

Crawford nodded. The media presence was unlike anything he had ever seen before in Palm Beach.

It was Rutledge's turn. "You've seen all the news vans, the helicopters. I saw one yesterday that said *BBC* on it. I mean, it's as bad as O.J. or the Manson murders."

"Yeah, I know what you mean," Crawford said, "but I don't need to tell you, we're on it around the clock."

Rutledge leaned in and put his hands on Crawford's desk. "Which, I don't need to tell you, does us absolutely no good until you got somebody."

"I know, Norm. Trust me, we get it."

"We've done a ton of interviews, but this woman had all kinds of relationships with a lot of different men," Ott said, looking first at Rutledge, then Chace. "I know you fellas don't want to hear this, but it takes time."

Rutledge looked at Chace as if he were taking his temperature. "What else did you want to say, Mal?"

"Nothing that I haven't said when we've been in this position before, except I don't recall ever being in a situation as bad as this in all my tenure." He turned to the detectives. "Look, I know I've got the best guys I possibly could have on this, but the case is—as I don't need to say—harmful to the public perception that this is one of the safest places in America. It's not like people are cancelling their reservations, or thinking it's a place to stay away from, but the longer it lingers without getting solved, the worse it becomes. As I said, and I know you know this, just do everything you possibly can, huh?"

It almost didn't require a response, but Crawford gave one anyway. A firm one. "We're on it, Mal. Believe me, we can't possibly be more on it."

ELEVEN

After Chace and Rutledge walked out of his office, Crawford glanced up at Ott, who was on his feet now. "I'm thinking it's time for you to call your friend DeeDee and ask her out."

Ott laughed. "You mean, it makes a lot of sense for our case—not for ol' Mort's love life."

"Yeah, well, look at it this way: we solve it, then you've got all the time in the world for your love life."

Ott laughed. "Question is, is it going to look obvious?"

"You mean, that you're trying to pump her for info?"

He nodded. "Yeah. You're a pro at it. You got the 'Charlie smooth' act down. I'm nowhere near as slick."

"Hey, nothin' to it. You just gotta ease into it. Ask her a bunch of questions about her life, then wait for your opening and slip in a question or two about Antonia. Oh, and bring her flowers."

"Good point. I noticed they got really good ones at Publix."

"They sell flowers at Publix?"

"Hell yeah, man, really nice bouquets for like ten bucks a pop."

Crawford shook his head. "Come on, Mort, go to a florist shop. Hell, the department'll pay. You can't cheap out on this."

Ott shrugged. "Okay, I'll do it. Know any good florist shops?"

"Yeah, there's one on South County, just north of the book-store there."

"I'm guessing you got flowers for either Dominica or Rose there?"

"Both, actually."

"At the same time?"

"Come on, Mort, despite what you may think, the *last* thing I am is a two-timer," Crawford said, tapping his desk a few times. "Speaking of Rose, you know what else I was thinking?"

"What's that?"

"It's time to pick her brain. I don't know why we didn't think of her sooner. That whole thing about the Poinciana Club and Antonia being a member got me thinking. Rose belongs and I'm sure she either knew our vic or knew of her."

"Good idea. She's been pretty helpful in the past."

"Are you kidding? She's like having a third partner sometimes."

*****

Ott had tried to reach Courtie Hiller several times but encountered the usual: no call-back. So, with Mal Chace's beseeching words echoing in his ears, he found out where Hiller lived and drove there. Soon he had parked in the Chattahoochee stone driveway, walked up to the porch and pressed the doorbell.

A minute later, the door opened and a tall man with slicked-back dark hair frowned out at him. "Yes?"

"Mr. Hiller?"

"Yes?"

"My name's Detective Ott, Palm Beach Police. I've left you several messages."

A look of panic spread over Hiller's face. "We can't talk here."

"All right. How 'bout we go to my station?"

"No, no, let's go to, ah, Starbucks… on Worth."

Ott nodded and returned to his car. Something told him that Hiller's wife was in the house, and Hiller didn't want her to get suspicious about what her husband was doing chatting up a cop.

Hiller arrived fifteen minutes later and was trembling with what looked like jumpy nerves. "What's this all about?" he asked, as he sat down, Frappuccino in hand.

"The death of Antonia von Habsburg," said Ott, taking a sip of his venti latte, which had set him back close to five bucks.

"And why would I know anything about that?"

"Maybe because you knew her. Had drinks at her house, in fact."

"One time. That's all. I would hardly say I *knew* her," Hiller said, taking a sip of his flavored drink, hand still shaking a little.

"But, you subsequently had dinner with a friend of hers by the name of DeeDee Dunwoody. At a place up in Jupiter, I believe it was."

Hiller's eyes flickered, and Ott knew he had caught him off guard.

"The woman mentioned she needed financial advice," Hiller said.

"So why couldn't you just meet her in your office?"

"Well, for one thing I don't have an office. I'm retired. I was just giving her some off-the-cuff guidance. She complained about having a stockbroker who churned her."

Ott cocked his head. "She tell you this at Antonia von Habsburg's?"

A few drops of sweat appeared on Hiller's upper lip. "No. When we were having dinner."

Ott held up a hand. "Okay, look Mr. Hiller, I'm going to cut to the chase. I suspect you didn't take DeeDee Dunwoody out to dinner to help her with her financial problems, which, according to you, you didn't even know about until she told you at dinner. My guess is you had an entirely different reason, and I have a pretty good idea what it was, but it's not in the least bit important to me. What *is* important to me is your relationship with Antonia von Habsburg. What that was all about. And unless you come clean with me, I'm going to have to drag your wife into this."

"My wife? What are you talking about? What the hell's she got to do with it?"

Ott shrugged. "I don't know the answer to that. That's why I'd have to question her."

Hiller's eyes seemed to darken, as if he'd like to take a swing at Ott. "This is dirty pool. You know damn well there's no reason at all to bring her into it."

"I need you to come clean with me. So, I'll ask one more time: what was the relationship between you and Antonia von Habsburg? You gotta level with me or I'm going to need to take that other course."

Hiller took another sip of his Frappuccino, then glanced away. "You're a real ballbuster, aren't you?"

"A ballbuster? Mr. Hiller, all I am is a man looking to solve a murder, and I need answers from you to see that happens."

Hiller sighed again and took another sip from his almost-empty cup. Like he was postponing the inevitable. "Okay," he said, hanging his head, "I'll tell you what you want to know. Antonia von Habsburg was fixing me up."

"And DeeDee Dunwoody was one of the women she was fixing you up with?"

"No, I thought she was. But... she turned me down."

"Was that after you offered her money?"

Hiller cast his eyes even lower and nodded.

"How much?"

Another sigh.

"Mr. Hiller, please don't make me drag your wife into this."

"Three thousand dollars."

Ott put up his hands. "All right," he said, "I don't get it. The way I understood it, you pay Antonia's company fifty grand to get a bunch of women's telephone numbers. But you're telling me in your case, it was just the good old-fashioned cash for sex thing?"

Hiller leaned closer to Ott. "I'm not telling you anything more until I have your assurance that you won't charge me with anything."

"Look, I have no big interest in a guy paying a woman for sex, or else I'd be up on Broadway in West Palm arresting hookers. All I care about is finding Antonia's killer. Got it?"

Hiller nodded.

"So what it's beginning to sound like to me is that maybe Antonia had two 'business models,' let's call 'em. One was the high road: fifty grand for a selected assortment of names and phone numbers, and two was just some guy calling up Antonia and saying, 'I want you to send a good-looking brunette to room 401 at the no-tell motel.' Or wherever. Is that about the size of it?"

"What do you think I am, her accountant? All I know is she introduced me to this woman, DeeDee, who I then asked out to dinner, and she wasn't interested in anything more than that. Period, end of story."

"But clearly Antonia would expect a cut or a commission if DeeDee said yes to the three grand?"

"I have absolutely no clue. The business between Antonia and DeeDee was of no interest to me."

Ott played a little drum solo on the tabletop with his fingers. "Okay, Mr. Hiller, that's all I need to know," he said. "Thanks very much, I appreciate your time."

"What about my wife? Are you going to leave her out of this?"

"Yeah, at this point I will," said Ott, "'cause the last thing I'd ever dream of doing is breaking up your happy marriage."

TWELVE

Ott felt as nervous as a teenager about calling DeeDee Dunwoody. He dialed her number twice and both times hung up before he put the call through. Finally, the shame of acting like a bashful high school kid became too much. He screwed up his courage and let it ring.

"Hello?"

Damn. He would have preferred leaving a message. "Hi, DeeDee, it's Mort Ott. You know, the, ah, detective?"

"You didn't need to add that, Mort, I remember."

"Oh good." *Full speed ahead.* "So I just wanted to see if I could take you out for, um, dinner?"

No hesitation. "Sure, when?"

He remembered Crawford's mantra: no time like the present.

"How about tonight?"

"Ah, sure, that works. Where were you thinking?"

"I don't know, there's a place near me on Dixie Highway called, what is it? Sean Penn's Nomad."

She laughed. "I think you mean Sean Rush's Nomad."

Okay, I'm a little nervous. "Yeah, yeah, that's it."

"Great," DeeDee said, like Ott wasn't the biggest dumbass in the world. "See you at seven?"

*****

Crawford now had a lot more to question LV Wurfel about, as he knew he would. When Crawford got to the house on El Cid, Wurfel was in his garage again, this time with another scruffy biker dude. The man was pure central casting: jeans, a black T-shirt with cut-off arms revealing bulbous but un-muscled arms, a turkey neck segueing into a Fu Manchu beard/mustache combo, and a red, pockmarked face.

"Dirt," Wurfel said, seeing Crawford approaching the garage, "say hello to my new friend, Officer Crawfish."

Crawford let it go, remembering Wurfel's self-described lame sense of humor.

"How ya doin', bro?" Dirt said, flipping Crawford a thumbs-up.

Crawford nodded at him, then turned to Wurfel. "Got a few more question for you, LV."

"Fire away, man. Dirt won't get in the way," Wurfel said.

"See, the thing is," Crawford said, shaking his head, "what I want to discuss is confidential."

Wurfel, working on something Crawford thought was the motorcycle's carburetor, grabbed a dirty towel from the floor and rubbed his hands. "I don't know what difference it'll make. I'll just tell Dirt what we talked about after."

Crawford didn't care that much. "Just do me a favor and step outside, will ya?"

Wurfel nodded; Dirt shrugged.

Crawford led Wurfel outside the garage to the shade of a scrawny tree on his lawn. "So," said Crawford, "there's a lot more to Distinguished Consorts than you told me about."

"There is? Like what are you referring to?"

Crawford leaned just over the edge of Wurfel's personal space. "I mean, men paying women for sex, provided by your ex-wife Antonia. It's called prostitution."

Wurfel looked down and pushed the right toe of his boot into a clump of grass. "That all happened after me. When I was there, we ran a clean operation. I had no interest in going back to jail."

"Okay, so let me get this straight, Antonia charged men fifty grand to have ten dates with women—"

"Not just women, but high-class, intelligent, very, very sexy women. Tens, man, every one of 'em was a ten. I can't tell you how hard we worked to have the best stable in the country." Wurfel slapped Crawford's arm. "Tell you the truth, that was my favorite part of the job."

"Recruiting for the stable, you mean?"

"Better believe it, man."

"Okay, so I get it from Antonia's angle, and I get it from the men's angle, but not the women's. Was it just that the women had the opportunity of snagging a rich man?"

"Pretty much. We provided those women a shot at landing a whale that they never would've had a shot at otherwise. Know what I mean?"

"Yeah, but their dates didn't always lead to marriage or even a long relationship. In fact, I'm guessing rarely."

"True that. In fact, only about one in ten. No… more like one out of twenty. But at least they scored a few really nice dinners out of it. Maybe a few extra bucks over and above."

"Okay, okay, so the 50K was the legitimate side of the business. Semi-legit at least… when you were still in it. What about the money-for-sex side hustle?"

"Okay," Wurfel said, "so as I understand it from Waverly after a long night of bikini martinis, a bunch of the girls got sick of going out to dinner with a guy and that was as far as it went. So, a few of them started griping to Antonia, and that's when Antonia changed the game."

"To good, old-fashioned sex-for-money."

"Make that a *shitload* of money for sex," Wurfel said. "Don't forget these were the cream dee la cream of broads. I mean a runner-up for Miss Universe, this hot soap-opera star, Miss Florida 2010, one of those babes on *The Real Housewives of Orange County*."

"How'd she end up in Florida?"

"Beats me. Anyway, you know what I'm sayin'. Like I said, the cream dee la cream."

"I got that," Crawford said. "So Antonia would set it up and… get a cut?"

"More than a cut. Wave told me she'd get half."

"So this was basically for guys who had no patience?"

Wurfel cocked his head. "What do you mean?"

"Men who didn't want to go through the song and dance of three dinners, five dates, whatever it took to have sex."

"Yeah well, look at it this way: some of 'em—the women—never put out 'til they had something solid. You know, living together with a guy or actually a ring on their finger."

"Really?"

"Really."

"So these women, the beauty queens and *The Real Housewives*—"

"By the way, Antonia put 'em up in a house up on Indian—the north end of Palm Beach."

Crawford nodded. "Yeah, I know where Indian is. I'm a Palm Beach detective, LV, case you missed that."

"Check." LV nodded. "So the girls had a regular sorority house up there."

"Gotcha," Crawford said, thinking, *that's certainly worth a visit.*

"They weren't allowed to bring guys there. One of 'em did once and Antonia tossed her ass out onto the street."

"Guess she ran a tight ship."

"Sure did."

"So, what else?"

"What else what?"

"Well, last time we talked, I thought you filled me in on everything there was to know about Distinguished Consorts. Turns out you only told me half."

"Well, now you know everything I know."

"You sure? You're not holding back on anything… again? Or forgetting something?" LV shook his head vigorously.

"Okay, well then what about this? A lot of people described the business as an executive headhunter business? What's that all about?"

"Oh, that? Well, see Antonia had a good job up in Manchester—New Hampshire, that is, where we came from—as a recruiter, so she wanted to try that down here."

"And?"

"It didn't fly."

"Why not?"

"Because recruiting a bank VP in Manchester for sixty grand was what they pay a trainee down here. As smart as she was, she was smart enough to bail on that. I came up with the girl idea, she came up with the name."

"And the rest is history," Crawford said. "What else, LV?"

"That's it."

"You haven't impersonated a police officer lately, have you?"

"Hell no."

"Or been up to any criminal mischief?"

"Come on, man. Like I said, the last place I want to end up is sideways with the law. You checked me out. You saw my sheet. I can't afford to add to it."

Crawford nodded at Wurfel. "Okay, well, thanks for filling me in. Now you can go back to your pal Dirt and spill the beans on everything we talked about."

THIRTEEN

Ott picked up DeeDee Dunwoody at her bungalow on Westminster Street, just south of the El Cid section of West Palm Beach. Ott, gentleman he was, opened the passenger door for her and she slid into the seat of his six-year-old white Infiniti. He had gotten it detailed an hour before picking her up.

"Nice car, Mort," DeeDee said, as Ott got in the driver's side.

"Thanks, an oldie but a goodie." He started to add, *like me*, but why draw attention to their age difference? He figured she was in her early thirties; he was forty-seven.

"So where are we going again?" DeeDee asked. "Oh right, Sean Rush's Nomad."

"Yeah, I went there once and liked it."

DeeDee nodded. "Cool place."

"And just so happens, tonight is bossa nova night."

"Is it now? Not sure I know how to do the bossa nova."

"Well, I'm *totally* sure I don't. I think it might be something in the samba family."

"I'll Google it," DeeDee said, pulling her iPhone out of her purse as Ott took a left onto Dixie Highway.

"Here we go," DeeDee said a few moments later. "So, according to Wikipedia, the bossa nova, 'is mainly characterized by a "different beat" that altered the harmonies with the introduction of unconventional chords and an innovative syncopation of traditional samba from a single rhythmic division.'"

Ott looked over at DeeDee, his brows furrowed. "Come again?"

She laughed. "Yeah, exactly. No clue what any of that means."

"Well, I guess we're about to find out."

*****

Ott and DeeDee had just stepped off the dance floor after doing their version of the bossa nova. If you took a look at a YouTube video of bossa nova dancing it would bear no resemblance to the Ott-DeeDee version, but they had fun and worked up a fierce thirst.

"You're a really good dancer, Mort," DeeDee said, as they sat back down at the table.

"Well, thanks, I'm not quite ready for *Dancing with the Stars*, but you definitely are."

She put her hand on his arm. "Flattery will get you *everywhere*."

"No, I mean it, you are really good. You got great moves."

The waitress came over and they ordered drinks. Rosé for her, a Yuengling for him.

"So are you making any progress on Antonia's murder?" DeeDee asked.

"That's a very good question and, as I'm sure you can appreciate, I can't tell you all that much. But, in general, what usually happens is we have to rule out a lot of suspects before we eventually rule someone in."

"I understand, but I read somewhere that if you don't catch the bad guy in the first forty-eight hours, it becomes a lot harder to ever catch him."

"That's the common belief, but my partner and I never seem to do it that way. I'm pretty sure we've only had one that we solved in the first forty-eight hours. In that case, we found a lot of good DNA samples and, boom, nailed the guy right away."

"You ever shot anybody, Mort?"

Ott laughed. "That's kind of a personal question," he said. "So, yes I have. One guy in the butt, another guy who was rushing me, in the stomach. They both survived, I'm happy to say."

"But never killed anybody, right?"

"No, not even close," Ott said, thinking about his partner, who couldn't say the same. "Can we talk about something other than shooting people?"

"Sure, I was just curious."

"So, let's talk about you… you said you've been looking for a job. How's that coming along?"

She exhaled. "Oh, I don't know. I've been doing a little with the real estate. I had this guy who was looking to spend up to $700,000 in the Northwood area. He said that was the only area he was interested in. We went around and looked at a bunch of different places, and I was sure he was going to make an offer on this one. So, I waited and waited and nothing. Then I called him a few days later and he told me he went and bought a FSBO in Flamingo Park."

"A FSBO?"

"Yeah, means For Sale By Owner."

"That's too bad. Thought he only wanted to be in Northwood."

"So he said. But there's this expression, 'buyers are liars.'"

"Well, sorry it didn't work out."

"Yeah, me too… sometimes I wish I had a bunch of other great-aunts dying off on me."

Ott laughed. "So tell me about that guy Warren," he said, immediately realizing there had to have been a better segue. But it was too late.

"Who?"

"You know, *Warren the pig.*"

She tapped her forehead. "Oh God, don't remind me," she said, her eyes narrowing. "Wait a minute, Mort, did you ask me out to talk about Antonia's murder?"

Yup, he had totally jumped the gun, and ignored Crawford's advice to go slow, ease into it.

"No, I asked you out because I thought we'd have a good time and you'd be a fantastic bossa nova partner."

"Well, good, then. As for Warren, do you like to talk about your bad dates?"

"Good point. And no, I don't. It's just that you brought up Antonia before so I didn't think it was off-limits."

"Fair enough. Warren's off-limits; Antonia isn't. How's that?"

"That's fair."

"So anything else on the job front?" Ott asked.

"I thought we were back to talking about Antonia."

"Whatever you'd like," Ott said.

"I'll tell you what I'd like," DeeDee said, standing up as a bouncy new song came on, "more bossa nova."

Ott was down with that.

They did a few fast ones; then a slower one came on. Ott put his right hand around her back and her right hand in his left.

"I also like cheek to cheek," DeeDee said, smiling up at him.

"Me, too," said Ott, and he moved closer, so their cheeks grazed.

"You're very warm," Ott said, meaning her cheek. "I started to say, 'you're very hot' but didn't think that would sound right."

She laughed. "I don't mind either."

The song ended a few minutes later. Before they broke the clench, Ott kissed her cheek.

"Why, Mort," DeeDee said, mock surprise.

Ott put up his hands. "I don't know what came over me."

"Whatever it was, I liked it."

*****

They stayed at Sean Rush's Nomad—dancing and talking—for another half hour and never got back to Antonia von Habsburg or the case.

At 10:35, Ott drove DeeDee back to her bungalow on Westminster Street. He parked in her driveway. "This is a nice neighborhood," he said.

"Yes, I like it. Pretty quiet, but pretty close to everything," she said. "Where do you live?"

"Grandview Heights."

"Oh, so just a hop, skip and a jump."

"Yeah, but not as nice as here."

"Okay, Mort, enough geography." She leaned toward him. "Kiss me."

And did he ever.

Like his dancing, it was a little rusty, but he picked it up again pretty fast.

After a few moments, DeeDee pulled back. "You're a really good kisser, Mort."

"You probably say that to all the boys."

She shook her head. "I don't kiss all the boys."

"Good to know."

She shook her head again. "All right, I better get out of here before this gets too intense."

"What's wrong with that?"

She leaned toward him, kissed him again and shrugged. "Blame it on the bossa nova."

*****

Crawford was in Rose Clarke's office at Sotheby's International Realty in Royal Poinciana Plaza. Rose was a tall blond, who had just turned forty, but sometimes she forgot that fact. She was the top real estate agent in Palm Beach—by far—because she was smart, savvy and hustled her shapely ass off. She also never forgot a name or a face. She and Crawford had had their romantic moments—more than two, less than ten.

"So, Charlie, why is it I never see you except when you need something from me?" she asked with her little smile.

"That's very cynical, Rose. What about that time I took you out to Malakor's for dinner? All I was after was your scintillating conversation and companionship, absolutely no ulterior motive."

"That was six, maybe eight months ago," she said.

He shook his head. "Couldn't a been that long ago."

"I remember… it was right before Thanksgiving."

"So, it *was* memorable though, right?"

"Anything with you is memorable, Charlie," Rose said. "So what do you want to know? Wait, I've got a guess… Could it be about Antonia von Habsburg?"

"Bingo. How'd you know?"

"Because that's the only murder in Palm Beach in the last six months, at least that I know of. And, boy, was it ever a grisly one."

"Sure was," Crawford said. "Hey, by the way, I have to pay you a compliment. Mort and I were talking and we decided you're like our 'third partner.'"

"Oh, I love that," Rose said. "Give Mort a kiss for me, will you?"

"Um, maybe just a fist bump," he said, raising his fist.

Rose laughed. "So Antonia von Habsburg, she's a bit of a mystery. What a horrible way to go. I actually liked her but never felt like I had that good a read on her. Totally self-made, I heard. Seemed intelligent, attractive… but, obviously, she really pissed someone off."

"Yeah, you can say that again."

"I remember when she came up for membership at the Poinciana, with the most bogus résumé you could imagine. I thought to myself, 'Well, she's got no chance.' But then, three months later, she was in."

"Bogus? How do you mean bogus?"

"Well, that her grandfather or great-grandfather was some kind of duke or count in Austria, grew up in a castle, and she was descended from *the* Habsburgs of... well, Habsburg fame. Went back there for Habsburg reunions or some nonsense. I mean the people on the membership committee aren't stupid. They check you out, vet the hell out of you."

"But, as you said, somehow she got through the process and became a member."

"There was speculation in my golf foursome that she was doing the president, but I think it had more to do with Janny Hasleiter."

"Who's she?" he said, remembering what Ott had heard about the president of the Poinciana.

Rose looked confounded. "Jeez Charlie, where have you been? You've never run across Janny Hasleiter?"

Crawford shook his head.

"Oh my God. Well, for starters she's one of the most powerful people in Hollywood. She's—I forget which—either a director or a producer, maybe both. She was one of the producers on, let's see, either the Spiderman or the Jurassic Park series. Also, one of the big series on Showtime, too, that's in like its sixth season. I forget the name of it, but it's huge. Oh, I remember now, it's called *Yellowstone*."

"So she and Antonia were friends?"

Rose glanced out her window. "You know, I'm not quite sure what they were. Antonia had that business, as you obviously know: matchmaking. For the most part, setting up rich men with good-looking women, but she also did a little of the other way around."

"Setting up rich women with good-looking young men, you mean?"

Rose nodded.

"So you're saying that was the case with Janny Hasleiter?"

Rose's eyes drifted back to Crawford's. "That's what I heard. I also heard Janny has a voracious appetite."

"For men, you're saying?"

"Men... and maybe women."

"Really?"

"Just to complicate things, she's also got a husband. Does the name Paul David Ranieri mean anything to you?"

"Wasn't he a big guy in Hollywood?"

"Yes, still is, but not like he used to be. Janny was his protégée and like all good protégées, she took over at some point."

"So, I wonder what ol' Paul David thinks of all her messin' around."

"What I've heard is he's like this world-class bridge player. Travels all around the world now. That's his passion, like movies and Janny used to be. Apparently doesn't mind so much that she's got... friends."

"Jesus, this *is* complicated," Crawford said.

"Aren't most of your cases?"

Crawford laughed. "Yeah, unlike New York, where things always seemed a hell of a lot more straightforward. A drug deal went awry, a gang power war, basic things like that."

"So who's your leading suspect at this point?"

"You know I couldn't tell you... even if I had one."

"So, you mean, you don't have one?"

"I didn't say that."

"Yes, but I know you. And you don't."

"So tell me more about Janny Hasleiter. Seems like a woman I should definitely talk to."

"Yeah, but you better be careful," Rose said. "She might eat you alive."

"Really? That bad?"

Rose laughed. "Some men think that's good."

He tapped his fingers on the side of his chair. "So is she just down here in season?"

"Yeah, I'm pretty sure. But I think she flies back and forth to L.A. a lot."

"How old is she?"

"Mm, I'd say around forty-five, maybe a little older."

"How about... is there anybody else you'd add to my suspect list?"

Rose thought for a few moments. "Do you know the name Courtie Hiller?"

"Yeah, I do actually. Mort interviewed him."

"All right. So, what I'm about to tell you is fourth hand. In other words, a long way from the gospel according to your normally reliable third detective, Rose Clarke. But Courtie's wife, whose name is Jean, supposedly discovered that he had mysteriously sold stock worth close to a million dollars from their joint account."

"To do what with? Do you know?"

TOM TURNER

"No, I don't. Neither did the woman who told me, who's a friend of Jean's. I just know that Jean's worth a ton of money. Speculation was Courtie might have spent some of that money on fast, expensive women."

"So, I guess it's a reasonable conclusion to reach that Courtie might have married Jean for her money?"

"Yes, I'd say that's a reasonable deduction. Supposedly, he was a car salesman who met her when she came in and bought a Bentley from him."

Crawford nodded and made a mental note to pass along this information to Ott.

"Okay... the president of the Poinciana, name's Morrison, right?"

"Yeah, George Morrison."

"Do you think maybe Antonia got in because of him?"

"I'd say that rumor has a credibility factor of... um, eight out of ten."

"Ten being the most credible?"

"Exactly."

"So, pretty high?"

She nodded.

"Morrison seems like a guy I should talk to, too."

"Just get to him before three."

"Why?"

"'Cause that's when he starts pounding the rum-dumbs at the club bar."

Crawford smiled at Rose. "That's a lot of good information, girlfriend."

Rose laughed. "Wait. I thought Dominica was your girlfriend."

Crawford leaned over to her and patted her arm. "Just a figure of speech, term of endearment. And, fact is, you both are."

"That works great for you, Charlie. For us, um, not so much. But then again, you're pretty much married to your job anyway."

"Only when I have a murder," Crawford said, standing up. He was way more comfortable talking about murder than girlfriends. He walked around Rose's desk and gave her a kiss on the cheek.

"That tells me a lot," she said.

"What does?"

"Where you kiss me."

"What do you mean?"

"Cheek means one thing, lips mean another... I prefer lips."

So without a moment's hesitation, he kissed her hard on the lips.

FOURTEEN

Ott's cell phone rang at 3:15 a.m. Whenever he received a call at that hour, he knew it wasn't a telemarketer.

"Hello," he squawked.

"Mort, it's DeeDee." Ott sat up straight. "I'm bleeding and I'm in really bad shape. He tortured me." Her voice was faint, barely above a whisper.

Ott threw his legs over the side of the bed. "Oh God, DeeDee. Where are you?"

"At home," she said weakly. "Help me, please."

Ott was already headed for his closet. "I'll be right there. Hold on, I'm on my way." He grabbed his pants, pulled them on, then did the same with a T-shirt. "Are you there?"

"I'm in bad shape… Come quick."

"I'll be there in five minutes; stay on the phone with me. I'm gonna put you on hold for a sec; gonna call Good Sam."

He called the emergency number at Good Samaritan Hospital and asked for a team of EMTs to go to DeeDee's address on Westminster. He had plenty of experience with them and knew they were thorough and fast. They might even beat him to DeeDee's house.

"DeeDee, I'm getting in my car right now, I'll be there in no time."

No response.

Ott was almost to his car. "DeeDee?"

Nothing.

He gunned the Infiniti and blew through a stop sign. The only good news was there was very little traffic at 3:20 a.m.

He squealed up to her house on Westminster minutes later. No ambulance yet, but he could hear a siren off in the distance.

He jumped out of his Infiniti and raced up to the front door. He turned the knob, but it was locked. He stepped back a few steps, put his shoulder down and rammed into the door. A thudding crash and the door gave way. He ran into the living room and saw DeeDee on the floor.

There was a pool of blood around her. He felt her wrist and detected a pulse.

Blood was dripping from both her arms and her neck. He ran to a bathroom and grabbed two white towels. He knelt down next to DeeDee's body and pushed the towel up against the cut on her arm that was bleeding the most.

"You're gonna be okay," he whispered frantically, then he moved the towel to stanch the bleeding of another laceration. He pushed it down hard and held it there with one hand as he grabbed the other towel and wrapped it around her neck, which had at least ten cuts that were bleeding, though not profusely.

It was then that it occurred to him what had been done to DeeDee. Something called *lingchi*, or *death by a thousand cuts*. He was relieved that there were nowhere near a thousand cuts and he was going to do everything he could to make sure she didn't die from them. He was so intent on applying pressure to her cuts and stopping the bleeding that he didn't hear the EMTs until they entered the living room.

"We're here," one shouted. "What happened?"

He pointed at DeeDee. "She's been cut," he said, turning to see three EMTs, "a lot of different cuts."

"We'll take over," said the EMT. "Who are you?"

"Name's Ott, Palm Beach Police."

"You look familiar," the EMT said, getting in a crouch with a blood pressure cuff in one hand, and what Ott guessed was some sort of portable monitor device in the other. The EMTs obviously knew what they were doing.

"I've been to Good Sam a few times," Ott replied, standing.

"You the one who called?"

Ott nodded. He took his cell phone out of his pants pocket and dialed.

"Hello," Crawford answered groggily.

"Charlie, someone tortured DeeDee Dunwoody. I'm at her house with paramedics. She's alive but hurtin'."

"What happened?" Crawford asked.

"She got cut up bad. Arms, neck, legs, I think."

"What's the address?"

"Not far from you," Ott said and gave it to him.

"Ten minutes," Crawford said.

Next, Ott called the West Palm Beach Police station. He had the front desk transfer him to a crime-scene tech who was on duty. Her name was Fran Boynton.

"Hey, Fran, my name's Ott, Palm Beach homicide," he said. "I need you to go to 215 Westminster. There was an attempted murder here about a half hour ago. Vic's alive but got a bunch of knife wounds. See what you can come up with, please. We're taking her to Good Sam in a few minutes."

"Roger that," Boynton said, "but how do we get in?"

"That's no problem—I kicked in the front door."

*****

Ott saw one eyebrow flicker, then her other eye open, then her mouth move, but no words came out.

"Relax, ma'am, you're gonna be all right," another EMT said. "We're gonna put you in an ambulance and take you to Good Samaritan Hospital. You're gonna be just fine."

The EMT looked up at Ott. "We'll get her stabilized; she's just gonna need some blood."

Ott nodded numbly and looked at the pool on the floor.

"Do you know her?" the EMT asked.

Know her? We were making out like teenagers a few hours ago. "Yeah, she's a friend." He dialed his cell again. "Hey, Charlie, go to Good Sam instead. We're headed to the ER momentarily."

"Okay. Will do."

A few minutes later, the EMTs rolled DeeDee onto a stretcher two of them had brought in.

Both of DeeDee's eyes were open now. She spotted Ott and did her best to smile.

"Hi, Mort," she said faintly.

Ott gave her a little wave. "You probably shouldn't talk," he said, and the EMT nodded.

She nodded weakly and mouthed the word, *Thanks.*

FIFTEEN

Crawford and Ott were in the emergency room of Good Samaritan Hospital; DeeDee was hooked to an IV with a team of emergency doctors and nurses hovering above her.

"So what's your gut tell you: whether or not this is related to von Habsburg?" Ott asked Crawford.

"I don't see how it can't be. What was done to her, I mean," Crawford said. "No clue why, though."

"Yeah, I agree," Ott said. "We'll know more when we speak to her."

Crawford shook his head. "Who the hell does a thing like that anyway?"

"Same person who killed Antonia?" Ott said, more a question. "Chinese invented it, is all I know about it."

"I remember watching that show, *Orange Is the New Black*. There was a scene, or maybe someone described it. *Lingchi*, I mean. My guess is, whoever did it was trying to get something out of her," Crawford said.

Ott nodded. "I think you're probably right."

Ott glanced over at DeeDee and the team of medical people surrounding her. "Her eyes are open; that's a good sign. By the way, I called for the West Palm techs to check out DeeDee's house."

Crawford nodded. "We should go there now. 'Cause we probably won't be able to talk to her for a while. We can come back later this morning or early afternoon."

"That's what I was thinking," Ott said, and they turned and headed for the emergency room door.

*****

They pulled up and parked in front of DeeDee Dunwoody's house on Westminster Road. The front door was open a crack, and it seemed very bright inside—almost as if the techs were using Klieg lights. Ott beelined for the front door. Crawford noticed an older couple across the street on a porch—the man in pajamas, the woman in a dark bathrobe—peering at DeeDee's house.

The man caught Crawford's eye. "What happened to DeeDee?" he called out to Crawford.

Crawford took a few steps toward the couple. "She's gonna be okay," was all he said. He started across the street, but the man spoke again.

"But I saw her taken away in an ambulance," the man said.

Crawford turned again and walked up to them.

"She's going to be all right," Crawford said again. "My name's Crawford, I'm a Palm Beach detective. Did either of you see or hear anything out of the ordinary at Ms. Dunwoody's house earlier tonight?"

"I saw a car I've never seen before parked in front," said the older woman with thick, Coke-bottle glasses.

"Do you know what kind of a car it was?" Crawford asked. "And the color?"

"It was black and it was big. One of those big SUVs like in the president's convoy. I don't know the make."

"And did you see anyone get out of it, or get back in it?"

"Sorry, I didn't," she said. "But earlier, between ten and eleven, I saw another car pull into the driveway and Ms. Dunwoody and a man get out."

"Can you describe the man?"

"Well, he was kind of bald, a little on the heavy side," the woman said. "He walked up to the front door, kissed her good night, went back to his car and drove off."

Attaboy, Mort, Crawford thought.

"But this big SUV, you didn't see either its driver or possibly a passenger?"

"No, sorry."

"Did you happen to see the license plate? Whether it was a Florida plate or another state?"

"I didn't notice that either," the older woman said. "I didn't want to be a snoop."

"You don't happen to have a doorbell camera, do you?"

The couple looked at each other, then shook their heads in unison.

"How long would you say the SUV was there? Parked in front of the house."

"I couldn't tell you. Sorry."

Crawford glanced over at the man. "And you, sir, did you see anything at all?"

"No. I was watching the game. Doris kind of likes to keep an eye on things. Neighborhood watch, you know."

Doris nodded.

"Well, thank you both very much."

"You're welcome," they said.

Crawford walked across the street to DeeDee's house.

Ott was already inside and had introduced himself to the two crime-scene techs, a man and a woman.

The man, bearded, bald and bulky, was standing, and the woman, black, thin and alert-looking, was in a crouch, a baggie in her left hand, tweezers in her right.

Crawford nodded to them both. "Any luck so far?"

The woman, Fran Boynton, pointed to two other bags on the floor. "I've got a bunch of hair follicles. Blond, brunette, black, take your pick."

"How 'bout a knife," Ott said. "I know, probably too much to ask."

"'Fraid so," Fran said, "but we haven't been through the whole house yet."

"We're going to look around outside, too," the man said. "Case the doer chucked it in the bushes or something."

"Yeah, it'll be light before long," Crawford said. "How 'bout prints. Anything?"

"Nah, not so far," said the man, "there's a beer can over there." He pointed to a coffee table not far from where DeeDee's body had been found. "I'm going to try it next."

"Yeah," Ott said. "I'm pretty sure she doesn't drink beer."

Fran perked up. "Oh, so you know her?"

"Yeah, a little."

"How's she doing?" Fran asked.

"I'd say as good as could be expected," Ott said, then glancing at Crawford who nodded, "for someone who's lost all that blood."

"Where'd she get stabbed?" the man asked.

"All over," said Ott.

"So, you mean, like *multiple* stab wounds," said the man.

"I mean, all over," Ott repeated.

"Jesus," Fran said. "like that Chinese thing?"

"Exactly."

SIXTEEN

It was 5:25 a.m. when Crawford and Ott left DeeDee Dunwoody's house on Westminster. They decided there wasn't much point in going back to their respective homes and trying to grab three or four hours of sleep. First of all, they had too much to do. Crawford needed to interview the woman Rose Clarke had told him about, Janny Hasleiter, and Ott wanted to go see if there were any security cameras at Sean Rush's Nomad. The reason for that, as Ott told Crawford, was that at one point in his time there with DeeDee, he felt that a man was paying undue attention to them, but he'd had more important things to concentrate on at the time: like his dancing and keeping a good flow to the conversation with the woman he was falling for so quickly.

Lastly and most importantly, they had to interview DeeDee when she had recovered sufficiently to talk. Would she have a description of the perpetrator? What had he said to her or asked her? Once they had answers to those and a few other questions, they'd know whether DeeDee's torture had something to do with the murder of Antonia von Habsburg. That was their hope, anyway.

*****

At 8:30, Crawford went down to where the Crime Scene Unit cubicles were. Gus Ochoa and Dominica McCarthy were in. He walked past Ochoa's cubicle and into Dominica's, which was as clean and neat as Crawford's office was cluttered. Dominica was nursing a large coffee from her neighborhood coffee shop up in the Northwood section of West Palm.

"Top of the morning, Mac," Crawford said.

He called her "Mac," short for McCarthy, when they were on the job, "Dominica" when he was being formal, and "babe" when they were alone.

"Hey Charlie," she said. "How's it going?"

"Mort and I had a little excitement in the middle of the night." He decided not to go into the Ott-DeeDee connection. "Know what *lingchi* is?"

"Sure. That Chinese knife torture thing."

"Well, someone did it to a woman over on Westminster Street last night."

Dominica cocked her head. "Jesus, really? But that's in West Palm, right?"

Crawford nodded.

"Why'd you catch it?"

"Mort knew the vic. A woman. She called him right after it happened."

"How's she doing?"

"She's alive. Got cut up pretty bad, though."

"Christ," Dominica said, shaking her head. "You want me to go check out the scene?"

"Yeah, if you would. I want to clear it with West Palm first."

"Gotcha. This have anything to do with the von Habsburg murder? I mean, two really nasty tortures?"

"That's an accurate description. The connection occurred to us, but we have nothing definitive yet."

"I mean, sounds like it might, right?"

"Yeah, it does," Crawford said. "You pretty busy?"

"Nah, things have slowed down."

"Nothing wrong with that, huh?"

Dominica smiled up at him. "No, but I'm like you, I like action."

*****

Rose Clarke had gotten Janny Hasleiter's cell phone number from the Poinciana Club. Only members could get other members' phone numbers and emails. So, Crawford dialed the cell number, expecting the usual routine: leaving five messages, then a pointed threat, before getting a call back.

Miraculously, though, a woman answered on the first ring. "Hello, darling," she said.

"Ms. Hasleiter?"

"Ah, no, this is her friend, Ms. Shamburg, but you can call me Lulu. Who's this?"

"My name's Charlie Crawford, Palm Beach Police Department."

"Well, hello, Officer. You want Janny?"

"Yes, please, is she there?"

"Yes, she is." The woman lowered her voice and dialed up a sexy purr. "Are you in uniform, Officer? One of those sexy blue uniforms with the silver buttons?"

"Well, actually—"

"Because Janny and I are skinny dipping here in Janny's pool and maybe you'd like to—"

"Gimme that, Lulu!" Crawford heard in the background, then another woman's voice came on. "Who is this?" the other voice demanded.

"Name's Crawford, I'm a Palm Beach homicide detective. Is this Ms. Hasleiter?"

"It is. What do you want?"

"I'd like to talk to you about your friend, Antonia von Habsburg. I'm one of the detectives investigating her murder."

There was a pause. "Ms. Hasleiter?" he said.

"Yes, I'm here. I'm checking my schedule," she said. "Can you come right now? Because tomorrow I'm flying out to Los Angeles, and tonight I have a dinner."

Not only first ring, but she was actually being cooperative.

"Sure. I can meet with you now. Where are you?"

"The Bristol. Penthouse A."

The Bristol was actually close to where he lived. "Your friend mentioned something about a pool. Are you down at the pool there?"

"No, no, we're at my pool… outside my apartment."

"Okay, I'll be there in ten minutes."

He heard the voice of the first woman, Lulu, in the background. "Don't forget your Speedo, Officer!"

The Bristol was a new, ultra-sleek building on South Flagler Drive not far from where Crawford had recently bought a condo. His building was called the Trianon. The Bristol, practically next door, put his building to shame. He had heard—from Rose probably—that a condo there had recently sold for thirty million dollars. Something told him it might just have been Janny Hasleiter's.

He walked out the back entrance of the station, got into his Crown Vic, and made the short drive over the middle bridge to the Bristol. What killed Crawford was how half of the condo buildings, not to mention office buildings, restaurants, and stores in West Palm made it seem like they were actually in Palm Beach. He remembered seeing a woman walking past the station with a blue and white canvas bag that said, *The Bristol, Palm Beach.* Well, no, actually it's in West Palm and there was a good-sized body of water called the Intracoastal in between the two. Not to mention, the Palm Beach Airport was in West Palm. Ditto the Palm Beach Zoo. *The Palm Beach Post* was in West Palm. The list went on. It seemed no one wanted to 'fess up that they were domiciled in lowly West Palm Beach.

He parked at the Bristol, went inside and stepped up to the stylishly-dressed woman at the main desk. He told her Ms. Hasleiter was expecting him, and she directed him to the elevator.

Janny Hasleiter met Crawford at the front door of her apartment in a fluffy white terry cloth robe and blue flip-flops. She looked to be in her mid-forties, had long, dark, shiny hair, and, something told Crawford, a well-toned body underneath the bathrobe. Crawford walked into the apartment, which seemed to have glass walls on all four sides. He got a quick glimpse looking east over Palm Beach and to the ocean beyond. It was what they used to call a million-dollar view. But now, it was more like a thirty-million-dollar view.

"Well," Janny said, after they'd done their introductions, "might as well work on our tans while you pepper me with questions." She led him through the luxurious apartment, dominated by white furniture and what appeared to be eighteen- to twenty-foot-high ceilings and out to the terrace and pool.

Crawford shaded his eyes from the sun.

And there in a micro red polka-dot bikini, stretched out in a double chaise lounge, was a woman who could only be the provocatively-talking Ms. Shamburg. She was blond, zaftig, and tan. Late thirties, he figured. Around his age.

"Aww," she said seeing Crawford, "no uniform with nice, shiny buttons."

"Sorry, I'm a detective, ma'am. We just wear regular clothes."

"And wear them *so* well," Lulu said.

"Christ, Lulu, leave the poor man alone," Janny said. "He just got here."

"I was just—"

Janny cut her off with a look.

Crawford was not surprised to see a half-empty bottle of Whispering Angel rosé on a table next to Lulu.

"Can I get you something to drink, Detective?" Janny asked.

"Ah, I'd love a Coke, please," Crawford said.

"What a sport," said Lulu. "Come on, it's after twelve."

Some people in Palm Beach, Crawford had noticed, started cocktail hour at six, others at five, but for the hardcore—noon.

Crawford glanced at Janny, who seemed to be waiting to see if Lulu had shamed him into changing his order. "Thanks. Just a Coke."

Janny walked back inside.

Lulu patted the side of the chaise lounge she was in. "Come have a seat."

"Thanks, ma'am," he said, pointing to a teak chair next to her, "I'm just going to sit there."

"Aww," she pouted, "and Detective, lose the 'ma'am', okay? Makes me feel like a fossil."

Crawford nodded. Closer up, she looked to be around forty-five and, clearly, no stranger to cosmetology.

"So you want to talk to Janny about Antonia?" Lulu said, pouring the last of the rosé into a plastic wine glass.

"Yes, did you know her?" he asked, remembering that tipsy women had always been a good source of information in the past.

"I just met her once. Terrible what happened to her."

Crawford nodded. "Did you know anything about her?"

Lulu took a quick pull on her wine. "Just that she had a lot of men in her life. Lucky girl. But, I guess a lot of that had to do with her job."

Janny walked back out onto the terrace with Crawford's Coke and a red drink in her other hand.

"You doing a Bloody?" Lulu asked.

"Uh-huh," Janny said.

"What a good idea. Think I'll switch over."

Janny handed the Coke to Crawford. "Here you go. What's your first name anyway? *Detective* has too many syllables."

"Charlie."

"Good. Only two," said Janny. "So what do you want to know about Antonia?"

Crawford glanced over at Lulu.

Janny shook her head and lowered her voice. "Don't worry about her. She'll forget everything in ten minutes."

Lulu laughed. "I heard that," she said. "Actually, only five."

Crawford eyes came back to Janny. "I'm told you were a pretty good friend of Ms. von Habsburg. Did she ever say anything to you about anybody she was scared of? Someone she may have feared? Or who may have threatened her? Anyone who, I don't know, wanted to do harm to her?"

"That's all kind of redundant, isn't it, Charlie?" Janny said. "I was actually a very good friend of hers. I always felt she was in kind of a dangerous business. I mean, it could have been a lot of people."

"What do you mean? A dangerous business, how so?"

"Well, she told me about this one man"—she paused to take a sip of her Bloody Mary—"who told her he was going to destroy her business. What happened was one of her girls got him drunk, took all his credit cards and charged up a hundred thousand dollars' worth of jewelry. Antonia, who always took great pride in how well she vetted the girls, was going to fire her anyway, but by then the damage was done and the girl was long gone."

"Any other incidents like that?" Crawford asked.

"Let's see, I'm sure you know about Luther King by now," Janny said. "He always strikes me as a man... I don't know, capable of bad things. Of course, it doesn't get any worse than that rat thing."

"Yeah, that was *so* horrible," Lulu piped in from her double chaise.

"Then, there's her ex-husband, LV. Figured he got screwed out of what was rightfully his. Saw his piece shrinking and shrinking. Antonia always told me that he was getting more than he deserved, but I don't know."

"Anybody else?"

Janny looked off in the distance, then her eyes returned to Crawford's. "Okay, and you didn't hear this from me,"—she glanced over at Lulu—"and if you tell anyone I'll kill you,"—Lulu put up her hands and shook her head mightily—"but I heard something through the grapevine that Antonia might have blackmailed a few men."

"Blackmailed them? What do you mean? How?"

"Telling them she was going to tell their wives about their little... indiscretions, unless they paid her a lot more money. But I want to make it clear, this was just a rumor. And if you put all the rumors in Palm Beach together you might end up with one whole truth. I also heard, she had photos too... very, very graphic photos."

"Was one of the men"—he glanced over at Lulu who had just stood up, and lowered his voice—"a man named Courtie Hiller?"

Out of the corner of his eye, he saw Lulu peel off her top. He mustered his willpower and didn't turn to look.

Janny nodded. "He was one."

"Who else?"

Janny sighed. "You know, I'd better not say."

"Ms. Hasleiter—"

"Janny."

"Janny. If I'm going to find your friend's killer, I really need your help."

She sighed again as, in the background, Lulu jumped into the pool.

"Finding her killer's not going to bring her back," Janny said.

"True. But don't you think *she'd* like her killer to be found?"

Janny glanced up. "Up there in heaven, you mean?"

"Wherever."

She lowered her voice. "George Morrison," she said, "the president of the Poinciana."

"Really?"

"Yes. They both had one thing in common. George and Courtie, that is."

"Antonia's girls?"

"Well, that too. But I was going to say, rich wives. Without them they'd have to go get a job or something."

"Hey Charlie!" Lulu called out from the shallow end of the pool.

He turned. The view was dominated by Lulu's bronzed and rather large breasts. She was beckoning him with a finger. He turned away.

"Oh, don't be so damn prudish," Lulu said.

"I'm conducting an interview," he said, keeping his focus on Janny.

"Okay, Charlie, interview's over," Janny said. "Take a swim with us. Party a little."

But Crawford stood up to go. "Sorry, I forgot my Speedo."

SEVENTEEN

"Thank you for meeting with me," he said to Janny, then turning. "Nice to meet you, Lulu."

Janny took a step toward him.

"Come on, stick around," she said. "Trade that Coke in for a man's drink."

He flashed to what Rose had said about Janny. He remembered the word *voracious*. Time to go.

He glanced down at his watch. "I really appreciate everything you've told me and assure you I will keep it all between us, but I've got a meeting with my boss that I can't be late for."

Awkwardly, he stuck out his hand to shake with Janny. "Let me know if you think of anything else relating to Antonia."

She took one step closer but didn't shake his hand. "You're very welcome, Charlie. And we'll still be here after your made-up meeting with your boss."

*****

He got out of there as fast as he could.

In the elevator down, his cell phone rang.

He imagined it was Janny asking, *Sure you don't want to reconsider?*

But it was Ott. "What's up?" Crawford asked.

"They let me speak to DeeDee at the hospital. She said we could come over. What are you doing?"

"You won't believe it. Tell you later," Crawford said. "I'll be there in five minutes."

"Make it ten."

"You got it."

*****

Crawford and Ott knew their way around Good Samaritan Hospital. They had been frequent visitors over the years, including when Rose Clarke was broadsided by a hit-and-run driver the year before. It had been intentional, and eventually they'd tracked down the driver. He was in prison now, no longer a threat to Rose.

DeeDee Dunwoody was on the same floor where Rose had stayed and, Crawford wasn't sure, but it might have even been the same room.

They walked in and DeeDee looked up from a paperback she had been reading. She had gauze bandages covering her face and arms. All you could see of her face was her mouth, nose and eyes. She had very pretty emerald green eyes.

She put the paperback down on her bed. "Oh, hi, Mort. Thank you for coming. Sorry, I haven't had a chance to put my make-up on yet," she said.

Ott laughed. "So good to see you, DeeDee," he said. "This is my partner, Charlie Crawford."

"Hi, DeeDee," Crawford said with a nod. "How you feeling?"

"Well, I've been better," she said with a sigh. "But… I'm alive,"—she glanced over at Ott—"thanks to you."

"I'd love to take credit, but thanks to the EMTs. They got there really fast."

Ott took out the trusty leather notebook he'd been using for twenty years, and Crawford took out his iPhone, which he took notes on.

Crawford looked at Ott. "Why don't you start it out."

Ott nodded. "So, tell us everything you can, so we can find whoever did this and put him away. What was the first thing you saw or heard?"

"Well, I was sound asleep when a noise woke me up. It was close, in my bedroom. I started to turn on my bedside lamp when I felt a hand on my mouth. A man's voice said something like, 'Don't scream or say a word or you're dead.'"

"That voice… what do you remember about it? Was there an accent or anything distinctive about it at all?" Ott asked.

"Oh God, Mort, I was just scared out of my mind. I didn't notice much… It was a deep voice. No accent or anything like that. Just scary. Kind of monotone."

"Understand," Ott said. "Then what?"

"Then I heard this ripping noise and felt him put something over my eyes. I realized later it was duct tape. After he put it on, he yanked me out of the bed, twisted my arm up around my back and walked me out to the living room. The funny thing was that it sounded like the footsteps of two people behind me. Next thing I remember was him lifting me up and putting me face up on my dining room table."

"Were there any lights on at this point?" Crawford asked.

"No, but he had a flashlight."

"Okay," Ott said, "so you were lying face up on your dining room table. Then what?"

"Do I have to go into all of it?"

"Just what you're comfortable telling us," Ott said.

She paused for a second. "Okay, well, I was wearing these baggy pajamas, um, bra and panties underneath. So, he took the pajamas off, then wrapped duct tape around my waist first, then my ankles, then around my... shoulders."

"Wait, did the duct tape go around you and under the dining room table?" Crawford asked.

"Yes, sorry, I forgot to mention that. Yes, around me *and* the dining room table. So I couldn't move. Plus, he put my hands together and wrapped the tape around my hands so they were... kind of resting on my belly."

"So, obviously you couldn't move," Ott said. "I mean you were duct-taped to the table."

"Yes, I literally couldn't move at all, then..." her eyes closed, as if the horrible memory had come rushing back.

"Take your time," Ott said.

"Yes, we've got as much time as you need," Crawford echoed.

Her eyes went to Ott. "He asked me, in that scary monotone of his, what I told the *detective*—that's what he called you, Mort—about Antonia."

"What did you say?" Ott asked.

"I told him you asked me about the time I was at Antonia's house when the two men and the other woman were there, but he didn't seem much interested in that. Then he asked me if you asked who I thought might have killed Antonia, and I said you never asked me that. You just wanted to know about those two men who were at Antonia's."

"Bob Jones and Courtie Hiller?"

"Yes," she said. "Then he asked me again if I told you who I thought killed her. He said something like, 'Come on, I know he asked you that.' I told him *no*, you definitely did not."

"Then what did he say?"

DeeDee paused for a moment. "This was a little strange... I heard him take a step or two away. My floors are hardwood, as you probably saw. And then I heard someone whispering and, I'm not absolutely sure, but it sounded like a woman."

"Really?" Crawford said. "So then what?"

"I heard a few more footsteps and I'm sure it was the man approaching. He asked me, 'Who do you think did it?' And I said, something like, 'I have no idea at all.' And he said, much louder and more, ah, forcefully this time, 'Goddamn it, tell me who you think did it!' And I really did—and still do—have no idea, but I had to say somebody, so I said, 'Either Luther King or Antonia's husband LV.'"

"And what did he say to that?" Ott asked.

"Nothing," DeeDee said. "He just started to cut me."

EIGHTEEN

"It was so painful," DeeDee said. "After I answered his questions, he put duct tape over my mouth. I could feel blood trickling out of me. I heard dripping, too."

Crawford and Ott did their best not to wince.

"Where did he cut first?" Crawford asked.

"My arm, my forearm actually," she said. "Then further up my arm. Then my face. I was screaming but nothing came out. I didn't feel like he cut really deep, but it was painful. I mean, he just kept doing it. The pain was everywhere."

"How long would you say he did it?"

"I would say fifteen or twenty minutes."

"Oh, that's all," Crawford said.

DeeDee laughed. "That's all? Have you ever had anyone cutting you for fifteen or twenty minutes."

"I am so sorry," Crawford said. "I didn't mean… for some reason I just thought it went on longer than that."

"When he was cutting you," Ott asked. "Did he say anything else?"

"No, and you know what? This was the other strange thing."

"What was?"

"He was humming."

"Humming?" Ott asked.

"Yes, humming. Like someone who was… enjoying their work. It was so bizarre… Oh, also, another thing: he breathed kind of loud, almost a wheeze."

Crawford noted that on his iPhone.

"And the other person who was there. A woman, you think possibly. She never said anything, or he never, you know, had another conversation or anything with her, that you could hear?"

"No, not that I remember. But after a while, I just passed out."

"What do you remember next."

"Coming to, and they were gone. I remember hearing a car out front driving away."

"But you didn't get a look at it."

"No."

"So somehow you got free," Ott said, "and called me."

She nodded. "My hands weren't tied all that tightly with the duct tape, so I just kept turning them from side to side, pulling them, twisting them and finally I got them free. Then I reached up and ripped the tape off my mouth and eyes, then the tape from around my shoulders and got free. Then I sat up and did the same with the tape around my waist, then my ankles. It was really bloody and I felt very weak, but finally I was able to get off the dining room table and went and called you on my cell phone. Then I guess I passed out again."

"That's amazing," Crawford said. "With all that loss of blood you were able to do that."

"*Really* amazing," Ott said. "I can't believe you got yourself free." He blew her a kiss. "I'd come over there and give you a kiss but I'd end up with a mouth full of gauze."

She started to laugh, then cried out in pain. "Don't make me laugh, Mort. It hurts everywhere."

NINETEEN

It was 1:45 p.m. now and Crawford had called George Morrison, the president of the Poinciana, earlier that morning and made an appointment to see him at his office on Royal Palm Way at two o'clock. He wanted to get to him before three when, as Rose had described, it was time to go "pound rum-dumbs" at the Poinciana Club bar.

Morrison's office was on the third floor next to one of the bank buildings on Royal Palm Way. The door to his office read: "Morrison Holdings, Ltd." Crawford didn't know exactly what a "holding" was but guessed it might be real estate, stocks and bonds, or maybe an orange grove or cattle ranch somewhere.

The office was small. A reception area, manned by a young brunette with stylish yellow-framed glasses and two uncomfortable-looking chairs facing her desk.

Crawford nodded at her. "Hello. Detective Crawford to see Mr. Morrison," he said.

"Yes, sir, I'll tell him you're here," she said, with an eyebrow flutter. "I'm Carolyn, by the way."

"Thank you, Carolyn."

A few moments later, a man with a prodigious pot belly, a handsome face highlighted by bright blue eyes, and reading glasses perched on top of his head lumbered out. Crawford's first reaction was a strange one: *how can a man with a gut like that—he had to have at least a fifty-five-inch waist—have sex?*

Morrison shook hands with him. "Come on in, Detective. I just got off a conference call."

"Thanks for seeing me on short notice."

"Hey, no problem. I always found it to be a good policy to be on good terms with you guys. Might help if you ever see me weaving down South County late one night."

Crawford didn't want to say, *it wouldn't*, so he simply nodded.

Morrison pointed to a chair facing his desk. He went around his desk and sat facing Crawford. "So, what is it you need to know?"

Crawford was dying to know about the naked Twister games at Morrison's cottage on the ocean but didn't go there. "I'd like you to tell me everything you know about Antonia von Habsburg."

"That's a pretty general question, Detective."

"I know it is. I just wanted to start out like that, then I'll narrow it down to more specific questions."

"Okay, well, I'll start by saying Antonia was, by no means, a typical member at the Poinciana."

Crawford nodded. "I kind of knew that, but exactly what do you mean?"

"Well, for starters, she kind of had this funny accent"—he laughed—"which was hardly the accent of an Austrian aristocrat. Second, she ran a business—she called it an 'executive headhunter' business—but I'm not so sure that's what it was."

"Not so sure... What do you mean?"

Morrison put one foot on his desk. "Charlie—you mind if I call you Charlie?"

"Not at all."

"So I looked into you, 'cause it's not every day a detective comes here to chat me up, and I found out you're a pretty sharp guy. Former New York hero detective, solved just about every murder case you ever worked on. Well, Antonia was killed six days ago, which means you probably know a hell of a lot by now. Got certain suspects on your list, ruled out other ones, know just about everything there is to know about Antonia von Habsburg. Am I right?"

"I know a fair amount, yes."

"Exactly, so an 'executive headhunter' she wasn't. A girl-provider was what she was. An... executive pimp, you might say," Morrison said, laughing at his word choice.

"Okay, so the question is, how did she ever get into the Poinciana? I mean last time I checked, you guys were all about doctors, lawyers, hedge-fund guys and, well, billionaires."

Morrison laughed. "You know what? I like you, Charlie. You're no bullshit," he said. "See, the reality is, Antonia had two members in her court who were very powerful. One was Janny Hasleiter, a name I'm sure you know by now—"

Oh boy, do I ever. "I interviewed her earlier today."

"I bet that was an experience. At her pool?"

"How'd you know?"

"That's like her office. She wearing anything?"

Crawford had to fight a blush. "Yes."

Morrison laughed again. "That didn't sound like much of a 'yes' to me."

"So who was the other powerful person?"

Morrison pointed at his chest. "Me."

"And why were you so supportive of her as a candidate for the Poinciana?"

"Because I'm so sick of these tight-asses from Greenwich and Locust Valley and Lake Forest. I mean, Christ, give me a little diversity. Everybody at the club's just so damn... *same-old, same-old.* Know what I mean? Like a production line of men and women in their pink pants or Lilly Pulitzer whatever. I mean, don't get me wrong, I got a pair of pink pants hanging in my closet, but all we have at the Poinciana are these damn conservative Republicans, and all they care about is their portfolio going up and their handicap going down. Christ, don't get me started. So, when I came in, suddenly we got a Turkish guy applying who's got a chain of urgent care medical drive-ins, a Russian who I guess you'd call an oligarch, not that I'm totally sure what an oligarch is—"

Crawford tried to hide his surprise. "They got into the Poinciana?"

Morrison sighed. "No, they got shot down, but at least we broadened the field of applicants a little."

"So you were, obviously, solidly behind Antonia."

"Sure was. I liked her spunk. I liked the fact that she was outspoken. I liked just about everything about her. I felt she'd make a hell of a good addition."

"Mr. Morrison, what else can you tell me about her? Or, specifically, your relationship with her?"

Morrison put his other leg up on his desk. "I know where you're going with this. Did I ever have sex with her or any of her girls is what you're asking, right?"

He was almost too direct for Crawford. "That *is* where I was going."

"I know that's what everyone thought, and that was the rumor going around. Just like those wild parties at my cottage after Friday night dances. And you know what I'm gonna do with that question?"

"What?"

"Plead the fifth."

"Mr. Morrison, I've got to tell you, that seems like an admission to me."

"Okay, that's fine with me. Assume it's an admission. Let's leave it like that, because we both know that any of that stuff is totally irrelevant to you finding Antonia's killer."

Crawford chewed on that for a moment. "You know what, I think you're right about that."

"Oh, I just remembered something else. I heard from a pretty reliable source that Antonia's ex-husband, I can't remember his name—"

"It's LV Wurfel. Larry Victor, to be exact."

"That's it. Anyway, I heard he's still pretty involved. Like a silent but very critical partner."

"Really? Where'd you get that?"

"I forget, but someone with credibility."

"Will you give me a call if you remember? My source said he's pretty much out of the picture."

"Yeah, sure, I'll let you know if I come up with *my* source," Morrison said, getting to his feet. "And on that note, Charlie, it's cocktail hour at the Poinciana for old George. Care to join me?"

Crawford smiled as he got to his feet. "That's the best offer I've had all day,"—actually it wasn't—"but I'm afraid I've got to go find me a killer."

TWENTY

While Crawford was questioning George Morrison, Ott drove to Sean Rush's Nomad restaurant on Dixie Highway in West Palm. He arrived at one thirty and went up to the bartender. "Hi," he said, "is the manager around, by any chance?"

"Well, there isn't really a manager, but the owner's here," the bartender said. "I remember you… you were here last night, right?"

"Yes, I was."

The bartender looked quizzical. "Well, was there any problem or anything?"

"Oh, no, I just need to speak to the owner."

"Okay, just a sec," the bartender went around the bar and disappeared into the back. Thirty seconds later, Ott saw him walking back toward the bar, a short man in his forties leading the way.

The short man walked up to Ott and smiled. "Yes, sir, I'm Sean Rush, can I help you? Everything all right last night?"

"Oh yeah, it was fine," Ott said. "My name's Ott, I'm a Palm Beach detective. I notice you have a security camera." He pointed to the camera mounted above the front door. "Would you mind if I have a look at the footage from last night?"

"You want to check out your moves on the dance floor?" Rush said with a smile. "I remember you. Fred Astaire's got nothing on you."

"Well, thanks," Ott said. "But, actually it's business."

"Business?" Rush said, a little alarmed.

"Something I'm working on. A case," Ott said, eager not to get into it.

"Sure," Rush said. "I can give you access to it. You want a place where you can look it over?"

"Yes, that would be good."

"No problem. I've got an office in the back you can use."

"Oh, great. I'd appreciate that."

*****

It took a while, but Ott finally found what he was looking for. It was a man in his sixties dressed in a tan suit and a turquoise tie, who seemed to be spending an inordinate amount of time watching DeeDee and him. The man was sitting alone at a table facing the dance floor but kept turning to look at him and DeeDee's table when they weren't dancing. Ott had noticed him the night before, but hadn't thought much of it. He took out his iPhone and clicked a few shots of the man from Sean Rush's monitor. It was small but he could enlarge it.

He walked out of the office to see if Rush could ID the man. Rush was behind the bar talking to two women. Rush spotted Ott, kissed one of the women on the cheek, and walked over.

"Find what you were looking for?"

"Yes, I did," Ott said, holding up a photo on his iPhone. "I wondered if you can identify this man?"

"Sure can. That's Luther King, playboy of the Western world. Comes here pretty regularly. You probably saw his limo out front last night."

Ott remembered seeing a long limo sticking out way past its parking space. And then he flashed back to Crawford describing his somewhat less than satisfying interview with Luther King. The man so intent on making the billionaires' list.

"Oh yeah, now that you mention it. What do you know about him?"

"Well, I'm sure you can respect the fact that I owe a certain loyalty to my customers,"—Ott nodded—"but Luther's a man who likes the ladies. I think I'll just leave it at that."

"He lives in Palm Beach, right?" He seemed to remember Crawford telling him on Middle Road.

"Yeah, over there somewhere."

"Was he here alone last night?"

Rush cocked his head. "You know, I'm actually not sure."

But Ott could tell he knew.

"Why are you so interested in Luther?"

Ott smiled. His turn. "I'm sure you can respect the fact that I can't go into much detail about my cases."

"Touché," Rush said. "I certainly can."

Ott put his hand out. "Well, I really appreciate you allowing me to use that office and letting me see that tape."

Rush shook his hand. "You're very welcome, Detective," he said, giving Ott a light pat on his shoulder. "And, may I say, sir, you have great taste in women."

TWENTY-ONE

Crawford called Courtie Hiller a third time, and this time Hiller answered.

"Yes, Detective," he said, irritably. "You know, I've already spoken to your colleague, Detective Ott… and, if I may say so, it was a less than satisfying experience."

"I'm sorry to hear that, Mr. Hiller. I'll try to make mine as satisfying as possible."

That didn't seem to satisfy Hiller. "What do you need to ask me that he hasn't asked me already?"

"Where are you at the moment, Mr. Hiller?"

"Classic Bookshop on South County. I was just about to leave."

"Perfect. Do you know where the Palm Beach Police station is?"

"Sure. That yellow, Spanish-style building."

"Can you stop by after you leave there?"

Hiller groaned. "Oh, Christ. Just what I need is my friends seeing me walk into the police station."

"Tell you what: there's a little park in front of the building, next to a fountain. Meet me there," Crawford said.

"Okay, I'll be there in a few minutes."

✳✳✳✳✳

Crawford was seated on a bench where he often had his lunch when he didn't go to Green's Pharmacy. Usually he'd buy an overpriced, undersized sandwich from a place just down the street whose clientele consisted of either rich Palm Beachers or tourists who fully expected to pay a fortune for two pieces of bread and something skimpy in between just to set foot on the sacred island.

In any case, it was a pleasant enough spot and a few minutes later, along came a man in yellow shorts, a blue Vineyard Vines sports shirt and loafers—sockless, of course.

He walked up to Crawford. "Detective Crawford?"

"Hello, Mr. Hiller, thanks for coming."

"Can we make this quick?" No handshake, no *nice ta meet ya*, no nothing… except a colossal scowl.

"Sure. I think we can." Crawford dived right in. "Did Antonia von Habsburg blackmail you?"

Hiller, on his feet, looked suddenly a little wobbly. "What in God's name are you talking about?"

"Exactly what I asked. Did she blackmail you? I'm told by a reliable source you made a large withdrawal from a bank account. Maybe to pay von Habsburg to keep quiet about a woman you were… let's just say, on intimate terms with."

Crawford, who prided himself on double-checking things before he made an assertion, had decided, pretty much spur-of-the-moment, that he would simply wing this one. See what came out of it.

Hiller folded his arms and stood up as straight as he could. "That, it just so happens, is patently untrue. Every word of it."

"So you didn't withdraw a large sum of money from a bank account of yours?"

Hiller glanced down at his loafers.

"Because I can get a judge to issue a court order to check your bank accounts." That was a bit of a long shot, Crawford knew.

"What the hell does my banking have to do with you?"

"A lot, if it has to do with my murder investigation."

Hiller sighed, exhibiting all the classic signs of a man who had little or no time for dealing with an inquiring, pain-in-the-ass cop. "All right. I'm going to come clean with you."

"Please do."

"So you'll leave me alone in the future."

Crawford just nodded.

"I have a gambling… issue."

"I'm sorry to hear that," Crawford said, "but to the tune of a million dollars?"

Hiller started scratching his chest like he wanted to rub the Vineyard Vines logo right off his shirt. "More."

"Do you mind if I ask… gambling as in going to Las Vegas or Monte Carlo, gambling as in betting on sports—"

"The latter. Horses, football games, baseball, soccer, hockey, tennis, you name it. But I finally did something about it. Haven't bet anything in almost a month."

"Gamblers Anonymous?"

"Something like it. I don't really want to go into it."

"I understand."

The man was either very quick on his feet or telling the truth. Crawford's guess was the latter.

"So, just to make sure I'm totally clear, you never gave any money to Antonia von Habsburg—"

"Not one red cent."

"Okay," Crawford said, pretty certain he could double check Hiller's gambling story somehow.

In any case, the interview was over. Crawford had heard enough. "Well, I appreciate you coming by, Mr. Hiller. I don't have any more questions."

Hiller nodded. "Okay. So, I trust everything we've just discussed—"

"—is between you and me… and my partner."

"That's what I was worried about, your partner."

"Don't be. We need to be very discreet in this business. And we are."

*****

Crawford went back to his office and placed a call to his friend David Balfour, considered to be one of Palm Beach's most eligible bachelors, though Crawford knew that he had been seeing one woman for a while.

"Hey, Charlie," Balfour answered, "what's new with you?"

"Not much. Work more, golf less. If you got a few minutes, I'd like to ask you a couple questions."

"Sure. Fire away."

"You told me once you have a guy you go to when you want to place a bet. Super Bowl, Kentucky Derby, World Series, whatever."

"Sure do. You want to bet on something?"

"Nah. Whenever I do, I always lose my shirt."

"I hear ya. The guy's name is Albie. You want his number?"

"Yeah, please."

"Just so happens, I got it memorized." And he reeled it off.

"Second thing is—I don't know why I didn't ask you this before—but what do you know about Antonia von Habsburg?"

"The *countess?* I always called her that when I ran into her, and she kinda liked it. So, Antonia… Antonia was one-of-a-kind. I liked her. She was a no-bullshit woman. Well, actually she was *all* bullshit, the whole von Habsburg thing, I mean. But no bullshit in speaking her mind. Always did what she said she was going to do, too."

"My kind of woman. So, my standard question: is there anyone you can think of who might have wanted to kill her?"

"You know, I've thought about that a fair amount after it happened. I haven't really come up with anybody. I'm sure by now you've figured out that the von Habsburg empire—hers, that is—was a lot more than her being a headhunter and a matchmaker, I forget what it was called—"

"Distinguished Consorts."

Balfour chuckled. "Yeah, gal had a way with words, too."

"What more was there?" Crawford asked.

"Well, let's see, there was 'the oldest profession in the world,' which I'm sure you know all about."

"A very, very high-end 'oldest profession in the world.'"

"Well, it *is* Palm Beach." Balfour said. "You know about the young bucks, too, right?"

"Young bucks?"

"Yes, Charlie. In case you haven't noticed, there are a lot of rich older women in Palm Beach, who either made it on their own or, in most cases, had rich husbands who died."

"Matter of fact, I had noticed that. Keep going."

"Yeah, they hang out at the Leopard Lounge at the Chesterfield. Sometimes on the early shift at Taboo. I see a lot of them at the Poinciana… So anyway, here's a real shocker, they get horny, too. And Antonia, who was never asleep at the wheel, saw an opportunity there."

"Young dudes for old babes."

"Exactly."

"So what more do you know about it?"

"Nothing firsthand. This is all via the Palm Beach rumor mill."

"Which is always cranking twenty-four/seven."

"Including Sundays and holidays," Balfour said.

"That's good info," Crawford told him. "I don't exactly know where it takes me, but there's probably something there. You wouldn't happen to know who any of these 'young bucks' are, by any chance?"

"Can't help you with that, Charlie. But I can ask around… discreetly, of course. See if I come up with some names."

"I would really appreciate that," Crawford said. "So, my last question is about you: are you still going out with…"

"Hadley? Nah, she cut me loose. Didn't really give me a good reason why,"—a long sigh—"I don't know, Charlie, sometimes I wonder about myself."

"Don't. She just wasn't the right one. Maybe you should try Rose again. You guys had a pretty good run, as I remember."

"Nah, she called me 'vacuous' once. A 'libertine' another time. I had to look that one up."

"What's it mean?"

"Come on, Charlie, you went to Dartmouth."

"I have no clue."

"It means a playboy, a roué. Another one I had to look up."

"What's wrong with that?"

"It was the word she used with it that hurt."

"Which was?"

"She called me a 'self-indulgent libertine.'"

Crawford laughed. "Well, I guess you're right. Maybe she's not the one."

TWENTY-TWO

Crawford clicked off with Balfour and dialed the number of his bookie, Albie.

"Prudent Wagers, Albie speaking."

"Yes, hi, Albie, my name's Charlie Crawford. I'm a friend of David Balfour. He gave me your number."

"Any friend of David's is a friend of mine."

"That's good to know. I'm a Palm Beach Police detective, just so you know."

Pause. "Oh."

"A very discreet Palm Beach detective. I just have one quick question for you."

"Is it going to get me in trouble?"

"No. I just want to know if you know the name Courtie Hiller?"

"Courtie the Whale? You bet I know him."

"So, he's like a big bettor?"

"Yeah, with me and a couple other guys around town. Dude'll bet on a tiddlywinks game."

Crawford laughed. "That's all I need to know. Oh, one more question: since when is wagering 'prudent'?"

Another pause. "I don't know, I just liked the sound of it."

*****

Ott was back at DeeDee Dunwoody's room at Good Samaritan Hospital.

"How you feelin'?" he asked. He almost added *honey*, but decided not to after only one date.

"It's only been a couple of hours since I saw you last, Mort," she said. "I'm not that quick a healer."

He chuckled. "But, it's not any worse, right?"

"No, they've been keeping me pretty doped up," she murmured.

"You look like a mummy, you know. A mummy with beautiful eyes."

And a sexy mouth, he started to say, but bit his tongue.

"Thank you, Mort. That's very sweet of you," she said. "Have you guys found out anything?"

"I went to Nomad, where we were last night. What can you tell me about Luther King?"

Her eyes closed for a moment. "Oh God, what about him?"

"He was there last night. At Nomad."

"He was? I never saw him. He must have been… lurking in the shadows. Like Dracula."

"Tell me about him."

"He asked me out once. Said Antonia gave him my number. He sounded nice on the phone, like a gentleman."

"But?"

"He took me out to a nice place, Bricktops. We had a drink, then a glass of wine and next thing I know, I feel his hand on my leg. I got up and bolted. That was enough Luther King for one lifetime."

"That was a little aggressive."

"Aggressive? Oh my God. Then I found out later that he and Antonia had gone out. But after a while, Antonia dumped him. I guess she gave him my number, maybe to get him off her back… so to speak."

Ott laughed, and so did DeeDee.

"Oh God, that was painful," she said.

"You okay?"

"Yup. It's just I've got these cuts on my stomach."

"No more jokes. So that's the whole story on Luther King?"

"Yeah, that's pretty much it. Except he called me again after what happened and apologized. But no way was I ever going out with that horny old bastard again. No matter how rich he is."

"Was that something he told you about? Being rich, I mean."

"Oh, boy, did he ever. Before he finished off his first drink, he told me he was a billionaire. About how he should have been included

114

in some article in the *Glossy* about all the billionaires in Palm Beach, but there was a misprint or something."

"Between that and the hand on your thigh, I get why you beat it out of there."

"Leg, not thigh. If it was my thigh, I would have kicked the wrinkly, old bastard in the... you know where."

Ott thought for a second. "Well, guess I'll never try that."

"Ha. You're different, Mort."

He smiled. "Anyway, I was just thinking maybe there was some connection between him like... almost stalking you at Nomad and what happened to you later."

She gently shook her head. "My guess is no connection at all. I mean, doing that to me would be a pretty extreme reaction to one bad date, don't you think?"

"I tend to agree with you," Ott said. "But I intend to have a nice long conversation with the man nevertheless."

TWENTY-THREE

Ott found out where Luther King lived and just went straight to his house.

A short man—Filipino was Ott's guess—opened the front door.

"May I help you, sir?" he asked.

"My name is Ott, detective with the Palm Beach Police Department. Is Mr. King in?"

"Is he expecting you, Detective?"

"Tell him it's important that I speak to him right away."

The short man gave Ott a frown, apparently not pleased about not getting an answer to his question. "Give me a moment," he said.

Ott nodded.

He stepped into the foyer, which was dark and had a funky smell. Before long he heard footsteps. The man following the short man was tall. Tall and frowning and around sixty-five years old. A little like Dracula in his dotage.

"I saw you last night," Luther King said, "with DeeDee. You're a detective?"

Ott nodded. "May I come in, Mr. King?"

"This is fine right here," King said. "What is it you want?"

"Ms. Dunwoody said you two had dinner together a while back," Ott said.

"I have dinner with a lot of women."

And do your grope all of them under the table? Ott was dying to ask. "So, Mr. King, I know you were at Nomad last night. Would you mind telling me where you went after?"

"It's a long list," King said. "I was making my usual rounds. Couple spots on Clematis Street, then I went over to Palm Beach. Finally, just before I was about to call it a night, I got lucky at The Honor Bar."

"Congratulations."

"Yeah, and man was she ever a hottie. Blonde, big whombos-"

"That's great. And can you get people at those places to say they saw you at specific times? Alibis are what I'm looking for."

"I can if I need to, but what the hell do I need an alibi for."

"Mr. King, did you know that DeeDee Dunwoody was seriously assaulted last night?"

King put his hand up to his mouth. "Oh my God, no. That's terrible, how is she?"

"She's in the hospital but she's going to be all right… in time. You know nothing about it?"

"No, not a thing. Please give her my best if you see her."

Ott stared down King for a few long moments.

He wanted so hard for King to be the guy.

But he wasn't. He just knew. And, despite all the things Ott had heard about King, his wishes for DeeDee rang genuinely sincere. Not to mention that Ott had many years of watching and assessing people's reactions to things he told them. King was genuinely surprised at his news about DeeDee, there was no question about it.

Seemed King was guilty of nothing more than unrelenting serial lechery.

Not pretty, but not against the law.

TWENTY-FOUR

For the third time in the past week, Crawford went to LV Wurfel's house on Sunset Road, and for the first time LV wasn't working on his Harley in the garage. So Crawford called him on his cell from his car, and Wurfel picked up right away.

"Hey, Charlie, I've missed our garage meetings," Wurfel said.

"Where are you?"

"Just about to get on an airboat in the Everglades. A little swamp tour with my buddies."

"When are you going to be back?"

"Tomorrow. Why?"

"We need to have another talk."

"About what?"

"You having a bigger role in Distinguished Consorts than you led me to believe and picking up where Antonia left off after she died."

"I told you I was a very minor partner at the time of her death."

"Yeah, *that is* what you told me, but I heard otherwise."

"Don't believe everything you hear, Charlie."

"I don't. When you get back, I want you to stop by the Palm Beach station."

"It would be my honor."

"See you tomorrow," Crawford said. "Watch out for hungry gators."

*****

Five minutes later, Ott stopped by Crawford's office. It was time to compare notes.

118

"So I had an interesting conversation with David Balfour," Crawford said.

"Oh, yeah, what did he have to say?"

"Among other things, that Antonia had a stable of men—'young bucks,' he called them—working for her."

"To service lonely women," Ott said. "That makes sense. That guy Bob Jones told me about women and their 'boy toys.'"

Crawford frowned. "Well, why didn't you tell me about it?"

"'Cause what he told me had nothing to do with Antonia von Habsburg. He was talking about guys, in general—like tennis and golf pros—who'd meet older women and, you know, hook up for a nooner or something. Antonia's name never came up in the conversation."

"Well, with Balfour it did."

"Which makes sense, because why just provide women for men? Why not the other way around, too?"

"Exactly. It was the first time I'd heard of it, though," Crawford said. "Another thing Balfour told me was that LV was a lot more involved in the whole operation than he claims he was."

"Well, when you think about it, why would he admit he was even involved at all?"

"Good question. I just bought it. What he said, I mean."

"That's unlike you, Charlie."

"I know, I'm slipping. What about you? Anything new?"

Ott told him about going to Nomad and finding out about Luther King being there and how DeeDee totally discounted King as anything more than a charter member of the Low-life Lechers of America club.

"Jibes with my take of the guy," Crawford said as his cell phone rang.

He looked at his display. It was a cop named Rob Shaw, who somehow had been blessed with the nickname Rude.

"Rude, what's up?"

"This is the weirdest thing I've ever come across, Charlie. You're the first guy I thought of to run it by."

"I guess I'm supposed to be honored?"

"I'll let you be the judge. Can I come down to your office?"

"Sure, I'm here with Ott."

"I'll be right there," Shaw said and clicked off.

"What's that about?" Ott asked.

"Beats the shit out of me. Shaw wants to tell us about something... weird."

Shaw walked in. "No," he said, "I want to *show* you something weird. Exhibit A." A young, tattooed man in his mid-twenties trailed along behind Shaw. "This is Nickie. Tell these guys your story, Nickie."

Nickie looked embarrassed at best, mortified at worst. "Well, uh, I was in bed last night. Sleeping. And next thing I know I heard this noise and feel this pain and see a guy with this yellow gun 'cause I left my bathroom light on."

"Yellow gun? Sounds like maybe a Taser," Ott said to Crawford.

Crawford nodded. "Then what?"

"Another guy behind him had like this big needle. Next thing I know, um, it was lights out. Then, I wake up later and it's morning. I look down and I've got these," —he pointed at his neck and his chest—"these tattoos all over me."

"Wait a minute, they weren't there before?" Ott said. "You're saying they tattooed you while you were out?"

Nickie was a good-looking kid with chiseled features, long dark hair and a fashionable three-day growth. On his neck was a tattoo— more like a banner—that read, "Loose," an image of two lips, "sink," then an image of two clipper ships. Then, on his forehead was a second tattoo of a large open mouth and below it the words, "Snitches get stitches."

"What the hell?" Ott said, his eyes boring into Nickie's. "You gotta have some idea what this is about."

Nickie looked down at his shoe tops, which, in this case, were expensive-looking kiltie tassel moccasins. "I got a pretty good idea," he said, almost in a whisper.

"What?" Crawford asked, thinking that Rude Rob Shaw was right: this was about the weirdest crime he had ever run across. *The question*, Crawford wondered, *was, what would the charge for something like this be?* He didn't have a clue. Something in the assault family?

Nickie looked up at him, then Ott. "It's kind of a long story."

"We got time," Crawford said, because he had a hunch—based on no hard evidence at all—that this might actually be related to the murder of Antonia von Habsburg.

Nickie's eyes shot back down to his shoe tops again. "Well... I don't even know where to begin."

"Take your time; no rush, son," Ott said.

"Okay. So, I've been having this relationship with this woman. She's older, see, and—"

"Let me stop you right there," Crawford said, cutting to the chase. "Does this have anything to do with a woman named Antonia von Habsburg?"

Nickie scratched the side of his face and smiled. "How'd you know?"

"Just a wild guess," Crawford said. "Keep going."

"Well, so like this woman is very possessive. She's also very, ah, demanding and likes to have a very active sex life. I mean, trust me, it's very hard to keep up with her."

"Let me guess again," Crawford said. "Her name is Janny?"

Nickie shook his head. "Nope. Danielle."

Crawford nodded and signaled for Nickie to continue.

"What I mean by possessive is she wanted me to be available like twenty-four/seven. But hell, man, I've got a job and everything."

"What do you do?" Ott asked.

"I'm assistant tennis pro at the Ocean Club. I'd get fired if I was on round-the-clock call with… the, uh, princess."

"The princess, huh?"

"Yeah, that was what I called her… not to her face."

"How much was the princess paying you, Nickie?" Ott asked.

Nickie batted his long eyelashes like it had suddenly dawned on him that male prostitution was against the law.

"Don't worry, you're not in trouble with us," Crawford said. "We don't care what your arrangement was."

"Well, the fact was, she was paying for my tuition at Palm Beach Atlantic," Nickie said. "See, I dropped out, still got a couple more years to go."

"Yeah, okay," Crawford said. "But what's all this got to do with those tattoos on your face?"

Nickie touched his forehead in distress, as if he had momentarily forgotten they were there. "Am I going to be able to get them removed?"

"I don't know much about tattoos, but I think there are ways to get rid of 'em," Crawford said, though he had no idea.

"I sure hope so. Anyway, she—Danielle—wanted me to act out these… guess you'd call 'em fantasies she had," Nickie said. "This one time she told me she was a casting director in Hollywood. You know, a person who—"

"Yeah, we know what a casting director is," Ott said, impatiently.

"Okay, and she said she could get me a part in this series she was casting. Another time she told me I'd be perfect in a certain role and we had to act out a scene to see whether I'd be right for it."

"Are you sure her name was Danielle?" Crawford asked. "Her real name?"

"That's the name she went by," Nickie said.

"But that could have been like... her stage name?" Ott asked Crawford.

"What did she look like?" Crawford asked. "And how old?"

"Late forties, but looks younger," said Nickie. "Smokin' body for her age, long dark hair, brown eyes."

Ott looked at Crawford.

Crawford nodded to Ott. "Sure sounds like Janny Hasleiter to me," he said, then to Nickie, "But you never heard that name?"

"Janny Hasleiter?"

Crawford nodded.

Nickie shook his head. "Just Danielle. Never said her last name."

Ott had been scrolling on his iPhone,

"Wait a minute," Ott said, showing Nickie his iPhone display, "is this Danielle?"

Nickie nodded. "Yup. Sure is."

It was Janny Hasleiter.

"So this role she wanted you to play," Crawford said. "What was it?"

"Yeah, let's hear more about that," Ott said.

"Well. Actually, there were several," Nickie said, pausing as if he weren't sure he wanted to proceed. "Okay, okay, I'll tell you. So, in this one, she said she wanted to play the role of someone named Catherine the Great. To be honest with you, I had heard the name before but didn't really know who she was. I guess she was like queen of Russia a long time ago and liked to mess around. So, one day, she wanted me to play the role of a guy named Potemkin and the next day a dude named, um... Karlov—"

Crawford thought back to his Russian history. "Sure you don't mean, Orlov?"

"Yeah, yeah, that's it. Orlov," Nickie said. "Tell you the truth, I couldn't keep it all straight, but it was clear that ol' Catherine had a shitload of lovers."

Ott chuckled. "Yeah, and as the story goes, a couple of barnyard friends thrown into the mix, too."

"I wouldn't know about that," said Nickie.

"Okay, we need you to bottom-line this for us," Ott said. "One, what are the tattoos all about and, two, what does this have to do Antonia von Habsburg?"

"I think I know the answer to number two," Crawford said to Ott. "Nickie here was in Antonia's stable."

"What does that mean?" Nickie asked.

"That Ms. von Habsburg hired you to be Danielle's, as you say it, escort."

"Was that it?" Ott asked Nickie.

Nickie nodded. "Yeah… I wish I had never met her."

"Okay, so let's go back to question number one, Nickie," Crawford said. "How come you got those tattoos? I bet you have a theory, because I sure do."

"What's yours?" Ott asked.

Crawford nodded at Nickie. "Let's hear him first."

"I… I… I…"

"You told somebody about 'Danielle,'" Crawford jumped in, "the things she made you do, all that role-playing stuff, right? And Danielle found out you were talking. That's my read on 'loose lips sink ships' and 'snitches get stitches.'" Crawford reached for his computer and hit Google.

"Except in this case it's 'snitches get tattoos,'" said Ott. "Is that how you see it, Nickie?"

"Um, yeah… I guess he's right."

"Okay, Nickie, well, thanks for coming in," Crawford said. "I found something here that might be helpful."

"What's that?"

"There's a doctor in West Palm, Dr. Goldberg, who specializes in tattoo removal," Crawford said, scrolling down. "Uses some kind of laser surgery called, ah, Picosure." Crawford turned his monitor around so Nickie could see. "That's the before and after. Might be just what you need."

Nickie smiled. "Hey, thanks a lot. I guess it'll cost a fortune."

"I don't know," said Ott, "maybe you can work something out with the doctor… give him free tennis lessons."

TWENTY-FIVE

Crawford and Ott had a conversation about Nickie and the tattoos after Nickie left the station. They theorized that Nickie must have been anesthetized for quite a long period of time, and probably taken to a tattoo parlor in West Palm Beach, where the inking was done. No way the job could have been done on the spot, at Nickie's apartment. They talked about getting Bettina on the case to try to track down the parlor where the work was done to get further information, but gave up on the idea when they saw there were over fifty parlors in West Palm alone.

Then Ott reminded Crawford that he never had gotten around to telling him about meeting Janny Hasleiter at her penthouse apartment at the Bristol. Crawford gave Ott the condensed version, leaving out any mention of lurid Lulu. Then Ott pressed him for details and complained how Crawford "always got the good jobs."

*****

Crawford was in the office later that afternoon when he got a call on his cell phone. The display said *Frank Lincoln*... Frank Lincoln? Oh yeah, the priest at the Five Wanderers of Gethsemane church in Royal Palm Beach and Antonia von Habsburg's son.

He nixed, *Hello, Father.* "Hey, Frank," he answered.

"Hi, Detective, I just wanted to tell you about something very strange," Lincoln started out.

What is it, Crawford wondered, *National Strange Day?* "Okay, I'm all ears."

"So I went to my mother's house on Dunbar to get a few things a while ago," Lincoln said.

"Okay?"

"And there's a wedding going on there."

Maybe not as strange as poor Nickie's tattoos, but right up there. "A wedding? And you knew nothing about it?"

"No, definitely not. At first I thought, maybe before she died my mother gave a friend permission to use the place. I mean, it is a beautiful venue for a wedding, I actually had my own there," Lincoln said. Then with a laugh, "A man came up to me and asked who I was. He had this puzzled look on his face and before I could answer, he said, 'Cause the priest is already here.' See, I was wearing my collar, which explained his confusion, and I said, 'This is my mother's house. Why are you all here?' He said, 'Because your father rented it out to us for my daughter's wedding… for a lot of money, I might add.' That was when I knew he meant Wurfel, who I can assure you is definitely *not* my father."

"No, I'm well aware of that," Crawford said.

"Then the guy said, 'He's here by the way, in the guesthouse watching TV. Your father.'"

"What did you do?"

"The last thing I wanted to do was confront Wurfel. I haven't talked to the man in years and wanted to keep it that way."

"So that's when you called me?" Crawford said.

"Yes, I had your card from when you came out to the church, so… what are you going to do?"

Crawford stood. "I'll go there right now. Hear what Wurfel's got to say."

"Oh, you know what he'll say," Lincoln said. "Something like 'Antonia told me it was okay. Felt that she didn't treat me right monetarily and wanted to give me a chance to make some money.' Or some such nonsense."

"Maybe she did."

"Are you kidding? She always told me she'd been too damn generous to that loser. That was her word for him."

"All right, well, I'll go there and get to the bottom of it," Crawford said. "I'm gonna get in my car and head over there right now."

"I expect to hear that he's in jail later today."

Crawford didn't want to make a promise like that. "Okay, well, thanks for letting me know about this."

"You're welcome."

Something triggered Crawford's memory about having seen something in the *Glossy* newspaper a few days before. He rifled through the piles on his desk and bookshelves until he found it. There it was, a large classified ad that had a headline that read, "Want Your Wedding to Look Like You're a Gazillionaire?" It caught his eye and he read on. "A twenty-five-million-dollar house and its spacious grounds, including a pool and a tennis court, are available as a location for your wedding. Call for details."

*****

Crawford decided not to disturb the wedding revelers who seemed to be getting their money's worth… whatever it was that LV Wurfel was charging them. Crawford watched a young man, who, judging by his costume, was one of the ushers, shove a woman holding a champagne glass into the pool. Beyond the pool he saw a tennis game in progress. Three women, who were dressed as bridesmaids minus shoes, were playing against a man who might have been the groom, also shoeless. He was wearing black tuxedo pants, a sweat-stained dress shirt, and an untied black bow tie and was running down tennis balls with great alacrity on the clay court. A DJ was spinning tunes on an outdoor flagstone platform and young and old, drunk and sober, were dancing, smiling and sweating. Most people had champagne glasses or cocktails in hand, whether they were playing tennis, dancing or just talking.

Crawford made his way to the guesthouse, where he had been exactly one week before after the discovery of Antonia von Habsburg's body. He opened the door and heard a TV upstairs. He climbed the steps and found LV Wurfel with a Budweiser in hand and, next to him, his friend, Dirt.

Hearing Crawford's footsteps, Wurfel swung around.

"What's up, boys?" Crawford said, walking into the room.

"Oh, hey, Detective, what an… unexpected surprise?" Wurfel said, suppressing a groan.

Crawford reached down for the remote on a table between Wurfel and Dirt and clicked off the sound of roaring car engines.

"So," Crawford said, "I understand that you rented out the premises for these nice people's wedding?"

"Yeah, the Houlihans, old family friends of me and Antonia's."

"Okay, LV, cut the shit. Frank Lincoln clued me in, plus I saw that ad of yours in the *Glossy*. I have to hand it to you, though, this whole thing is a pretty slick racket. Only reason I really care about it is how it may have something to do with Antonia's murder. But, at the moment, I can't see that it's got anything at all to do with it. So talk to me."

"Trust me, Detective, it's got nothing to do with it. It's just me trying to make a buck to make up for getting, well, royally screwed."

"Yeah, I know, LV, I've heard that song and dance," Crawford said. "So who are these people, the Houlihans?"

"Just met Mel—that's the father of the bride—three days ago. Gave me a nice deposit. Runs a construction company down in Delray, I think it is. Just wanted to have a nice, fancy wedding at a big house. They were all set to have it at some Catholic church down there, but his wife saw my ad and… well,"—he threw up his hands—"here they are."

Crawford nodded and glanced over at Dirt. "What's your role in all this, Dirt?"

"My role? Nothin'. LV just asked me over to watch the race, have a couple of brewskis."

"Okay, boys," Crawford said, turning back to Wurfel. "I wouldn't want to spoil your fun, so you can watch the end of the race, then get the hell out of here. Because, Larry Victor, as much as you may think you have a stake in this house, you don't. Not that easy chair you're sitting in, not even that Budweiser in your hand, because I saw a whole case of the stuff in the refrigerator here a week ago. We clear?"

Wurfel and Dirt nodded.

"Oh, also, you two better expect to spend a fair amount of time cleaning up outside and in the main house after the wedding breaks up. This crowd seems kind of rowdy. I hope you got a good security deposit from Mr. Houlihan."

Wurfel nodded. "Yeah, I did."

Crawford clicked the remote in his hand and the sounds of roaring engines filled up the room again. "Well, enjoy the race, boys," he said, walking away. Then he turned and glanced at the TV screen. "Is Mario Andretti still driving?"

TWENTY-SIX

"By the way," Wurfel said, as Crawford was at the door, "as you may have gathered, there is no love lost between me and Junior. That's what I call Frank, that pain-in-the-ass son of Antonia's."

"Yeah, matter of fact I did gather that," Crawford said. "Exactly what's the problem there?"

"Problem is, dude's a total pain in the ass."

"You said that already."

"Yeah, okay, the problem is that everything he's ever done in his life, including that half-assed church of his, is because Mommy gave him the money. Never accomplished a goddamn thing on his own. I get that mothers are supposed to help their kids, but he'd be a bum on a street corner if he didn't have her. I mean, the Five Wanderers of... whatever. Gimme a frickin' break!"

"Gethsemane," Crawford said. "I kind of like the name. So, what else about Lincoln?"

"Well, okay, I'll give you a scoop. Ol' Frankie's in for a little shocker."

"What do you mean?"

"Well, see, Antonia has a daughter."

Crawford straightened up. "What are you talking about?"

Wurfel nodded. "I knew about it all along. Guess I forgot to tell you. She told me one time after a couple glasses of wine that the father's some rich guy at the Poinciana. Knocked her up right after we split."

"Really?" Crawford didn't sense that LV was joking this time.

"Seriously. The kid lives with Antonia's cleaning lady down in Lake Worth. I think the cleaning lady may have actually legally adopted her. Anyway, I got a call from this attorney who said he's representing

Carmen—that's the cleaning lady's name—asking if I knew the name of the attorney handling Antonia's estate. I told him the name's Perry Jastrow, but I wasn't totally sure. Then he asked me if Antonia had any other 'offspring'—and I told him about Frank."

"So presumably this attorney is going to be making a claim on behalf of the daughter, is that what you're saying?"

"Not only that, he told me he was in possession of a will naming the daughter as the primary... whatchamacallit?"

"Beneficiary?"

"That's it," Wurfel said. "So I go and Google this guy and see he's one of those ambulance-chasing injury lawyers."

"What's his name?"

"Somebody Westerling. Firm is Westerling, Westerling and Westerling."

"That's a lot of Westerlings," Crawford said. "What's the cleaning lady's last name."

"Uh, something like Carmen Bodega. No wait, Ortega. Yeah, that's it, Carmen Ortega. Honduran, I think. Husband's name is Fortune or Fortunato, one or the other. Antonia's daughter is Lauren."

Crawford nodded, then locked his eyes on Wurfel's. "That's good info, LV. You got anything else you been holding back?"

"No, man, but how about taking it easy on me. The wedding thing, it's kind of, what you might call a victimless crime. Antonia probably would have been okay with it. Using her place to make people happy? And what could be a happier cause than holy matrimony? Even though it didn't really work out for me."

"How much did you get for it?" Crawford asked.

"Uh, ten grand."

"Oh, cut the bullshit. This is a wedding in Palm Beach. What did you *really* get for it?"

"Twenty-five."

"I'll let it slide, but only because you got a record and you'd probably go back to jail if you got prosecuted for this."

Wurfel nodded dolefully.

"So, what you're going to do is make a contribution of twenty grand to your favorite cause. Or causes. You know, something like taking care of the homeless in West Palm. The Lord's Place, I think it's called. Or maybe the vets—that's another good one. Then once you've decided on who you want to give the money to, I want you to give me the name. I'll call 'em up and make sure you really gave it. Not that I don't trust you or anything, but just to make sure. You can keep five grand for your creativity in dreaming this whole thing up."

"Gee, thanks, five grand for all the work I did?"

Crawford chuckled. "All that work has a name, LV. It's called fraud."

Wurfel put up his hands in surrender. "Okay, okay."

"I also want you sticking around. No trips up to Daytona or airboats on the Everglades."

"Why not?"

"I just want you where I can keep an eye on you."

"What if I just go on a quick ride?"

"Then I'll charge you for the wedding scam."

Wurfel let out a deep sigh. "You know, Charlie, you can be a real ballbuster."

"So it's been said."

TWENTY-SEVEN

After leaving Antonia von Habsburg's house and LV Wurfel to decide what good cause he would donate twenty thousand dollars to, Crawford went back to the station and stopped by Ott's cubicle. Ott, on his computer, looked up and flashed Crawford a big grin. "Have I got one for you, Chuck."

"Whatever you got, I can top it."

Ott stood and looked over the top of his cubicle and into a detective who specialized in burglary's space. His name was Kendrick and he'd just clicked off his cell phone. "Okay, Ken , we need a little levity," Ott said. "So you be the judge of who's got a better story. Me or Crawford."

Kendrick smiled. "Okay, I'm listening."

Crawford raised his arm. "Wait, Mort, you're not going to tell him about the kid who woke up with the tats all over his face."

"Nah, not Nickie, that was bizarre all right, but this one tops that by a mile."

"Can't wait," Crawford said.

Ott turned back to Crawford and opened his hand. "Okay, you go first," he said. "This better be good."

Crawford told Ott and Shaw about LV Wurfel's wedding scam and added another wrinkle that he had discovered belatedly: that Wurfel had already run another ad in the latest *Glossy* with the headline: "Throw Your Wedding at Casa Villamer, One of the Great Estates of Palm Beach!" Crawford had to grudgingly give Wurfel credit, knowing that he had invented the name Casa Villamer. He reminded himself to call Wurfel and tell him to cancel any new wedding bookings that resulted from the second ad.

At the end of Crawford's presentation, Kendrick clapped enthusiastically and asked, "That really happened?"

"You think I'm creative enough to make up something like that?" Crawford said.

Kendrick shook his head. "Amazing." Then turning to Ott: "Okay, whatcha got, bro?"

"I gotta admit, Charlie, that's definitely Hall of Fame material. And in Palm Beach, that's saying something. Anyway, here goes... So, I'm driving down South County, just past Jungle, and I see this jogger up ahead. She's kind of hogging the lane a little so I go wide on her and I look back in my rearview and damned if she ain't naked from the waist up."

"Bullshit," said Kendrick.

"Swear to God. She had to be around seventy, seventy-five, and my first instinct is to just keep going. Ignore it, you know. But I figured if some old geezer came along, he might drive into a tree or something checking her out, so I pulled over about a hundred feet past her and got out of my car."

"She comes flapping up to me, and I say, ''Scuse me, ma'am, but you're not allowed to jog topless.'"

"And she looks down and goes, 'Oh my God, I didn't even notice. I got dressed in such a hurry and just'—big shrug—'forgot my top. She kinda looked at me like, *Hey, shit like that happens all the time at my age.* I mean, what am I s'posed to say? So I go, 'Why don't you hop in the back of my car. I'll take you back to your house. You live close?' And she says, 'Thank you very much, but I live all the way up on Barton.'"

Both Crawford and Kendrick burst out laughing.

"You mean she's been jogging topless for like twenty blocks already?" Kendrick said. "Right through the commercial section, all the way down to Jungle?"

"Yeah, must've been," Ott said. "I didn't exactly ask her to give me her whole route. But no way I was the first one to spot her."

"But no 'concerned citizen' phoned it in or anything?" Crawford asked.

"Not that I heard."

Both Ott and Crawford looked at Kendrick like contestants in the finale of *America's Got Talent.* "You got a tough decision to make," Ott told him.

Kendrick tapped his desk top. "Yeah, no kiddin', I gotta think about this a little."

"Let's just call it a tie, Mort," Crawford said, suddenly losing interest in tales of Palm Beach bizarreness. "We gotta get back to work. All this weird shit is taking us away from the damn case. Which, by the way, we're still nowhere on."

"Yeah, I hear ya, but distractions aren't a bad thing every once in a while."

"Every once in a while? Are you kidding, we're getting 'em every five minutes."

Ott nodded and gave a deep sigh.

"All right," Crawford said, "to make the case even more complicated, I just found out Antonia has an illegitimate daughter living with her cleaning lady down in Lake Worth."

Ott threw up his hands. "Come on!"

Crawford shook his head. "You believe that shit?"

His partner shrugged. "In this case? Hell, yeah, I'd believe just about anything."

TWENTY-EIGHT

"Westerling, Westerling and Westerling," said the voice.

"Yes, hello, I'm trying to speak to the Westerling representing the daughter of Antonia von Habsburg?"

"Okay, I think that's Ed," said the voice. "Let me connect you."

The phone rang a few times. "Ed Westerling."

"Hello, Mr. Westerling, my name is Detective Crawford. You're representing Antonia von Habsburg's daughter, correct?"

"Incorrect. That's my brother, Sam. I'll connect you."

More rings.

"Sam Westerling."

"My name is Detective Crawford. Are you representing Antonia von Habsburg's daughter Lauren?"

"I'm representing Antonia von Westerling's daughter Esmerelda."

"Esmerelda?"

"Same person. What is it you'd like to know, Detective?"

"I'm trying to find out who the beneficiary is of von Habsburg's estate."

"Esmerelda is."

"Not according to Frank Lincoln, her son."

"Frank Lincoln is a fraud," Sam said. "Not to mention a religious quack."

"I saw the will, Mr. Westerling. There was no mention of either Lauren or Esmerelda."

"You saw the fraudulent will. The one that Frank Lincoln fabricated. I have a copy of the real one."

"Why is it that Antonia's daughter is known as both Lauren and Esmerelda?"

"That's a long story."

"So how do you know with certainty that Lincoln's will is bogus and your client's will is legitimate?"

"Look, I'd be lying to you if I said I saw Lincoln's copy. But I've seen a lot of wills in my day and know that my client's is the real deal."

"That probably has something to do with your compensation, doesn't it?"

Westerling laughed. "That's a little cynical, Detective."

"I've been around, Sam," Crawford said. "I have another question: who's the father of Lauren/Esmerelda?"

"I don't know the answer to that. It's not really relevant because whoever the father is, he's not getting a dime."

"So you say, but I've seen situations where a father can prevail on a daughter to give him a good chunk of the money the daughter inherited."

"*That* is *really* cynical."

"There's a big difference between cynicism and reality."

"Well, as I said, I have no idea who the father is."

"Okay, well, thank you, Mr. Westerling. If I have any more questions, I'll give you a call back."

"Sure, happy to help," Sam said. "Hey, by the way, I know you guys are involved in high-speed car chases every once in a while. If you ever have an accident and get injured, Sam's your man."

Crawford nodded to himself. "Seems like I've heard that line before."

"I sure as hell hope so. I advertise all over nighttime TV. Wouldn't want to think I'm wasting my money."

*****

Crawford called Frank Lincoln next, who answered his cell phone with a question. "You got Wurfel in the slammer?"

"No. But he won't be profiting from his little enterprise at your mother's house."

"He should be in the can. Isn't that at least a misdemeanor?"

"Tell me about your baby sister, would you please?"

136

"Oh God," he said, taking his boss's name in vain, "somehow I knew she'd raise her ugly head."

"That's not very Christian. I get the sense she's just a little kid and doesn't know the first thing about any of this," Crawford said. "Fact is, she's being represented by a barracuda attorney claiming that the will naming you as the sole beneficiary is fraudulent."

Lincoln groaned. "So, I guess this whole thing is going to end up in court now?"

"Good chance," Crawford said. "Do you know who her father is?" He was now contemplating the theory that the man who sired Antonia's daughter might have an ulterior monetary motive to want Antonia dead. So the man could cozy up to his daughter and wangle her inheritance out of her.

Lincoln made a whooshing sound which Crawford interpreted as a sigh. "Let me put it to you this way, Detective: my mother was not terribly discriminating about who she had sex with. The ones I've heard most often rumored to be the father are Malcolm Chace, David Balfour and the Duke de Montpelier."

Whoa, thought Crawford. Two out of three he knew well, the third he had never heard of before. Balfour, of course, was his good friend and sometime golf partner, and Chace was the mayor of Palm Beach who was urging him to find Antonia von Habsburg's killer *yesterday*. Then he remembered back to somebody mentioning a duke before. He thought it might have been Waverly Bangs. Then, he surmised, half in jest, that maybe Antonia was looking to produce a royal son or daughter so the offspring would have royalty on both sides? It didn't exactly jibe that Lauren/Esmerelda was living in Lake Worth or had been adopted by Antonia's cleaning lady.

"Does this come from a reliable source?" Crawford asked. "These supposed fathers?"

"Is *anybody* reliable in Palm Beach?"

It was a good question.

*****

David Balfour was Crawford's next call. He felt like he was churning in circles with no real strategy at work at the moment, simply hoping something would fall into place the more calls he made and the more people he interviewed.

"Hey, Charlie," Balfour said, a friendly lilt in his voice.

"Hello, David. Remember when, a while back, we were talking about the ever-active Palm Beach rumor mill?"

"I sure do. Why? What's the latest?"

"You."

"What?"

"That you were the father of Antonia von Habsburg's daughter."

"Not guilty."

"You sure?"

"That's something one can be sure of. As Bill Clinton would say, 'I never had sexual relations with that woman,' except in my case, it's true. Not that I wouldn't have been tempted, but the opportunity never presented itself. You got any other rumors hot off the presses?"

Crawford balked at first, but then decided to ask. "How about Mal Chace? Think he and Antonia ever—"

"Funny you should mention that. I actually did hear that once. Why don't you ask the man himself?"

"Why don't you? You and he are friends and members of the Poinciana."

"But you and he are both members of our local government."

"I'm not real comfortable in posing that question," Crawford said. "What about a man named... or rather a duke named the Duke de Montpelier. You ever heard of him?"

Balfour burst out laughing. "First of all, your pronunciation is really bad. It's not Montpelier, like the capital of Vermont, it's *Mon-pell-yay* like... I don't know what."

"Okay, *Mon-pell-yay*. By the way, David, I'm impressed that you knew Montpelier is the capital of Vermont."

"Just so happens, I know all the state capitals," Balfour said. "So, how's your history, Charlie?"

"Not bad. Why?" Crawford said. After all, he had pulled Catherine the Great's lover out of thin air.

"Okay, well, back in the late 1800s or maybe early twentieth century, rich American heiresses used to hotfoot it over to the UK and marry these titled English guys. It worked for both. The American woman got a title and the English guy got her cash. Well, the duke, Nigel—of course, it had to be a name like Nigel or Angus or Percy, one of those bullshit limey names—figured he'd try that routine all over again in the twenty-first century. So, he came over here with his title and his upper-class accent and his snazzy Turnbull & Asser shirts, but no dough, looking for a wife. And damned if it didn't work yet again."

"Landed himself a rich woman?"

"Well, so it seemed anyway. Wendy Moffett had just gotten divorced from a big, hedge-fund guy in Connecticut, and she and Nigel were going at it hot and heavy. Dinners at Le Bilboquet or La Goulue every night, flying to St. Barts for the weekend, you know the drill."

"No, I don't, but I've heard of those places."

"Yeah, so then after a month or two of this, Nigel finds out to his dismay that, like all good hedge-fund guys from Connecticut, Clifford Moffett got Wendy to sign a pretty tight pre-nup ten years back. So, Wendy, who's used to the high life, all of a sudden has to tone it all down and start eating bologna sandwiches instead of foie gras. She tells Nigel about the pre-nup and, of course, Nigel is out of there in a flash. So, I guess then he hooks up with Antonia, but I don't know anything more about it than that."

"How long ago was this?"

"Oh, maybe four or five years ago," Balfour said. "I think Nigel's still around, but I don't know where. Something tells me he never quite hit the home run. Probably over in West Palm somewhere."

"A fate worse than death," Crawford muttered in reference to his own neighborhood.

"Oh, sorry Charlie, I didn't mean—"

"No offense taken, but hey… it may not have occurred to you but we can't all live in Palm Beach."

TWENTY-NINE

Crawford decided to take the back-door approach with Malcolm Chace. He couldn't very well walk into the office of the mayor and ask, *Hey Mal, just curious, but were you banging Antonia von Habsburg? Oh, and while I'm asking, did you have a kid as a result of it? Sweet little thing down in Lake Worth?* Even if he posed the questions obliquely, it would likely upset the very same man who hired him five years before.

So, instead he went to the man who sometimes did a very convincing impression of being Chace's lackey, Chief of Police Norm Rutledge. Rutledge, who favored brown suits and orange ties, was wearing a seersucker suit that could best be described as "close to stylish" if it weren't for a blue and white striped tie that made his whole look… well, *busy* was a charitable way to describe it. Crawford decided to stay away from any fashion comments, and just go with a simple: "Hey, Norm."

"Hey, Crawford," Rutledge said, indicating for Crawford to have a seat on the other side of his desk. "You got good news on von Habsburg for me?"

"Well, matter of fact, that's why I stopped by," Crawford said. "But I doubt you'd call it good news. More like a question."

Rutledge shook his head in obvious disappointment. "You know, those TV news vans haven't gone away, and the reporters still got the story plastered all over the front pages of all their papers."

"I know, I know. There's nothing I can do about that." Crawford realized at that moment that he'd awkwardly stumbled into a Rutledge trap.

"Nothing you can do about it? Nothing you can do about it?" he repeated. "How 'bout catch the son of a bitch. Solve the goddamn thing. That would be nice."

Crawford ignored Rutledge's ire as he had done so many times before. "Let me ask you a question, Norm: you know anything about a relationship between the mayor and Antonia von Habsburg?"

Rutledge's face twisted into a severe frown. "The mayor, as in Mal Chace?"

"Well, yeah, I don't know another one."

"Is that what your so-called investigation has come to? Getting the skinny on the victim's sex life."

"Look, Norm, I can think of at least three cases in the last five years where that had some bearing. And one case where an ex-lover of the vic was the perp."

"Yeah, yeah, I know what you're referring to, but it's totally outrageous to even suggest that Mal Chace could have had anything to do with what happened to von Habsburg."

"Christ, that's the *last* thing I'm suggesting. I'm just asking if you know if Mal might have had a relationship with the woman. It's just one of the many roads I need to go down to solve this thing."

Rutledge looked down at his clashing tie and straightened it. "So the answer to your half-assed question is, I have no idea if the mayor had ever even met that woman. And I can assure you this, I'm sure as hell not about to ask him, any more than I'd ask you if you ever had sex with a certain crime-scene tech."

"All right, I can see this is going nowhere."

"Which is exactly where it should go," Rutledge said. "Now what I suggest is you and your... corpulent friend zero in on real suspects and get to the bottom of this so I don't have to look at all those TV vans crawling all over the streets of Palm Beach."

Corpulent, huh? He guessed Rutledge had gotten his thesaurus out recently to spice up his normally mundane speech.

Crawford stood. "Okay, Norm, matter of fact my 'corpulent' friend was going to be my next stop. I'll give him your best."

As Crawford walked away, he had another thought: maybe George Morrison, the president of the Poinciana Club, was the father of Esmerelda. Then he decided it actually didn't matter much who was the father. He had a much bigger mystery to solve than that.

*****

It was Ott's third trip in two days to visit DeeDee Dunwoody at the Good Samaritan Hospital.

If one could smile with their eyes, that's what he thought he detected in DeeDee's.

He walked up to her and gave her a light pat on the head. "How ya feelin'?"

"Better. It's still painful, but less so."

"Good to hear. You'll probably be out of here before you know it."

"I hope you're right. They're still not telling me when, though," DeeDee said. "So let me tell you about my call."

"What call?"

"From Waverly Bangs. I was able to answer my cell and put it on speaker. Clearly, she didn't know what happened to me because she asked me if I wanted to go on a date with a man."

"Really? So, I guess she's trying to keep Distinguished Consorts alive."

"Yeah, definitely. My guess is that she's got Antonia's Rolodex. Can't blame her, given how successful it was."

"I get it. Did she say who the date would be with? Or didn't it get that far?"

"No, it did. A man named Bart Resor. Never heard the name before."

Ott shrugged. Nor had he. "What else did she say?"

"Well, so I was curious about that. About her continuing Distinguished Consorts, I mean. So, I said something like, 'I'm not interested—even after I've fully recovered—but I have a friend who might be.' 'Cause I do. So, she asked me all about her—specifically, what she looked like. I told her she's a beautiful woman. Then she said, 'We'd definitely be interested.' I said, 'Wait, who's *we*?' To which she quickly said, 'Sorry, I meant me.'"

"Sounds like that little slip might mean she has a partner," Ott said.

"Which was exactly what I thought. I mean, that's not a mistake you'd make. You don't say 'we' unless you're thinking 'we.'"

"Did she say anything else that might be helpful?"

"Sorry, I think that was about it."

Ott stroked her hair gently. "Well, is there anything I can get you when I come back next time? Anything you'd really like to eat or drink?"

"I'll tell you what I'd really like: a Texas margarita."

"A Texas margarita, huh?"

"Yes, twice as much tequila."

"Somehow I don't think that's a good combo to go with your IV," Ott said, pointing at the IV in DeeDee's left arm.

"How about ice cream?"

"I think that'll fly. What's your flavor of choice?"

"Breyers Heath Bar."

"Something else we have in common. I love that stuff," Ott said. "Tell you what, I'll come back tonight with a half gallon; we can try to polish it off together."

She raised her thumb. "You got yourself a deal."

*****

Crawford had left a Post-it on Ott's desk. "Need to talk."

Ott went straight back to Crawford's office.

Crawford told him what he'd learned from the attorney, Sam Westerling, and his subsequent conversations with David Balfour and Norm Rutledge.

"I got the address of Antonia's cleaning lady, where her kid lives. Gonna take a run down there a little later."

Ott agreed, then filled his partner in on what DeeDee had to say.

"That's huge," Crawford said. "I mean, someone sliding into a business that's making a million a year. Gotta be a few people out there who'd find that worth killing for."

"Amen," Ott said. "Definitely worth us having another conversation with Waverly. Find out who the 'we' is. Could just be the man-woman team we're looking for."

"I'll go see the daughter first, then swing up to North Flagler afterwards and pay Waverly a visit," Crawford said.

"You gonna call her first?"

"I don't know yet. The surprise element might be the way to play it. I'm a big fan of the surprise visit. Never know what you'll find."

Ott nodded. "But didn't you tell me they got a doorman? Won't he have to like... announce you?"

"It's a guy at the front desk," Crawford said. "But I spotted a way to sneak onto the elevator without him seeing me."

*****

There was only one Fortunato Ortega in Lake Worth, located at 2335 Fifth Avenue, so Crawford GPSed his way down to his address. 2335 Fifth Avenue bore no resemblance to the avenue of the same name in New York City, but the neighborhood where Antonia's cleaning lady lived was well-kept, clean, and felt like a place that was relatively crime-free—something that could not be said of certain sections of Lake Worth.

A silver Toyota Tercel was in the driveway, which was good because Crawford had figured beforehand it was fifty-fifty that both Carmen and Fortunato would be at work. It was, however, four in the afternoon, so he guessed Esmeralda would be home from school and someone would need to take care of her.

He got out of his car, walked up to the porch and pushed the doorbell. A few moments later the door opened and a pretty Hispanic women with dark skin and gleaming white teeth looked out. "Yes?"

"Hi Carmen, my name is Detective Crawford and I'm investigating the murder of Antonia von Habsburg. You are Carmen, right?"

The woman nodded. "Would you like to come in?"

"Thank you," Crawford said. "Is your daughter here?"

"Yes, she's playing in the back yard," Carmen said, opening the door. "Why do you want to know about her?"

"Because I spoke to Sam Westerling. He told me about the will."

Carmen nodded noncommittally and pointed to a small living room. The furniture looked like pieces picked up at a yard sale, but a Palm Beach yard sale, not a Lake Worth one.

"Nice room," Crawford said, as he sat down.

"Thank you," Carmen said, sitting down across from him. "You know, Ms. Antonia told me to get a lawyer if she died. And tell him about the will she gave me."

"So Ms. von Habsburg actually gave you the will."

"Yes. In a manila envelope."

"How long ago was that? That she gave it to you?"

"About a year ago."

"Do you have a copy?"

"I have the original and a copy. I made a copy for the lawyer, too."

"Just out of curiosity, how did you choose the lawyer, Sam Westerling?"

"To tell you the truth, I saw him on TV."

Crawford smiled. "Sam's the man."

Carmen smiled back at him. "I sure hope he is."

"Would you mind if I took a look at the will. You said you have another copy?"

"Yes, sure, that's fine. I actually made three copies."

Crawford heard footsteps. Little footsteps, the opposite of thudding Norm Rutledge footsteps.

He looked up and saw a little girl. No one had mentioned her age. He guessed she was around eight. She had blond hair, dark skin, and a winning smile.

"Es, this is Detective Crawford," Carmen said. "Shake his hand."

The little girl walked up to Crawford and, making full eye contact, shook his hand, and did a little curtsy.

"Pleased to meet you, Esmerelda," Crawford said with a smile.

"Pleased to meet you, sir," she said.

"You have very good manners," Crawford said. "Your mother taught you well."

"And my dad," she said with a smile.

He didn't quite know where to go from there. "Do you see your dad a lot?"

Carmen shot him a look.

"Every day when he comes home from work," she said.

Oh, Christ. He'd almost blown it.

"Where's your dad work?" Crawford asked, recovering.

"At the car place," she said.

"He's a mechanic," Carmen explained.

Crawford glanced back at Esmerelda. "I bet he's a very good one."

Esmerelda smiled and nodded.

"You can go back outside now, Es."

Esmeralda looked up at Crawford. "Okay, bye Mister..."

"Detective," said Carmen.

"Bye, Mister Detective," Esmeralda said, giving him a wave and walking toward the back door.

"I know what you were thinking," Carmen said. "But we have no idea who her real father is. I'm not too sure Ms. Antonia did either."

"Let me ask you about something completely different."

"Okay."

"How long were you the housekeeper at Ms. von Habsburg's house?"

"Eleven years."

"So in that time you must have seen a lot."

"What do you mean, 'seen a lot'?"

"Well, I mean, seen different men. As I'm sure you know, she did have lots of men in her life."

Carmen's eyes flicked away like they were trying to find a place to hide. "My job was to keep her house clean and well-organized."

"I know that and I see that you were, and are, very loyal to Ms. von Habsburg, but she's dead and the best thing you can do for her now is help me find her killer."

"But if you want me to talk about her... love life, I will not do that."

"No, you don't need to do that. My interest is what you may have overheard. Or seen. Like maybe a man who mistreated her. A man you may have heard threaten to harm her."

Carmen thought for a few moments. "I can't think of anyone like that." Then she cocked her head and raised a finger. "Do you know Mr. King?"

"Yes, I've interviewed him. Why, what were you going to say about him?"

"I just never thought he treated her very well. What is the word... grouchy. He always seemed so grouchy. I never knew what she saw in him."

"But, did you ever see him do anything physical to her. Slap her or hit her or anything."

Carmen shook her head.

"What about... did any of the men ever stay at her house? I mean, did you ever go to the house and see Ms. von Habsburg, say, having breakfast with any of them?"

"Yes, sometimes. Mr. King, for one. A few others, too, but I never heard their names. Except for her daughter and her husband."

Crawford's head jerked back. "Daughter? I never heard about a daughter except Esmerelda?"

Carmen nodded. "Abby. She lives up north. Her husband's name is Steve."

How had they missed this?

"Do you know if she and Antonia were close? Had a close relationship, I mean?"

"I don't think they really did. They were just down here staying with Antonia on vacation."

"They were? When exactly?"

"They were here for a week and left... the day before Ms. Antonia was killed."

"Do you know where they live up north?"

"New something?"

"New York?"

"No."

"New Jersey?"

"No."

"New Hampshire?"

"Yes, that's it. That's up there, right?"

Crawford nodded. "About as far north as you can get," he said. "What's their last name?"

"Swain."

"And do you know where in New Hampshire they live?"

Carmen scratched the side of her head. "Something like Whop-O, I think it is."

"Whop-O?" Crawford said with a smile. "Doesn't exactly sound like the name of a New Hampshire town. See, I actually spent four years up there."

Carmen shrugged. "Sorry, that's the name I remember."

Antonia's family, Crawford was thinking, was growing and growing. From just a son who was pastor at an odd church, it had now tripled. Were there yet more offspring out there somewhere?

"So, Carmen, Ms. von Habsburg had three children— Esmerelda, Frank and Abby—correct? Were there any others?"

"No, just those three."

"You're sure?"

"I'm pretty sure."

"Back to the men in Ms. von Habsburg's life, are there any one of them who, after you heard about her murder, you thought might have been capable of killing her?"

"No." Absolutely no hesitation on Carmen's part.

Crawford stood up and went for his wallet. He took out a card. "Well, thank you for meeting with me. If you think of anything that might be helpful to my investigation, please give me a call."

"I will. I certainly will," she said. "And if you'll wait a moment, I'll get you a copy of the will."

A few minutes later, Crawford walked out of the house, got in the Crown Vic, reached for his cell phone, and dialed.

Bettina, at the station, answered. "Hi, Charlie. I'm bored. Got a job for me?"

"Just so happens I do. I need you to see what you can find out about Steve and Abby Swain from a town in New Hampshire called Whop-O, except that can't be the real name. Something like that, though."

"Okay, Charlie, once again, I'm on it. Anything else I should know?"

"Yes. They were down here right before Antonia von Habsburg's murder. Call the airlines and find out the exact times and dates."

"That's it?"

"Yep. Let me know what you find out."

"I'm on it, Charlie."

"Thanks." He clicked off and dialed Ott's number.

"Hey, Chuck."

"Antonia von Habsburg's family just got bigger."

"Oh, yeah?"

"Turns out she's got a daughter up in New Hampshire."

"Where's she was originally from, right?"

"Uh-huh," Crawford said. "I got Bettina on the case. You got anything?"

"Nothing much. I'm interviewing DeeDee's neighbors but not coming up with anything. Where you headed now?"

"Waverly Bangs."

"Okay, catch you back at the station?"

"Yeah, I'll be there later. Hopefully with something that helps crack this goddamn thing."

THIRTY

Crawford drove onto Dixie Highway, headed north, and for the next twenty minutes seemed to hit every red light on the busy commercial street. He drove past Good Samaritan Hospital and wondered whether Ott was visiting his favorite patient. Five minutes later he pulled up to the Portofino building at 2600 North Flagler Drive. He had decided not to try to sneak onto one of the elevators after all and instead walked right up to the man at the front desk. He flashed ID to the man, who had slicked-back hair and a friendly smile.

"She just went out a little while ago," the man answered when Crawford asked if Waverly Bangs was there.

"She didn't happen to mention when she'd be back, did she?" Crawford asked.

"No, but I think she was going for a run."

One of Crawford's life observations was that if you gave a man who had a boring job a chance to unburden himself, you often ended up with a helpful scoop. This man's job could certainly be described as boring: *good morning, Ms. Bangs, good afternoon, Ms. Bangs* and *good evening, Ms. Bangs*—this multiplied by a hundred people or however many residents there were in the building. That could hardly be described as scintillating. Receiving packages from the Amazon man, the Federal Express man, the UPS man, and the occasional pizza delivery dude must get old too.

"Nice building," Crawford said, giving the man one of his most hated ingratiation devices, a wink. Then he lowered his voice. "Job like yours, bet you see and hear a lot."

"You better believe it."

"What's your name?" Crawford asked.

"Roy."

Crawford nodded and shot him his best, winning smile. "So Roy... Ms. Bangs, does she have a boyfriend?"

"Last time I checked, two," Roy said with a muffled chuckle.

"Tell me about 'em."

"Well, let's see, we got Lamborghini Lou and Easy Rider."

"Can you be a little more specific."

"Sure, Lou—don't know his last name—has a bitch of a time getting out of his Lambo and the condo board is trying to get Easy Rider banned from the premises because his Harley makes such a racket."

"Wait," Crawford said, bending down closer to Roy. "The Harley guy,"—he touched above his upper lip—"he got a reddish mustache, by any chance?"

Roy laughed. "Yeah, that looks lopsided."

Crawford nodded. "I know what you mean. So, he comes by a lot? Larry Victor Wurfel's his name."

"Yeah, LV, he comes over quite a bit. Day, night, middle of the night."

"Middle of the night... what do you mean?"

Roy looked to his right and left, like he didn't want anybody catching him gossiping. "Well, the guy on the graveyard shift here told me he and Waverly got caught skinny-dipping in the pool at three in the morning. One of the old bats on the condo board couldn't sleep, it was a full moon and she spotted 'em. I guess they were just swimming around at first and then they started gettin' it on."

"Wow, wild place you got here."

"Yeah, sometimes it gets like that place, the Villages."

"Where's that?"

"You don't know about the Villages?"

Crawford shook his head.

"Oh, man, talk about wild. It's for old people—you gotta be sixty or so to live there," Roy had lowered his voice way down now, "but it's like one big swingers club. They sell Viagra on the black market there and it's got the record for the most STDs in Florida."

"STDs?"

"Man, Detective, you got a lot to learn: *sexually transmitted diseases*," he whispered dramatically.

Crawford straightened out. "Okay, well, thanks for all the info, Roy. I really appreciate it."

Out of the corner of his eye, he spotted Waverly Bangs coming toward the glass double doors. Then Roy turned and spotted her, too.

The doorman looked disappointed, as if he'd only begun to shovel the building gossip.

Like he had stories about the Villages and God-knows-what-or-where that he could keep Crawford spellbound with for the rest of the afternoon.

Crawford walked toward the front door. Waverly Bangs was wearing running shorts and a Chanel T-shirt with the interlocking Cs logo. When she saw him, she smiled. But he got the sense she didn't mean it.

"Hello, Detective, welcome back to the Jackhammer Arms," she said.

"Seems pretty quiet today," Crawford said. "Is there somewhere we can talk?"

"Sure," she said, going past Roy and giving him a finger-flutter wave, "the lovely Mediterranean Room. Follow me."

She took a right down a hallway. "Any progress on Antonia?"

"We're getting closer," Crawford exaggerated.

"That's good to hear," Bangs said, turning into a room on her left. At the far end were bookcases lining the walls. To the right were mail boxes for the tenants. In between was brightly colored bamboo furniture, circa twenty years ago.

"Want to sit over there?" Bangs said, pointing to a circle of chairs.

"Sure," said Crawford, waiting for Bangs to sit, then pulling out a chair so it faced her.

He leaned back in it, getting the sense it wasn't the sturdiest chair he'd ever sat in. "So I understand that Distinguished Consorts is still going strong?"

"Not as strong as when Antonia ran it, but I'm doing the best I can. I figure I owe it to her to wrap up a bunch of loose ends before it shuts down."

Crawford turned his head to one side. "I would think that like any business where the owner dies, the business would be inherited by its beneficiaries. Unless, of course, she willed it specifically to you. Which I don't think she did, right?"

Bangs thought for a few moments. "I don't disagree with you, but I heard there might be a dispute about who the beneficiary, or beneficiaries, are, and until that's all sorted out I might as well keep the business running. As kind of a caretaker. Know what I mean?"

"You say *I*, but I have reason to believe it's really *we*. That you're running it with a man, now."

"What if I am? As long as it's being run professionally and competently and lawfully, would it matter if I was running it with a... a chimpanzee?"

"I guess that makes sense. Since LV Wurfel does have quite a few years' experience in the biz."

Bangs didn't react.

"What occurred to me, though, is you and Wurfel could basically... well, steal the business from whoever the beneficiary turns out to be."

She shot him a massive frown. "Steal? What are you talking about? I'm not a thief."

"Okay, I apologize for using that word," Crawford said. "What I meant was, you could change the name, keep Antonia's Rolodex and whatever names and numbers you have, and do exactly what she was doing. But with Antonia around, you couldn't. So you see, that presents a strong motive for someone to kill Antonia. To take over her business and make a million bucks a year. Do you see what I mean?"

Waverly shook her head long and slow. "I got news for you: I didn't kill Antonia nor do I know anything about it. Same goes for LV."

"I know. That's why I said *someone*. But you do see how *someone* might regard you two as people with strong motives?"

"Look, Detective, if *someone* thinks either me or LV had anything to do with Antonia's death, why don't you just come out and say it?"

He gave her a friendly smile. "I'm just asking questions."

"Okay, well, in case I haven't made it loud and clear, me and LV had nothing to do with Antonia's murder."

"So you've said a multitude of times. But how can you be so sure about LV?"

"I just am. He's certain things, but hardly a murderer."

Crawford decided to let her denial sit there.

The sound of a jackhammer and electric drill broke the silence.

"Wow, that is loud," Crawford said. "What did you call it, the Portofino Philharmonic?"

Waverly didn't seem in the mood for banter. "Do you have any more questions?"

He was thinking. Waverly broke the silence.

"You know, you should maybe go talk to that... Janny what's-her-face."

"Hasleiter?"

"Yeah."

"Why do you mention her? She and Antonia were friends."

"Until they weren't."

"Okay, Waverly, you're being a little too mysterious for me."

"Isn't that what you do? Solve mysteries."

Crawford put up his hands. "Okay, okay, so tell me about her."

"I will... So, during Covid, the *ten names for fifty grand* thing slowed way down for us. 'Cause, you know, men were a little reluctant to go out with women—even beautiful women—for fear of getting sick, so the business kind of dried up."

"Okay, I think I'm getting it," Crawford said. "Antonia jumps to Plan B. Or maybe it's Plan C. Just flat-out blackmailing men, but in this case, Janny Hasleiter. Is that what you're saying?"

Waverly nodded. "Based on what little I know about it... maybe. I mean, Antonia knew that Hasleiter wouldn't be too thrilled if word got around she was doing teenage boys. That would raise a few eyebrows, even in Hollywood."

Crawford nodded. "Do you have any idea how much she was after?"

"From Hasleiter?"

Crawford nodded.

"I wouldn't be surprised if it was really big bucks."

"Which you define as what?"

"Um, a million or more. I know she had gotten that much from this one man who *really* didn't want his rich wife or the world to know what he was doing in his spare time."

Crawford thought for a moment. "Sounds like what you're saying is, #MeToo in reverse."

"What do you mean?"

"Well, all the #MeToo publicity and all the press about Bill Cosby, Harvey Weinstein, and Kevin Spacey? This would be the opposite. A big name in Hollywood, but a *woman* this time, using the casting room couch to seduce and sexually harass young guys. Promise them roles and jobs for sex."

"Never thought of that."

"What else do you know about it?"

"Like I told you, I don't know for sure that Antonia ever did that with Hasleiter. She just kind of mentioned it once in passing when the main business had slowed down."

"But you don't know for sure that she *didn't* do it, right?"

Waverly nodded. "Right."

THIRTY-ONE

C rawford called Ott's cell from his car.

"Hey, Charlie."

"Where are you?"

"The station."

"Stay there. I'm gonna get LV Wurfel to come by. Got a bunch of questions for him. I'll fill you in when I get there. I got some more intel on Janny Hasleiter, too."

"Can't wait," Ott said, and clicked off.

Crawford dialed Wurfel.

"Hello, Charlie," Wurfel said, sounding uncharacteristically apprehensive, "What did I do this time?"

"I'm sure Waverly's called you by now. I need you to come by the station."

"When?"

"Now."

*****

Bettina buzzed Crawford to say LV Wurfel was in the reception area.

Crawford went out to get him while Ott waited in Crawford's office.

"This is much nicer than any police station I've ever been to," Wurfel said, as Crawford led him back. "Course it is Palm Beach."

Crawford turned to him. "You been to quite a few, have you?"

"More'n three and less than a hundred."

His humor was getting marginally better.

They walked into Crawford's office. Ott was standing on the other side of Crawford's desk.

"This is my partner, Mort Ott."

"Heard a lot about you," Ott said, shaking Wurfel's hand.

"All of it good, I'm sure," said Wurfel.

Ott just smiled.

"Have a seat, LV," Crawford said. "I'm going to just cut right to the chase."

"That is your MO," Wurfel said, sitting next to Ott.

"As I'm sure you know, I had a conversation with your, ah, partner, Waverly,"—Wurfel nodded—"and I told her that someone who has taken over Distinguished Consorts, a million-dollar-a-year business, after the death of its owner, has to be regarded as a prime suspect."

Ott nodded. "I can't think of anyone more prime," he chimed in.

"That so, Mort?" said LV.

Ott just chuckled his throaty Ott-chuckle.

"Okay, well, first of all," Wurfel said, "as we all know, it's just a temporary gig. Meaning, once the will's… what you call it?"

"Probated?"

"Yeah, once that happens, Distinguished Consorts goes to the will's beneficiary."

"True," Crawford said. "But two things: one, that could take a long, long time. 'Cause, as I'm guessing you know, it looks like the will is going to be contested, and that could take forever to resolve. And, two, as I said to Waverly, with your combined knowledge, the two of you could start an identical company with what you already have: that being Antonia's Rolodex and all her contacts."

"Yeah, just call it Prominent Companions or something," Ott said. "All you gotta do is print new business cards."

"I like Distinguished Consorts better, if it's all the same to you, Mort," Wurfel said.

"Your clients aren't gonna care," Ott said. "They know what you're selling."

"Okay, so I get why you're trying to make me out as a prime suspect. Now what?"

"Well, you could confess," Ott said.

"You're a funny guy," Wurfel shot back. "Only problem is I didn't do it. See, as I told Charlie, I was a hundred miles away. With witnesses to prove it."

"Yeah, but you could get your biker buddies to lie for you," Crawford said.

"I'm surprised at you, Charlie," Wurfel said. "Don't you realize by now I'm just a guy looking to make a buck? Last thing I am is *any* kind of killer. Yeah, okay, you may not approve of the ways I like to make that buck, but let's face it, it's pretty harmless."

"Actually, yeah LV, that *is* pretty much my take on you," Crawford said. "I just wanted to give my partner a chance to look you over. You know, kick the tires. See what he thinks."

Wurfel turned to Ott. "So what *do* you think?"

"I haven't decided yet," Ott said.

Wurfel nodded. "Okay, well, do you boys have any more questions for me?"

Crawford glanced over at Ott. Ott nodded.

"Where were you three nights ago at about two in the morning?" Which was when DeeDee had been assaulted at her home.

Crawford followed up on that. "And, how 'bout, do you own a sharp knife?"

Wurfel thought for a moment. "In the middle of a crazy dream, in answer to the first question. And no, the knife I have is dull as hell. Could barely cut a piece of string."

"Got anyone to alibi you on the first one?" Ott asked.

"You mean, did I have a bedmate, Mort?" Wurfel said. "Nope, no such luck."

Ott's nod lacked enthusiasm.

"Okay," said Crawford. "That does it then."

Though he was tempted to ask Wurfel about his nocturnal skinny-dipping at the Portofino pool.

Wurfel got to his feet. "You're welcome. Nice to have met you, Mort."

"Yeah, same," Ott said with a phlegmatic nod.

Crawford walked Wurfel out to the front desk, where he saw Bettina with a big smile on her face. It could only mean one thing: she found out where Whop-O, New Hampshire, was and had the skinny on Abby and Steve Swain.

He turned to Wurfel. "No more shenanigans, huh, LV?"

"Like I said, it's all harmless stuff, Charlie," he said. "See ya around."

"Hold on, wait a minute," Crawford said. "What about your twenty-grand charitable contribution?"

"Oh, yeah, I forgot to tell you," Wurfel said. "Half is going to that homeless group, the Lord's Place, the other half to Wounded Warriors. I'll show the receipts as soon as I get 'em."

Crawford gave him a pat on the shoulder. "Good man, LV. Money well-donated."

Wurfel nodded and walked away as Crawford went over to the amped-up Bettina.

"It's name is Walpole, a little town on the Connecticut River." Crawford could remember seeing the name on a highway sign when he drove up to Dartmouth on Interstate 91 twenty years before. "And wait 'til you hear about this guy Steve Swain."

Crawford shrugged. "Tell me."

"He was a big basketball star in high school, then went to play at UConn—University of Connecticut—"

He nodded. "I know. Then what?"

"His senior year, a year after he married Abby, he got booted for stealing a car when he was drunk."

"When was this?"

"Three years ago," Bettina said. "So he never graduated."

"What happened to him?"

"He ended up getting a job as coach of the Walpole High School basketball team, but apparently had kind of an anger-management issue and got into a serious fight with a rival team's coach."

"And when was that?"

"Earlier this year. Lost his job. And was charged with aggravated assault."

"For the fight with the other coach?"

"Yes. The Walpole team forfeited the game, too."

"Wow. And what do you know about Abby, other than apparently, she made a poor choice in husbands."

"Nothing. Not a thing," Bettina said. "Oh, but I did find out that they were supposed to leave Palm Beach the day before Antonia's murder, but they missed their flight home."

"They weren't on the plane?"

"No, they spent that night at the Economy Inn near the airport here. Left late the next day."

"So presumably after Antonia was killed."

Bettina nodded.

"Where were they flying to?"

"Bradley Field in Hartford."

Crawford nodded. He knew Bradley was a little over a two-hour drive to Hanover, where Dartmouth was, which meant it would be less to Walpole.

"It's a ninety-minute drive from Bradley Field to Walpole," Bettina said, as if reading his mind.

"You do good work, Bettina," he said. "But you didn't find anything at all about Abby?"

Bettina shook her head. "I looked everywhere. Nothing. Sorry."

"Don't be."

She cocked her head and smiled. "If Mort ever retires, you know where to find me."

He patted her on the shoulder. "Good job," he said. "Oh hey, one last thing. Make reservations for me and Mort on the first flight out tomorrow to Hartford, please."

"You got it."

He went back to his office where Ott was waiting for him.

Ott had his feet up on his desk, reading something on the internet. He looked up when he heard his partner's familiar footsteps.

"Ever been to New Hampshire, Mort?"

"No, but I've been to Vermont. Same thing, right?"

"Similar." And he proceeded to tell Ott what he had learned from Bettina.

"I'd say those are two people we definitely should be checking out," Ott said. "I mean, he sounds like a guy who's capable of violence. Oh, hey, what were you going to tell me about Janny Hasleiter?"

Crawford nodded. "That's the other person we need to talk to."

"Why? What's the story?"

"According to Waverly Bangs, she might have been the female version of Harvey Weinstein."

"Except with... guys, you mean?"

"You got it," Crawford said, and told Ott about Waverly Bangs suspecting that Janny Hasleiter might have been blackmailed by Antonia von Habsburg for big money.

"But maybe Waverly told you that to take the spotlight off of her," Ott said.

"Yeah, I thought of that and could be. But Hasleiter... I've already put in a call to her. I mean. I'd like to try to see her before we go north."

"Maybe if she turns out to be our killer, we can skip the trip north."

"Yeah, maybe, but I still think the Swains look like good possibles," Crawford said. "In any case, I'm gonna talk to Norm. Get him to authorize us going up there."

"Is it cold up there this time of year. I mean, do I need a parka or anything?"

Crawford laughed. "It's summer, man. Even in New Hampshire, it's nice in the summer."

"Want me to go with you to talk to Norm?"

"Nah, the whole thing'll probably cost less than a thousand bucks. I think he'll be good with that."

How wrong he was.

THIRTY-TWO

"New Hampshire? What? You going skiing or something?" Norm asked. "I mean, you really think they got guys up there creative enough to have done this job?"

"Creative? What are you talking about? How about sadistic?"

"Well, okay, that too. You know how some guys feel about their mothers-in-law."

Crawford shook his head. He wondered if maybe Rutledge had had a few pops at lunch. "Are you trying to be funny, Norm? I mean, I come to you with a credible perp and you're cracking mother-in-law jokes."

"Hey, relax, will ya. I just can't see a guy from New Hampshire doing this job."

"What difference does it make where he's from? It's all about motive."

"So you're saying because he's after his mother-in-law's money?"

"That's exactly what I'm saying. And now that I think about it, there's a possibility that he and his wife might have taken a bunch of her very expensive jewelry. And possibly fenced it around here somewhere."

"How do you come up with that?"

"Because they missed their flight back up north the day before her murder. Maybe intentionally. And when Ott and I went through von Habsburg's house, we got the sense a bunch of jewelry was missing. So, my theory is, they might have gone to a few places around here and fenced it. Probably a hell of a lot more places to do it around here than in Walpole, New Hampshire."

"What about Hartford? I'm sure they got places there."

Crawford nodded. "Yeah, that's a possibility."

"So this is the best guy you've come up with in a whole week? No, make that eight days, now."

"We got others, but I also have a hunch that Steve and Abby Swain might just show up in one of Antonia von Habsburg's wills."

"Wills... plural?"

"Yeah, there're already two, with two different beneficiaries."

"No shit?"

"No shit."

Rutledge put his hand to his chin in an imitation of *The Thinker*, as if perspicacious thoughts would course through his brain now. Crawford couldn't wait for them.

"I'm going to call Perry Jastrow, von Habsburg's lawyer, and find out if he's heard anything about a third will."

"From a lawyer representing these people the Swains, you mean?"

"Yeah, exactly."

"Let me think about this for a minute," Rutledge said.

Crawford could practically hear the clanking.

Finally. "All right. But do you really need Ott?"

"Course I need Ott. He's my partner."

"Yes, I'm well aware of that. But this seems like a one-man job."

"Norm, I need him. Okay?"

The customary Rutledge theatrical sigh came next. "All right."

Then he had an afterthought. "I don't s'pose this is 'cause you want to go up there for some reunion at that fancy ivy-league college of yours? Figured you needed a wingman."

Crawford thought it was a toss-up as to who had the worse sense of humor: Rutledge or LV Wurfel.

THIRTY-THREE

The earliest flight Bettina was able to book to Hartford was one that left at eleven thirty in the morning. For Crawford and Ott, it was a pretty uneventful flight. No unruly passengers which seemed to be the "new normal" post-Covid. Bettina had rented them a car at Enterprise and they were pulling out of the lot now. Ott, who it had been decided a long time ago was the better driver of the two, was at the wheel of the Chevy Cruze. They crossed the Connecticut River and got onto Interstate 91.

"I'll be giving you a travelogue since we'll be approaching my old stomping grounds," Crawford said.

"Oh, goodie. Can't wait," Ott said, flipping on his blinker to pass an eighteen-wheeler. "We ever get out to Cleveland, I'll repay the favor."

"You can point out that burning river you got out there," Crawford said.

"Oh, yeah, the good ol' Cuyahoga."

"So, the Connecticut River, when we get further north, divides Vermont and New Hampshire."

"I did not know that," Ott said. "Okay, geography quiz: What river divides Ohio from Kentucky and West Virginia."

"West Virginia? Ohio borders West Virginia?"

"Sure does."

Crawford thought for a moment. "Um, I'm going with either the Allegheny or the Ohio?"

"Okay, which one?"

"The Allegheny."

"*Ahhhnn!*" Ott made the *Jeopardy* buzzer sound. "Sorry. The Ohio."

Crawford shook his head. "Okay, I got one for you. If the Pro Football Hall of Fame is in Canton, what's in Springfield, Massachusetts, which we're about to drive through in about fifteen minutes."

"What do you mean, 'If the Pro Football Hall of Fame is in Canton'? There's no *if* about it, *it is.*"

Crawford laughed. "Okay, okay, it's a figure of speech. What's in Springfield, Mass?"

"Ah, the Bowling Hall of Fame?"

"Come on, man, don't insult Springfield. The Basketball Hall of Fame."

"That was my second guess."

They rode in silence for the next ten miles. "Lotta of hills in this part of the world," Ott said.

"Yeah, mountains, too."

"So I'm guessing you were a skier, along with all your other athletic conquests."

"Yup. We had this place twenty minutes away from college called the Dartmouth Skiway. Broke my leg there. Trying to impress this girl."

"Show-off."

There it is," Crawford pointed as they passed through Springfield: a big white pillar with an oversized basketball and a sign that read: "Naismith Memorial Basketball Hall of Fame."

"Maybe check it out on the way back if we got this Swain dude in the back seat in handcuffs."

Crawford nodded. "Yeah, that would be nice. Get Rutledge off our backs."

Crawford's cell phone rang as they were on the outskirts of Springfield.

He looked down at the display. "Oh, good," he said, "this is Perry Jastrow, von Habsburg's attorney." He clicked the green button and put it on speaker. "Thanks for getting back to me, Mr. Jastrow."

"Sure, Charlie. What do you need to know?"

"Just one question: have you heard from Ms. von Habsburg's daughter or attorney about yet another will?"

"No, I haven't. Abby Swain, you mean?" Jastrow said.

"Yes, that's her."

"I just know about the ones naming Frank Lincoln and Esmerelda Ortega as beneficiaries. We've got to find out which is legit."

"What happens if they're both legit but have different dates on them?" Crawford asked.

"I've had that happen before and it's a real mess. The probate judge makes the call and, I can guarantee you, somebody's always pissed off and ready to sue when it's all said and done."

"I hear you," Crawford said. "Well, thanks for getting back to me. Let me know if you get anything that might help me."

"Will do." He clicked off.

"I'm thinking we just show up on the Swains' doorstep rather than call," Crawford told Ott. "The usual MO."

"Yeah, I agree. Otherwise, they could be conveniently busy or heading out of town."

Crawford's cell rang again. He looked down at it. "Speaking of Bettina," he said, putting her on speaker. "Hey, Bettina, what's up?"

"So in my never-ending quest to keep you and Mort up to speed, I have a scoop for you."

"Let's hear it."

"Guess who lives in Walpole, New Hampshire?"

"Besides the Swains?"

"Yes, and your clue is *the king of documentaries*."

"Ken Burns?" Ott said.

"Bingo," said Bettina, "Very good, Mort."

"What's he doing in a little burg like that?" Crawford asked.

"I don't know, but scoop number two is he's got a restaurant there, too."

"Called?"

"Burdick's, and it sounds really good. Put it this way: where in Palm Beach can you get a fourteen-ounce steak for thirty-three bucks?"

"Nowhere."

"Or there's something called Ken's Salad—grilled salmon, Bibb lettuce, avocado, lemon vinaigrette—twenty-three bucks."

"Make us a reservation, will ya?" Ott said.

"One step ahead of you. Six o'clock tonight. It was either that or eight."

"Yeah, that's too late. Thanks, you're a doll," Ott said. "What's the address?"

"47 Main Street."

"Which may be the only street in Walpole," said Ott.

"No," Bettina said, "there's at least one more because the Swains live on Prospect Hill Road. Number 33, to be exact."

"Right," Crawford said. "We should be arriving there in about a half hour. We're outside of Brattleboro, Vermont, at the moment."

"Brattleboro? That's a real name?"

"Yup. It's a thriving metropolis," Crawford said.

Bettina laughed. "All right, well, let me know if you need anything else."

"You've been calling that number for Janny Hasleiter I gave you, right?" Crawford asked.

"Sure have. Left four messages, but no call back."

"Okay, try to get the number of the studio in Hollywood she works with. Or a West Coast number. She might be out there."

"Okay, I'm on it."

"Thanks," Crawford said. "When do you have us leaving tomorrow, again?"

"At 3:40 p.m. out of Bradley."

"Good deal."

"Tell Ken, Bettina sends her regards," she said.

THIRTY-FOUR

They drove into the driveway of the house at 33 Prospect Hill Road twenty-five minutes later. It was a large white Georgian with black shutters and a porte cochere in front. Straight ahead was a three-car garage and what appeared to be a two-story guesthouse; to the right, a pool and a vast garden.

"This is really nice," Ott said. "I'd say the Swains are doing all right for themselves."

Crawford pointed at a black BMW. "Yeah, no kidding. Car's pretty new."

Ott, car guy he was, nodded. "Last year's Bimmer."

They got out of the Cruze and walked up to the front door. Crawford looked down at this watch. It was 4:10 p.m.

Ott hit the buzzer and a few moments later a woman in her late twenties, with nice skin and unfashionably thick glasses, opened the door.

"Mrs. Swain?" Crawford asked.

"Yes," she said quizzically, as if seeing two men in ties in her little town was as rare as an alligator on the back lawn.

"My name is Detective Crawford and this is my partner, Detective Ott. We're from the Palm Beach Police Department and we're investigating the death of your mother."

Abby Swain nodded. "Wow, you've come a long way," she said. "Want to come inside?"

"Yes, thank you," Crawford said.

Abby turned and they followed her inside.

The living room looked like something you'd inherit from your conservative Yankee grandmother, with the exception of what looked to be some kind of contemporary shrine in the far left corner. Crawford spotted a silver statuette of a basketball player taking a shot and knew that this must be Abby's husband's memorial to his glory days as a star high school hoopster.

Abby pointed to two easy chairs and a sofa. "Have a seat, gentlemen."

They did. "Is your husband at work?" Ott asked.

"Yes, he should be home shortly."

"Does he work in Walpole?" Crawford asked.

"No, Keene. It's about twenty minutes away."

"Are you okay answering some questions without him here?" Ott asked.

"Oh, sure," Abby said. "Ask away."

"Well, first, we understand that you visited your mother a week or so ago in Palm Beach," Crawford said. "And that you were scheduled to fly back the day before the day she was killed, but ended up flying back the following day. The day she was killed, that would be."

A look of panic or possibly anguish cut across Abby's face. "Yes, well, something... came up."

"Can you tell us what that was?" Ott asked.

Abby shut her eyes. "Oh God," she said, like that was all she wanted to say on the matter.

"Please, Mrs. Swain, it might help in our investigation. Help us find your mother's murderer."

"I doubt it," she said with a deep sigh. "All right, what happened was Steve got in a fight at a restaurant. He actually was arrested and had to spend the night in the West Palm jail."

"No offense," Ott said, "but it must have been a pretty bad fight."

Abby nodded and dropped her eyes to the floor. "The man he had the fight with was hurt pretty bad."

"Sorry to hear that," Crawford said. "So you got a flight back the next night."

"Yes, we were lucky. It ended up that Steve just had to pay a fine. No charges were filed."

"Did you see your mother the next day?" Ott asked.

"No, I just spoke to her on the phone as I waited to get Steve out of jail," Abby said. "It was not easy telling her about what had happened."

"And when did your husband get out of jail?" Crawford asked.

"Around twelve noon, after the, ah... arraignment."

That let Swain off the hook, since the ME had pegged Antonia von Habsburg's death at between 9:00 and 11:00 a.m.

They heard the sound of a car driving in. "Speak of the devil," Abby said.

"Where does your husband work, Mrs. Swain?"

Abby's eyes fell back down to the floor. "He's a teller at a bank in Keene."

The front door opened and they heard footsteps, then a very tall man appeared. "Entertaining again, huh, Abby?" he said.

Abby didn't laugh as Crawford and Ott rose to their feet. "Steve, these are two detectives from Palm Beach investigating Mom's death," she said, pointing. "Detective Crawford and Detective Ott."

"All that way for nothing," Swain said, shaking Crawford's and Ott's hands.

"Well, we hope not," Crawford said. "Mind if we ask you a few questions, Mr. Swain?"

"Nah, ask away," Steve said. "If I don't like one, I'll just lie... JK."

"JK?" asked Crawford.

"Just kidding."

Crawford nodded, wanting to cut to the chase. He looked back at Abby. "Your mother, it appears, left at least two wills. One naming her son, your brother Frank as her sole heir—"

"My half-brother," Abby corrected him.

"Okay, half-brother... and the other will names your mother's daughter, your... half-sister Esmerelda Ortega as sole beneficiary."

"Frank's is bullshit," Steve blurted.

"What?"

"He forged it. That will he came up with."

Crawford glanced back at Abby. "Could you please explain?"

Abby sighed. "It's kind of a long story."

"Tell you the truth," Crawford said, "we didn't come all this way for short ones."

Abby glanced at her husband. "You want to tell them?"

"No, it was your mother," Steve said. "You got the floor, honey."

Steve shook his head, and Abby took a deep sigh again. "Okay, well," Abby said, "the good news, I guess, is there isn't going to be a third will naming us as beneficiaries."

"Can you start at the beginning, please?" Crawford asked.

"Sure, let me give you the big picture," Abby said. "When my mother was alive she was very generous. Both to Frank and Steve and me. You probably know already that she basically paid for that church of his in Royal Palm Beach. I mean, all of it. She was also very generous to us. Bought us this house, in fact. Paid a lot of bills of ours when we were going through hard times,"—she gave Steve a quick glance—"which actually we're still going through."

"Come on, hon," Steve said, "it's not so bad. At least I got a job."

"Yes, you do," Abby said. "And I'm proud of you for that."

Steve chuckled. "She's just saying that for your benefit."

"So, the point is, my mother told us when we were visiting that she was going to leave whatever she had to that little girl—"

"Esmeralda?"

"Yes, Esmeralda, Lauren, whatever you call her, because she had given Frank and us over three million dollars each."

"Betcha Frank was closer to five million," Steve said.

"Whatever. Mom wasn't keeping track of everything so it wasn't exactly a penny for Frank and a penny for us."

"But, so what you're saying, in your opinion, is that the real will is the one in which Esmeralda is named beneficiary—"

"— and Frank's is a total phony," Steve said, "which is why I'd maybe look into Frank a little harder. As a suspect, I mean."

Ott was nodding. "So, knowing what you know, Mr. Swain," he said, "Frank Lincoln would get your vote for the one who did it?"

"Yeah, definitely," Steve said, turning to his wife. "What about you?"

Abby shrugged. "I don't really know. Tell you the truth, I haven't spent a lot of time sitting around thinking about it."

Crawford shot Ott his "got anything else?" glance. Ott gave him a quick head shake.

Crawford started to get to his feet. "Well, thank you both very much, you obviously have a bulletproof alibi, which your wife explained to us," he said to Steve. "You have our cards. If you think of anything that you think might be helpful, please give us a call."

"Will do," Steve said, as he shook Crawford's and Ott's hands and his wife nodded.

They walked out of the house, got in their car and headed down Prospect Hill Road to Ken Burns's restaurant Burdick's.

Ott was reading something on his iPhone as they walked in.

"Says, of this place: 'a little piece of the big city in an historically well-heeled tiny country town,'" Ott read to Crawford, then looked up as they approached a stylish, white-haired woman who was clearly the hostess.

"Gentlemen," she said, "you must be Mr. Crawford and Mr. Orr."

"Ott," said Ott, "Ts not Rs"

"I'm sorry about that," she said. "May I show you to your table?"

"Please," Crawford said.

They followed her to a corner table and sat.

"Nice place," Ott said, looking around.

"Yeah," Crawford said, glancing at the menu, "with prices to match."

"I don't even have to look," Ott said. "That fourteen-ounce steak for thirty-three bucks has my name all over it. What about you?"

"Well, I'm thinking that when at Ken's, maybe do a Ken's Salad."

"The salmon one, right?"

Crawford nodded.

"Where does Bettina have us staying up in Hanover?" Ott asked, just as Crawford's cell phone rang.

Crawford looked at the display and picked up. "All Ott has to do is mention your name and you call… Hey Bettina, what's up?"

"I finally got to speak to Janny Hasleiter, and she is in L.A. We had about a twenty-second conversation. Guess she's got no time for the little people. Bottom line is she'll be back in Palm Beach day after tomorrow and said she can talk to you then."

"Good work," Crawford said. "See you day after tomorrow."

"Bye, Charlie."

Crawford turned back to Ott. "What'd you ask me?"

"Where are we staying in Hanover?"

"Place called the Hanover Inn. My parents used to stay there."

"You mean, when they came up to watch junior perform his heroics on the Dartmouth athletic fields?"

Crawford laughed. "Or lose to other teams, which happened a lot of the time."

"*You*, Charlie? You actually lost? Can't believe it," Ott said, as a waiter approached their table and took their drink and dinner orders.

"So what was your favorite sport?" Ott asked, as he handed the waiter the menu.

"Lacrosse. I loved it."

"Old Indian sport, right?" Ott asked.

"Yeah, the Hurons and the Mohawks started it up in Canada somewhere."

"I think they had club lacrosse at Cuyahoga Community College, but there was too much running for a lard-ass like me."

"I saw a picture of you back in the day. You weren't a lard-ass."

Ott laughed. "Well, I sure as hell wasn't a hard-ass."

"Okay, how 'bout a pudgy-ass or maybe a... roly-poly-ass?"

"Yeah, that's about right," Ott said. "So you liked lacrosse better than football?"

"Yeah, liked the fact that lacrosse was pretty much constant action; football was start, stop, time out, injury, half-time..."

*****

The steak and salmon did not disappoint. Crawford was paying the bill as Ott talked to the waiter. He had just asked him what Ken Burns was like.

The waiter lowered his voice. "We're s'posed to pretend we never met him if people ask, but he comes in here like three, four times a week."

"Nice guy?" Ott asked.

"Very nice guy," the waiter said. "Good tipper, too."

"Well, next time you see him, tell him Bettina from Palm Beach, Florida, is a big fan," Ott said.

"I'll pass that along," the waiter said as he handed Crawford his Visa card back. "Thank you, gentlemen, have a nice evening."

It was only seven fifteen when Crawford and Ott got back to their rental car.

"How far to Hanover?" Ott asked, as he opened the driver's side door.

"Um, I guessing fifty minutes if we get on 91 and maybe an hour, ten if we go the slow, scenic route."

"I vote for the slow, scenic route."

Crawford nodded. "You're driving. Your call."

*****

They were pulling into the Hanover Inn at just past nine fifteen. They had an unexpected adventure on the "slow, scenic route" just south of Lebanon, New Hampshire: a flat tire. Ott tried to claim that as driver, he couldn't both drive and change a flat, that job always fell to the man riding shotgun. He added, "Besides, if I ever got down near the ground to change it, I'd never get back up. Bad knees and all."

Crawford shook his head and chuckled." That is the lamest thing I've ever heard." But he ended up putting the donut spare on the right rear anyway. Then, after that, they had a ten-minute wait for a very slow moving train.

"You know," Ott said as they waited, "I was just thinking… did it ever occur to you that waiter was never gonna tell us that Ken Burns was the biggest dipshit in the world, even if he was?"

Crawford watched the last few train cars rumble by slowly. "What?"

"That waiter was never gonna tell us… never mind."

"Were you about to make a profound observation?"

"No, just making conversation while we watch this train hump along at ten miles an hour."

After they checked in to the Hanover Inn, they went to the bar. It was nine thirty.

It was half-full with mainly couples who seemed to be in their forties and early fifties. Crawford guessed they were mostly parents there to visit their sons and daughters and make sure they were going to classes instead of nights full of keggers followed by hungover days.

They were going to have a nightcap, then lights out by ten o'clock when Ott's cell phone rang.

*****

"Hey, DeeDee," Ott answered.

Crawford shot him the thumbs-up.

"I've missed your visits," DeeDee told him. "I also called cause I heard something you might be interested in if you haven't heard already."

"What's that?" Ott said, tapping on the speakerphone.

"A girlfriend told me Luther King got arrested for assaulting a woman."

"You're kidding. Do you know anything more about it?"

"Just that it happened in his car."

"He got arrested by the Palm Beach Police?"

"No, my girlfriend said it happened in West Palm."

Crawford pulled out his iPhone.

"Okay, well thanks, we'll look into it. How you feeling anyway?"

"Better. You know, every day a little better."

"Good to hear. Well, I'll come see you tomorrow."

"I missed seeing you today."

"I would have been there today, but I'm up in New Hampshire."

"New Hampshire? What are you doing there?"

"It's the leaf-peeping season, I never miss it."

DeeDee laughed. "No, seriously?"

"The Antonia case."

"Well, good luck."

"We need some. See you tomorrow."

*****

Crawford dialed his phone the second he overheard about Luther King. He knew a homicide guy in the West Palm Police Department.

"Hey, Ronnie, sorry to call so late, it's Charlie Crawford."

"Hey, Charlie, what's up?"

"You know anything about an assault somewhere in West Palm. Perp's name is Luther King from Palm Beach."

"Matter of fact, I do. One of my guys investigated. He slapped around a woman 'cause it seemed like she wouldn't put out for him in the back of his limo. Class acts you got in Palm Beach."

"How bad was she beat up?"

"Not real bad. Her name is, ah, Justine Burroughs. Sustained some cuts and a black eye. We got King in the jug."

"Do me a favor, see if you can get the vic's number. I want to talk to her."

"I'll see what I can do, Charlie. That's all you need?"

"Yeah, for now. Thanks, Ronnie."

"You got it. I'll get back to you."

Crawford clicked off and looked up at Ott. "You got the gist of that?"

Ott nodded. "Guy likes to beat up women."

"Question is, does he like to kill 'em," Crawford said, taking a sip of his bourbon.

Then out of nowhere, he heard a voice behind him. "Charlie? Charlie Crawford, is that you?"

Crawford turned and saw an older man with a blond crewcut and military posture smiling at him.

"Holy shit," the man said, "it *is* you. Greg Bork, your old lax coach."

"I'll be damned," Crawford said, shaking his hand. "How the hell are you, Coach? Nice to see you again, man."

"Same," Bork said, then pointed to a man next to him. "And this is Miles Crennfield. I'm trying to recruit his son. He's a big star at Manhasset High on Long Island."

"Hey, Miles," Crawford shook his hand, then turning to Ott. "And this is my partner, Mort Ott."

"Wow, Charlie, I would never have guessed—" Bork shook Ott's hand.

Crawford burst out laughing. "No, no, not that kind of partner. We're detectives, down in Florida."

"No shit, really," Bork said. "I figured you were headed to Wall Street."

"I was, but… Anyway, back when I was playing, you were assistant. I heard you got the head coach job… what, like ten years ago?"

"Twelve actually, we've had a hell of a lot of good teams. Won the Ivies three years in a row."

"Nice going," Crawford said. "So where's your son, Miles?"

"That's a good question," Crennfield said. "I think some of Greg's players might be leading him astray at one of the frat houses."

"Oh God, which one?" Crawford asked.

"Theta Delta Chi," Bork said.

He turned to Ott. "That's my old house,"—then to Crennfield—"a bunch of notorious badasses."

Crennfield nodded. "Then Connor will fit right in."

Crawford laughed. "Hey, if it's any consolation, I survived."

Ott patted Crawford on the shoulder. "We might have to check out your old stomping grounds, Charlie. The Theta Delta Chi house."

"It's your kind of place," Crawford said. "You're never gonna want to leave."

THIRTY-FIVE

Greg Bork bought Crawford, Ott, and Miles Crennfield a round of drinks while the four—excluding Ott, who was clueless on the subject—talked about lacrosse. They talked about some of the great players in lacrosse history—Jim Brown, the star football player, among them— and some of the great games, then Bork reminisced about a few of Crawford's glory moments, which Crawford had long since forgotten.

"I remember when you had a fight with a Harvard player, knocked the bastard out. Your senior year, I think it was," Bork said.

Ott cuffed Crawford on the shoulder. "Lucky punch, huh Charlie?"

Crawford cringed. "You must have me confused with someone else, Greg."

Greg Bork laughed. "No, it was you."

"What position does Connor play?" Crawford quickly changed the subject.

"Attack," said Crennfield.

"Kid's fast as hell," Bork said.

Crawford nodded and snuck a peek at this watch. It was 11:05.

Greg Bork clapped his hands. "All right, you boys ready?"

"Ready for what?" Crawford asked.

"Go have a pop at Theta?"

Crawford shook his head. "I'm ready for bed."

"Come on, Charlie, I gotta see your old hangout," Ott said.

Crawford groaned. "All right, but just one drink."

"Come on," Greg said, "when was the last time you hung at Theta and had just one drink?"

"Never, but this is the new me. The grown-up Charlie."

Ott glanced at Bork, smiled and lowered his voice. "The boring Charlie."

*****

"There you are," Greg Bork said, pointing at Crawford's name in gold letters on a brown wooden plaque. The four men were in a hallway of Theta Delta Chi house. Crawford's name was next to the year he graduated—1999—on a plaque that read, in larger, raised gold letters, "Athlete of the Year."

"Wow, my hero," Ott said.

The other men laughed as Greg Bork led them to a stairway that led downstairs.

"This is what's known as the descent to hell," Crawford warned Ott, as they went down the stairs.

The frat party room had three distinct areas: a bar area, a dance floor, and a game room. All of which were occupied by drinking, laughing, sweating, smiling, dancing, flirting boys and girls—they all looked so young to Crawford, there was no way he could think of them as men and women. The game room had a beat-up foosball game, a pool table, several console games, and an area where a group of kids were playing a game which Crawford recognized as beer pong, aka Beirut.

"Hey, Dad," one of the kids yelled as the four men got close to the pong game in progress.

"Hey, Connor," Miles shouted back to his glassy-eyed son, who had a big red plastic cup of beer in hand. "That your first beer of the night?"

"Yeah, if you don't count his first six," said another boy, who Crawford guessed was one of his lacrosse-playing hosts.

*****

It was an hour later and somehow Ott had wangled Crawford into playing a game of pong with the losers of the previous game, two girls by the name of Cynthia and Fiona.

"You're the first Fiona I've ever met," Ott said giving her a gentle fist bump.

"And I think you're my first Mort," she said.

"So, this is my first time playing," Ott said to her. "Since it wasn't around in my college days, but, look out, my partner's a ringer."

"In different sports," Greg Bork, now a spectator, added.

"All right, ladies first," said Crawford, handing Cynthia a ping-pong ball.

Cynthia, who looked a little wobbly, tossed the ball at the sixteen-ounce Dixie cups full of beer. It bounced on the rim of one of the cups and dropped in.

"Nice shot," Ott said, glancing up at Crawford. "So now we have to drink what's in this cup?"

Crawford nodded. "Yup, eight ounces for you, eight for me."

Ott took the ping-pong ball out of the cup and drank half of the beer in it. Then he handed the cup to Crawford.

"Wow," Ott said to Crawford. "I just did the math. So, there are ten cups times sixteen ounces, that's 160 ounces or... Jesus, that's over two whole six-packs."

Crawford nodded. "Yeah, let's just hope the girls aren't so accurate next time."

"No kiddin' or we'll be crawling back to the Hanover Inn."

"I've done that before," Crawford said, then downed his half.

"Okay, boys," said Fiona, "less talking, more tossing."

"Sorry, sorry," Ott said, flipping the ping-pong ball at the ten cups in a triangular formation in front of the girls. It, too, bounced off a rim but fell to the floor.

Then Cynthia lined up her toss.

It landed squarely in a cup. "Yes!" said Cynthia with a fist pump. "Down the hatch, boys."

Crawford groaned, took the ping-pong ball out of the cup, took a long pull, and handed the cup to Ott.

"You only drank a third."

"Close enough," Crawford said, then he tossed the ping-pong ball. It went in a cup.

"Okay, girls, your turn. Drink up," he said.

"Nice toss," Ott said, then lowering his voice. "You know, Chuck, I haven't added it all up yet, but between Burdick's and the Hanover Inn bar and now here, this is more than I typically drink in a... month."

"Yeah, and you got a nice little slur I've never heard before, except maybe at Mookie's," Crawford said, looking over at the two girls. "Okay, Cynthia, you're up."

Cynthia did a couple practice motions, then dunked the ball into another cup.

"Who's the ringer?" she said, rubbing it in.

Crawford looked over at Greg Bork. "Will you drink some of this for me, Greg?"

"Sorry, Charlie, you know the rules."

Crawford and Ott downed their halves of the Dixie cup.

This time Crawford did the math: two bourbons at Burdick's, three at the Hanover Inn, twenty-four ounces of beer at Theta Delt… He stifled a burp. "Hey, Mort, I think we better concede."

"I heard that!" Fiona said. "Just for the record, it is very unmanly to concede."

"Yeah, you gotta take your punishment," Cynthia chimed in.

Ott smiled at Crawford. "Yeah, Charlie, you some kind of pussy."

*****

Fifteen minutes later, after he and Crawford had downed three more cups of beer, Ott swayed forward and bumped into the table, knocking a considerable amount of beer out of the Dixie cups and knocking one over that was now dripping over the side of the table.

First, Fiona and Cynthia laughed, then they accused Ott of doing it on purpose.

"Honest, I didn't," Ott protested. "I just don't have full control of all my motor skills at the moment."

"Oh, good," Fiona said. "So you're ready to dance then?"

Ott burst out laughing as he looked off in the distance of the cavernous room and saw dancers thrashing on the dance floor to an old Culture Beat tune.

Ott shook his head. "Sorry, but I only do the bossa nova."

Nobody got the reference.

*****

Crawford didn't exactly bounce out of bed. He got up slowly, got dressed slowly, and took the slow elevator down to the ground floor of the Hanover Inn. Out of the corner of his eye he saw Ott in the large dining room across the lobby, a silver pot of coffee in front of him.

He walked over to him. "Whose idea was that?" he croaked.

"What?"

"Going to Theta Delt."

"Yours. You wanted to show me your name on that plaque."

Crawford laughed. "What are you having?"

"A stack and a pile of bacon. Proven hangover killers. What about you?"

"A large bottle of Bayer aspirin."

THIRTY-SIX

Crawford and Ott were in the fourteenth row of a JetBlue flight from Hartford to the West Palm Beach airport.

"You feelin' any better?" Ott asked Crawford.

"You mean since I killed half that bottle of aspirin?"

"Shit never worked for me."

Crawford shook his head. "I had to try something. I was near death. In that Beirut game alone, I figured I had at least a six-pack."

"That was nasty beer, too. I figured your frat bros could do a little better."

"What kind was it?"

"Keystone."

"Never even heard of it."

"Pure piss water."

"All right, Mort, we gotta do our best to pull it together and talk about the case."

"Okay," Ott said. "You never heard back from your friend at West Palm PD, did you?"

"Yeah, when I was getting the aspirin. He gave me the number of the girl Luther King beat up. I called her and left a message."

Ott nodded. "So in no particular order, we got Frank Lincoln—never had a padre before as a suspect—and Janny Hasleiter, and now Luther King's back in the running 'cause of his assault charge against, ah, Justine Burroughs, plus Waverly and LV, despite how innocent they both claim to be. I miss anybody?"

"I wouldn't call him a suspect," Crawford said, "but I want to at least talk to this guy David Balfour mentioned, Lord whatever, Nigel somebody, who, by process of elimination, might be the biological father of Antonia's daughter Esmerelda."

"What do you think you'll find out from him?"

"I don't know exactly, but according to David, he was a Brit looking to snag himself a rich American wife. It didn't quite work out, to the point where the guy didn't have two nickels to rub together. So, if I was him, and suddenly I found out my daughter was about to inherit fifteen million bucks, I would sure as hell want to come forward as her loving papa."

"To relieve her of some of that fifteen mil?"

"Yeah, I mean she lives with Antonia's cleaning lady in a pretty basic bungalow in Lake Worth. I never told you about her."

"No. Just that you met with her. No specifics."

"So, anyway, yeah, add ol' Nigel to your list."

"Okay, five suspects all together. But nobody's jumping out."

"I don't know about that. If you're Frank and used to your mother shelling out a couple hundred thou a year on you and all of a sudden it dries up and she says, 'That's it,' that might be a motive to go to her and beg. And if she says, 'No, that's all you're getting, business has slowed down,' then maybe you lose it and kill her and create a new will on the spot."

"Yeah, but the whole torture thing?"

"I know, I know. Not exactly something I see a son doing to a mother, especially a son who's a padre. The torture doesn't fit what we know of any of them. But we don't really know much about Luther King, except when he gets mad, he gets violent," Crawford said, with a shrug.

"Okay," Ott said, "but what's his motive? With all the others it could be money, but with Luther, being a few bucks short of being a billionaire, it clearly isn't."

"Back to Janny Hasleiter. Antonia goes from being her dear friend who she put up for membership at the Poinciana Club to a woman who's maybe blackmailing her. Course we don't know that for a fact, just something Waverly threw out there."

"To maybe take the heat off of her and LV?"

"We got too many maybes, Mort."

"No kiddin'," Ott said. "So what's our next move?"

"That's a hell of a good question. All I can see doing is asking a bunch of new questions to all of 'em. Press 'em all a little harder."

"You think it's one of 'em?" Ott asked.

"Put it this way, I'm confident enough that we've done our job to the point where it's highly unlikely some new suspect is gonna come out of the woodwork."

Ott nodded. "I agree."

The captain announced that they were about to land in West Palm and that they were ten minutes ahead of schedule.

"I hope this is a soft-landing pilot," Ott said.

"What do you mean?"

"'Cause this hangover of mine is not gonna be able to handle any bounces."

"Why'd you have to remind me? All that talk about suspects made me forget."

Ott shook his head. "That frat house of yours is an evil, evil place."

"I guess I never mentioned something."

"What?"

"It was the real-life inspiration for *Animal House*."

THIRTY-SEVEN

As Crawford and Ott were walking through the airport, Crawford got a call on his cell.

"Antonia's attorney," Crawford told Ott, then answered the phone.

"Hi, Charlie, it's Perry Jastrow. Boy, do I have a scoop for you."

"Can't wait to hear it."

"Okay, so does the name Nigel Ballantrae mean anything to you?"

"If he also goes by the name The Duke of Montpelier, it does."

"Yes, same guy," Jastrow said. "Is that how you pronounce it, *Mon-pell-yay*?"

"Yes, it is. So tell me."

"Okay, so I got a FedEx envelope this morning. In it were two things: the first was a promissory note, allegedly from Antonia von Habsburg to the duke. Cut through the legal bullshit, it says that Antonia owes the guy three and a half million bucks because she bought a painting from him for four million, of which she, again, allegedly, paid him $500,000 in cash."

"Meaning she still owes him three and a half million?"

"Exactly."

"And what was the other thing?"

"A letter to me from Nigel Ballantrae explaining that he sold her a painting of his called, *Untitled (Machinations)* by an artist named Cy Twombly, and that their agreement was—as stated in the promissory note—that she make three more payments on March 1 of each of the next three years to pay it off."

"Incredible," Crawford said. "And I was told, by a pretty reliable source, that Nigel Ballantrae, the Duke of Montpelier, was down to his last dollar and living on PB&Js."

"I didn't know what to make of it," Jastrow said. "It came with a photo of the painting, and the signature was either Antonia's or a damn good forgery."

"My money's on a forgery," Crawford said, as he and Ott walked out the main entrance of the airport.

"I just thought you'd want to know," Jastrow said. "I don't know what this does to the distribution of Antonia's assets. I suppose I'm going to need to freeze 'em—put three and a half million dollars in escrow, at least until this painting thing gets resolved."

"Then there's the whole issue of the two conflicting wills, right?"

"Yeah, I mean I strongly suspect Frank Lincoln's is bogus, but it's got some credibility in that you and your partner found it in Antonia's house."

Crawford held up his hand to Ott and stopped walking. "Do me a favor, Perry, will you put all that stuff you got from the duke into an email, including, if you can, a copy of the painting?"

"Sure. You got it. I'll get it over to you as soon as possible."

"Thanks. I think what I'm going to need to do first is go to Antonia's house and see if the painting is there. She had a fair amount of artwork but it wasn't as though I was checking out each artist's name."

"I'll take care of it," Jastrow said. "Will you get back to me as soon as you've had a chance to check this all out?"

"Yeah, definitely. We'll talk soon." Crawford clicked off.

"What was that all about?" Ott asked, as they walked to the bus stop for short- and long-term parking.

"Just the latest chapter in the most bizarre, convoluted case you and I have ever had to try to wrap our badly impaired minds around."

THIRTY-EIGHT

Crawford dropped off Ott at the police station on South County at 6:45 that night. He had a mission before he could call it a day. He drove up to Antonia von Habsburg's mansion and was happy not to find a wedding in full swing or LV Wurfel and his friend, Dirt, sitting around and drinking beer and watching NASCAR. What he did find to the right of von Habsburg's eight-foot-high marble fireplace was a painting by the American abstract artist, Cy Twombly. Crawford knew it was a Twombly because he had found a website that displayed many paintings of Twombly's and what prices they had fetched. The one hanging on Antonia von Habsburg's wall was of what appeared to be scribbled white letters on a blackboard-colored background. The letters didn't spell anything and, on closer inspection, weren't actually letters at all but more like dashed-off scrawls.

Of course, Crawford had the reaction that probably many people before him had about Twombly's multi-million-dollar paintings: *What's all the noise about? Hell, an eight-year-old kid could have done that.* But, admittedly, Nigel Ballantrae's story seemed to be holding up—there was a Cy Twombly hanging in Antonia's house—but there was a lot more that needed to be determined before Crawford told Perry Jastrow that he better get ready to write Ballantrae a three-and-a-half-million-dollar check.

At 7:20, Crawford arrived at his apartment at the Trianon. He made himself a tuna salad sandwich and a giant smoothie using leftover fruit, plus some chunky peanut butter and a large scoop of protein powder and propped himself up in front of his Samsung. He got halfway through a movie, which he had no intention of finishing, and was in bed by 9:15.

He slept like a baby and didn't wake up until 7:15.

*****

Nigel Ballantrae wasn't too difficult to track down. Crawford just Googled him—1437 Lake Crystal Drive, Unit J, to be exact. Sure didn't sound like the snappy address of British royalty. Crawford briefly debated with himself whether to call the man—a number was listed—or to go with the tried-and-true *just show up* strategy, which Ott and he had been employing a lot lately.

He went with the latter, drove into the complex, and searched around for numbers. He finally found 1437 Lake Crystal Drive, Unit J, and spotted a man on a second-floor balcony just to the left of a Unit J sign.

He got out of his car, shaded his eyes, and looked up at the man, who was reading a book.

"Are you Mr. Ballantrae, by any chance?" he called up to him.

"I am, and who might you be?"

No doubt about it, the man was a Brit.

"Name's Detective Crawford, Palm Beach Police. Mind if I have a word with you?"

The man had reddish hair, parted pretty close to the middle of his scalp, and tortoiseshell glasses. "Why don't I come down to you," Ballantrae said. "My flat's a mess."

"Sure, come on down."

A minute later Crawford was face-to-face with Nigel Ballantrae, the Duke of Montpelier, on a badly cracked sidewalk.

"Thanks for coming down," Crawford said, seeing a woman with a dog coming toward them on the sidewalk. "I'm one of the detectives investigating the death of Antonia von Habsburg."

"I figured as much and was pretty certain you'd eventually get around to me."

"Yes, well, I recently had a conversation with Perry Jastrow, Ms. von Habsburg's attorney, who told me about receiving your claim for three and a half million dollars from her estate."

Ballantrae scratched his cheek. "I bet that came as kind of a shock to Mr. Jastrow."

"Yes, it definitely did. There have been a few other shocks in the case as well."

"I'm not surprised to hear that," Ballantrae said, as the woman and the dog walked past them. The dog started to give Crawford's right leg a sniff, but the woman tugged on its leash.

"He liked you." Ballantrae smiled.

Crawford smiled back. "So can you tell me about the transaction between you and Ms. von Habsburg?"

"Absolutely," Ballantrae said. "It's relatively simple. Antonia and I became friends, and I found out about her interest in contemporary art and simply asked her if she might be interested in purchasing a Cy Twombly of mine."

Crawford glanced at Ballantrae's plain white brick building and couldn't imagine that he had a lot of million-dollar paintings hanging on his walls.

"I know exactly what you're thinking, Detective: 'How is it that this man, living in this… not so grand apartment building, ends up with a four-million-dollar Cy Twombly?' Well, I'll be happy to tell you: about thirty years ago, I lived in Rome where, it so happened, Cy Twombly lived with and was married to an Italian painter named Tatiana Franchetti. I got to know him a little, though he was much older, as I was a student at an art school there. I admired his art enormously, and one time he asked me if I wanted to visit his studio. Of course, I jumped at the chance and fell in love with this one painting he was finishing up. He asked me, totally out of the blue, if I wanted it and naturally, I said yes, but told him I only had a thousand pounds to my name. He said, 'Fine, you just pay me a thousand pounds a year, for twenty years.' I was thrilled at the idea and said I'd pay him a thousand pounds a year for the rest of my life. He just laughed and said, 'Twenty years is long enough.' I read later that he had sold a painting earlier that year at a Christie's auction for 5.5 million, so… I guess he really didn't need the money."

"That's a pretty amazing story," Crawford said. "So where did you go to school in Rome, Mr. Ballantrae?"

Ballantrae smiled and raised a finger. "Aha, you're trying to check my story, aren't you? See if I just made this whole thing up?"

"Just curious."

"It's called the Accademia di Belle Arti di Roma."

"So you had the painting for thirty years before you sold it to Ms. von Habsburg?"

"Yes, I did."

"And it seems like she got a pretty good deal. I saw some of the prices other paintings of his sold for."

"Yes, she did, and I let her pay for it over a period of several years, just like Cy had done for me."

"You call him Cy."

"Yes, he was a very down-to-earth, simpatico man. He was named after an American baseball player, Cy I-forget-the-last-name."

"Cy Young?"

"That's it," Ballantrae said. "I'll tell you a quick story about him... if you have time?"

Crawford found himself suddenly very interested in this painter he had barely heard of before. "Sure, I've got time."

"So,"—Ballantrae thought for a moment—"I guess it was about fifteen years ago at a show of Cy's works in France—Avignon, I think—when a French woman came up to a triptych of his and kissed it. Well, it was a white canvas and now it was smudged with the woman's bright red lipstick. She was arrested on the spot and later charged in court with—I remember it word for word—'voluntary degradation of a work of art.' I always reckoned that seemed a little harsh. Anyway, the woman did, in fact, go to trial and defended her act by saying something like, 'It was just a kiss, a loving gesture. I kissed it without thinking; I thought the artist would understand.'"

The woman with the dog passed by them again, the pup now in the woman's arms.

"Hello, again," Crawford said, and she gave him a business-like nod.

"So what finally happened?" Crawford asked.

"Well, the prosecution demanded that she pay a big fine and go to some kind of behavioral modification class."

"Never heard of that before."

"I know, so what finally ended up happening is the woman was ordered to pay the owner of the painting a thousand euros, then another five hundred euros to the owner of the gallery, and to Cy, one euro."

Crawford shook his head. "That's a pretty incredible story. Now going back to the painting you sold Ms. von Habsburg: I'm assuming that you're intending to get the remainder of what she owes you—$3.5 million—after the will is probated."

"Yes. Correct."

Crawford nodded and paused for a moment. "On a completely different subject, Mr. Ballantrae, what do you know about Ms. von Habsburg's children?"

"I just know that she didn't see them very often, but it seemed she was very generous with both of them."

"Both of them?"

"Yes, a man named Frank, who lives down here, and a daughter named... Abby, I think, who lives up north somewhere."

"And it was just those two?"

Ballantrae nodded.

"And you never heard the names, either Lauren or Esmerelda?"

"No, who are they?"

"It's just one. A little girl."

Ballantrae shrugged. "That's news to me."

The Brit's story was pretty convincing and clearly he knew the subject, Cy Twombly, well, but Crawford still had a niggling doubt. Usually in situations like this, his reaction was, "Okay, I buy it," or "The guy's lying through his teeth." This time it was something in between.

"Well, thank you, Mr. Ballantrae," Crawford said, not able to call someone *Lord*. "I appreciate your time and learning so much about Cy Twombly. That ought to do it."

"You're very welcome, Detective, and I hope you catch whoever killed Antonia. That was such a horrible thing."

"Sure was. Oh, can you give me your phone number in case I have any more questions?"

Ballantrae did.

Crawford nodded, turned, and walked down the sidewalk.

When he got back to the police station, he went into Ott's cubicle.

"Hey, how's it going?" Ott asked.

"I just got back from interviewing Nigel Ballantrae, either Antonia's last or next-to-last boyfriend."

"And?"

"Do you remember any files of hers that had to do with art she owned?"

"Not really. Why, do you?"

"I vaguely remember seeing one. I never opened it, though."

"So what are you gonna do?"

"Make a couple of calls, then go back to her house. What about you?"

"I've got Luther King coming up. He got sprung from the West Palm jail and he's coming here. Gave me some bullshit about how he wants to know what his 'inordinate' taxes are being spent on."

"Let me know," Crawford said, turning to go.

"You got it."

*****

Crawford found what he was looking for in a file labeled "Paintings." It was a pretty thin file, but he quickly found a piece of paper that proved Nigel Ballantrae, Duke of Montpelier, was a flat-out liar, despite all his impressive-sounding knowledge about Cy Twombly. It was a receipt and something called a "Letter of Provenance" from Christie's at 20 Rockefeller Plaza in New York that showed that Antonia von Habsburg had paid four million dollars for the painting, *Untitled (Machinations)*, back in 2018. At least Ballantrae got the price right.

Crawford dialed Ballantrae's number immediately and he answered.

"Hello, Detective, what did you forget to ask me?"

"Whether any of what you told me was true," Crawford said. "I'm at Antonia von Habsburg's house now looking at a file that says she bought that Cy Twombly from Christie's back in 2018—"

"Well, there must be some mistake, I—"

"No mistake. The painting is called, *Untitled: Machinations* and there's a photo that it came with that matches the photo you sent to Perry Jastrow *and* the painting on the wall here. So, the question is, did you kill Antonia von Habsburg after you came up with this whole scam, or did you come up with it after someone else killed her?"

Silence.

"Mr. Ballantrae, I asked you a question."

Long sigh. "I had absolutely nothing to do with Antonia's death. I was very distressed to hear about it. She was a friend, a very dear friend."

"Whose estate you intended to profit from in a very despicable way."

Silence.

"I'm just curious, did you ever lay eyes on Cy Twombly in Rome?"

Faintly. "No."

"Did that woman actually kiss Twombly's painting."

"That is true. That really *did* happen. I read about it on Wikipedia."

"Hm. Well, what you were attempting to pull off is a third-degree felony."

"Oh, please, Detective. I was a desperate man. This was something that wouldn't really hurt anybody. Please, be merciful on an old man."

"Tell that to Ms. von Habsburg's heirs. Or in this case, heiress."

Even more faintly. "What are you going to do, Detective/"

"I'm going to talk to Perry Jastrow, then I'll decide."

"Will I go to jail?"

"You might, if you're charged."

"Oh, please. I can't go to jail. I couldn't possibly survive there."

Crawford put the file back in the file cabinet. "Should have thought about that before you tried to pull off this whole elaborate swindle."

THIRTY-NINE

Bettina, at the front desk, called Ott, then lowered her voice. "Mort, guy in a limo as long as the state of Florida just walked in, says he has an appointment with you."

"I'll be right out."

A few moments later, Ott walked up to Luther King.

"Hello, Mr. King," Ott said to him, skipping the handshake, "come on back with me, please."

King looked around. "I thought police stations were supposed to be much... shabbier. They are on TV anyway."

"Yeah, those are big city ones: New York, L.A., Chicago. Palm Beach doesn't do shabby. You ought to know that, Mr. King."

Knowing Crawford was out for a while, Ott was going to borrow his office. "This is my partner's office," Ott said as they walked in, then he gestured. "Have a seat."

"This is a lot nicer than I expected. A little messy, though."

"Yeah, mine's even messier. Shabbier, too."

King frowned. "So what are we doing here? Are you still looking at me as a suspect?"

"We've got quite a long list."

"Look, Detective, you need to take me off it. I—"

"I heard about your assault charge last night."

King's face went red. Clearly anger, not embarrassment. "That was such bullshit. I slapped the woman, that's all, not even hard."

"That constitutes assault and, more importantly, tells me you're capable of assaulting a woman."

"What happened to Antonia was way beyond assault."

"I'm well aware of that. But people who assault sometimes have different levels of assault."

"Okay, okay. So, is that why I'm here, because of what happened last night, where I was provoked?"

Ott cocked his head. "Provoked? How were you provoked?"

"Well… she wouldn't…"

"Yeah, that's what I thought."

"Look, Detective, Antonia and I still had… feelings for each other when she was killed."

"Spell that out for me."

"Okay, fact is, we were going to have dinner together the day she died to celebrate my birthday. I had asked her out a couple of days before."

"Any way you can prove that?"

"Yeah, as a matter of fact, there is. Just call the Beach Club and ask them if I had a reservation for that night."

Ott pulled out his cell phone. "If this is true, why didn't you tell me this before?"

"I don't know, 'cause I didn't know you were seriously looking at me as a suspect. To begin with, that is so totally farfetched. I just thought you were talking to shady people who knew Antonia."

"We were. Do you know the number there, at the Beach Club?"

King gave him the number of the Beach Club on North County Road and Ott dialed it.

"Yes, my name is Detective Ott with the Palm Beach Police. I'm hoping you can check something out for me." He gave them the date and time when Luther King said he had made the reservation for dinner.

"Yes, sir. I see it right here. Mr. King's reservation."

"And what exactly does it say?"

"Seven thirty that night. Mr. Luther King, Ms. von Habsburg and an unnamed guest."

"Thank you very much," Ott said. "That's all I need. Goodbye."

He turned to King. "An unnamed guest? I guess you must have forgotten about… *her*, I'm assuming?"

King shrugged. "She was just one of Antonia's… friends."

"What was her name?"

"Um…."

"Come on, Luther, think real hard."

"Justine."

"Justine who?"

"I… I didn't catch her last name."

Ott nodded slowly. "There's a real coincidence here, Luther, because it just so happens that it was Justine Burroughs who lodged that assault charge against you eight days after your scheduled dinner with Antonia von Habsburg."

King shrugged. "Um, maybe that's who it was."

"Okay, so clearly that night at the Beach Club, Antonia was going to introduce one of her women to you."

"So? What if she was?"

Ott inhaled deeply, slowly shook his head, and stood up. "Get out of here," he said, with a shooing motion. "Creeps like you disgust the hell out of me."

FORTY

While Ott was meeting with Luther King at the station, Crawford paid a visit to Frank Lincoln at his church out in Royal Palm Beach. Again, Lincoln was outside working in his vegetable garden.

"How's everything with the Five Wanderers, Pastor?"

Lincoln smiled. "Last time I checked, still wandering."

"I'm reading a book now. The protagonist always seems to be wandering."

"Is it Jack Reacher, by any chance?"

Crawford nodded. "Sure is. You a reader?"

"I am. One time in a sermon, I actually mentioned him."

"No kidding. Still bugs me Tom Cruise playing him," Crawford said. "So, I'm still trying to understand something."

"What's that?" Lincoln said, pulling up a tomato.

"The two wills your mother left behind. Obviously, only one is legit."

"I don't know what to tell you. You found the one naming my church as the beneficiary at her house that day she was killed."

"Yes, I know, but your brother-in-law Steve Swain seems to think that one was bogus. And your sister said that your mother told her she had given both you and your sister enough money. You weren't getting any more from her."

"When did she tell her that?"

"Right before she died. Your sister and brother-in-law visited her just days before."

Lincoln scratched his head. "Doesn't that make you suspicious at all?"

"You mean, that they were down here from New Hampshire right before she died?"

Lincoln nodded.

"No, it doesn't make me suspicious, because they seemed to accept the fact that your mother wasn't going to give them anything more. That her entire estate was going to go to her young daughter."

"Her young, *illegitimate* daughter."

Crawford smiled. "Just like you. Except you were her illegitimate son. And she would hardly be the first illegitimate child to inherit money."

Lincoln looked blank for a few moments.

"I don't know what to tell you," Lincoln said again after a few moments. "I've got a church and over $200,000 in the bank. I live a low-key life,"—he opened his hand to his garden—"eat vegetables from my garden, go to Applebee's once a week; fact is, I couldn't spend that $200,000 if I tried."

Crawford shrugged. "I don't know what to tell *you*," he echoed Lincoln. "There's no way to explain why your mother would have two wills."

"Except maybe she changed her mind."

Crawford shook his head. "That doesn't fly."

"Why?"

"Because they were dated five days apart."

"Some people change their minds five times in the same day."

"Not about something as important as this."

It was Lincoln's turn to shrug. "Well, sorry. I just can't help you."

Crawford was out of questions. "Okay, well, thank you for your time once again. I appreciate it."

"You're very welcome," Lincoln said, the tomato still in his hand.

He handed it to Crawford. "Just give it a little wash. Best tomato you'll ever eat."

The ride back to the station house gave Crawford a lot of time to think. The best idea he came up with was long overdue. He would ask Dominica McCarthy out for an early dinner at a restaurant they both liked. Then have her over to watch a little TV with him. He badly needed to unwind.

FORTY-ONE

"I need to borrow your brain for a couple of hours," Crawford said to Dominica as he clicked on his Samsung in his condominium.

"Okay, it's available, I guess," Dominica said, no idea what he was referring to.

Earlier they had dinner at a place on Clematis called Hullabaloo, which on its website was billed as a "gastropub." Crawford had no clue exactly what a gastropub was, but liked the food and also the music that they played there. He had the chicken parm, something he felt you could never go wrong ordering; Dominica was more adventurous and had the ratatouille.

It had been a while since they had dinner together and the activity that usually followed it. He thought he saw anticipation in her eyes, and he knew for a fact that's what he was feeling.

"Okay, Charlie, what exactly are you going to pick my brain about?" Dominica said, as she nestled close to him on his couch.

"Have you ever heard the name Janny Hasleiter?"

"No. Who's she?"

"Well, she's been both a producer and a director of movies, some of them you've heard of. Even was credited with being a writer on a few of 'em. She's married to a guy named John David Ranieri, who used to be a big deal in the movie business but doesn't seem to be involved much anymore. May be retired, I think. Anyway, Janny was friends with Antonia von Habsburg and, according to someone who I wouldn't say is one hundred percent reliable, used Antonia's little black book of eligible bachelors. But when I say 'eligible bachelors,' I mean guys who are like in their late teens, early twenties."

"And how old is Janny?"

"Somewhere between forty-five and fifty?"

"So she's what used to be called a cradle robber?"

Crawford laughed. "Yeah, a cougar nowadays."

"Have you met her? Janny?"

"Yeah, I have. But I'm way too old for her," he answered, rather than go into detail about meeting her.

Dominica smiled and stroked the back of Crawford's neck. "Even though you're ten years younger."

"Yup."

"Okay, so you still haven't told me why she's a person of interest."

"I was just getting to that. So, according to this woman who used to work for Antonia, when times got tough for Antonia's business during Covid... by the way, have I even told you what Antonia did?"

"I heard she was basically a high-end matchmaker. Charged like fifty grand—"

"Or more."

"—to fix up rich guys."

Crawford nodded. "So apparently Covid was tough on her business 'cause men were reluctant to go out with women they didn't know anything about."

"I get it."

"So Antonia might have created a side hustle which can best be described as blackmailing married men—her past clients—with photos of them messing around with Antonia's girls."

Dominica frowned. "Yuck," she said. "But I can see how that might have been pretty lucrative."

Crawford put his arm around Dominica's shoulder. "Lucrative, but potentially very dangerous."

"You mean, if one of those men wanted to put an end to Antonia doing it?"

"Yeah, permanently."

"Okay, so what you're saying is Antonia also had a little black book of men... for older women looking for younger men."

"In Janny Hasleiter's case, much younger men."

"Gotcha."

"So—"

"Let me guess," Dominica said, "Antonia had fixed up her friend Janny with young dudes and when times got tough, 'cause of Covid, Antonia may have gone to Janny and said, 'I need a hundred thousand to keep quiet about young—pick a name—or John David whoever's gonna find out about what you've been up to.'"

"You're a very smart woman."

"Isn't that why you asked me out in the first place?"

"Among other things."

"You mean it was not all because of my steel-trap mind?"

"That was a major part of it," he said. "But I'm thinking you're low."

"Low?"

"Instead of being a hundred thousand, I'm guessing it was a lot more."

Dominica nodded then stroked the side of his face.

"Okay, the brain-borrowing session is now officially over," Crawford said leaning into her and kissing her with passion.

She kissed him back with equal passion.

Moments later he reached behind her and unsnapped her bra. She unbuttoned the top three buttons of his shirt.

His hand came up inside her blouse and cradled her breasts. She lifted his shirt over his head.

They had done this before and were pretty adept at it.

Within a minute they both were naked except for his socks.

They never made it to his bedroom.

*****

She looked up at him twenty minutes later. "I've really missed that, Charlie. It's been too long."

"I know. You never call; you never write."

She laughed. "Oh, yeah, blame it on me."

He kissed her on the lips again. "Well, we're going to make up for it. There's lot of night left."

"And morning."

He nodded. "And morning."

*****

They decided to leave their clothes off and watch TV naked. Well, except for a comforter he brought back from his bed. It was still only 7:45 p.m.

"Okay, so I need to explain a little more what we're going to watch."

"Yeah, I don't feel as though I'm totally up to speed on it."

"Do you know what IMDb is?"

"Yes, it gives a list of movies or TV shows actors and actresses have been in."

"Exactly. Writers, producers and directors, too," Crawford said. "And I made a list of ones that Janny Hasleiter has done."

He reached down on the carpet for his pants, then pulled out his wallet. "Here's the list."

Dominica glanced down at it. "Wow, it's pretty long."

"I told you, she's been around," Crawford said. "So a lot of her shows, most of 'em I'd say, are on either Netflix, Amazon, Hulu, HBO, or one of the streaming services. I'll explain more as we go along."

"Okay, but tell me why you want to watch just her shows?"

He rubbed his chin. "Um, that's a very good question... Maybe because she's right up there on my list of suspects. Maybe because, I don't know, I'll learn more about her somehow. I don't know."

"Not your most articulate, Charlie," she said with a smile, "but you kinda piqued my interest."

"All right, so the first one is called *Maladjustment* with Halle Berry. You might remember it, but I don't. Seems like one that did well at the Sundance Film Festival, but not at the box office."

"I vaguely remember the name."

Crawford flipped to it on Netflix. It was pretty short—an hour and a half—and neither one of them loved it when it ended at 9:15.

"Too much talk, not enough action," Dominica said.

"Yeah, I agree. Lame ending, too."

Dominica laughed. "What's next?"

"*The Warlord*," Crawford said, flipping to Hulu. "An oldie but a goodie from 2007. Set in China, during some war there. Janny was the writer and her husband the producer."

Dominica nodded and pulled up the comforter. "Okay, I'm up for it."

Dominica had started to doze off just before a quite graphic scene close to the end. It was of one of the main characters being executed... by *lingchi*. Crawford was wide awake and sitting ramrod straight when the death scene arrived.

"Holy shit," he whispered to himself. It wasn't something he felt he needed to wake up Dominica for. But he said it again... "Holy shit." He almost replayed it but figured he got the gist. It sure seemed realistic enough. He couldn't wait to tell Ott about it. He almost called him, but decided it could wait. It was now just past eleven.

Crawford figured he had maybe four—max five—hours left in him before he crashed. Dominica was snoring lightly now, in a cute kind of way. He tucked the comforter around her. She stirred and mumbled something.

A rom-com came next, which Crawford remembered seeing with his ex-wife. It had been popular as hell, like the ones that always took place in the Hamptons and had either Jack Nicholson or Meryl Streep, or both, in them. He drifted into a light daze during a wedding scene that dragged on too long. It ended at 12:45.

Next was one with Bruce Willis, past his prime but still worth watching. Crawford fast-forwarded a few times and it ended around two in the morning. Then came one called *The Marked Man* on HBO Max, which he remembered was also popular and had won a few awards, but which he had never seen. It was about gangs in the barrio—L.A., circa the late nineties—and was intensely violent. He was on the verge of skipping ahead when in one scene one of the gangs took a rival gang member hostage and proceeded to press a branding iron to, first his neck, then both cheeks. The sizzling sounds were particularly squirm-inducing and made Crawford wonder what it must have felt like to the young gigolo Nickie, who woke up with strange tattoos on his face, having made the mistake of spreading the word about having kinky sex with Janny Hasleiter.

Now Crawford was absolutely convinced: Janny Hasleiter had ordered the tattoos on Nickie's face and *The Marked Men* was where she had gotten the idea. The only missing piece was who had helped her. Because what happened to Nickie had clearly not been a one-woman operation. And DeeDee's assault had been done by a man, but a woman had apparently been in the background. Then he remembered a recent scene from the Kevin Costner streaming series *Yellowstone*, in which cowpokes were branded with a big *Y* for being loyal to Costner's ranch. It meant they were integral members of a select fraternity of badass cowboys, similar to a mafia man becoming a 'made' man. But in Nickie's case it was the opposite. Nickie's tattoos were a punishment, pure and simple.

He couldn't wait to tell Ott.

FORTY-TWO

Crawford got up at 6:00 a.m., having had at most three and a half hours of sleep. His mind was hopped up with things to do that day.

At some point in the night, he had picked up Dominica and given her a gentle lift to his bed, where she now remained sound asleep.

He left her a note on the bedside table: *I had a very nice time with you last night. But when don't we have a nice time together? Interesting things came up viewing the Janny Hasleiter films. Fill you in later.*

He did the requisite Dunkin' Donuts stop, though he had taken to stocking their coffee at his condo. But that was only half of his purchase, blueberry donuts and glazed sticks being the other half. At quarter to seven, he got to his office and thought over his next moves for a half hour.

At seven thirty, he called Ott. It was a ten-minute conversation in which Ott said very little. Just "You're shittin' me…" three times.

At quarter of eight, he dialed the phone number of Nickie, the tattooed boy.

"Hello," said a groggy voice.

"Nickie?"

"Yeah, who's this?"

"Detective Crawford. We met after you got tattooed. 'Member?"

"What did I do now?" he asked, nervously.

"Nothing. I need to talk to you, though. What's your address?"

Nickie gave Crawford an address in West Palm.

"I got an extra donut for you. I'll be there in fifteen minutes."

"Okay, but the place is a mess."

Crawford chuckled. "I was twenty once."

"I'm only nineteen."

*****

The place *was* a mess, and a girl was sleeping in a couch in the living room that had two empty wine bottles and an ashtray full of cigarette butts and what Crawford recognized as a stubbed-out joint.

Nickie was wearing grey cargo shorts and a T-shirt that read, "The Cadavers." But his tattoos were what Crawford noticed first.

Crawford pointed at the T-shirt. "That a band or something?"

"Yeah, my friend plays bass in it."

"Catchy name… if you like dead people."

Nickie smiled, but Crawford wasn't sure he knew what a cadaver was.

Crawford opened up the iPad he had brought with him and looked over at the girl who was either sleeping soundly or faking it convincingly. "Why don't we go outside? This won't take long."

Nickie nodded and followed Crawford toward the door. They walked out to the wooden front porch.

Crawford turned to him. "I want to show you someone. You IDed her before. But I want you to be absolutely sure about it."

"Okay."

"Tell me if she's the older woman you were fixed up with. The one you said liked to do kinky things."

Nickie squinted. "Oh God, her. Why?"

"It's part of an investigation."

Crawford showed him the picture of Janny Hasleiter from her IMDb page. It was one of those hand-under-the-chin poses that seem to be intended to convey gravitas.

Nickie glanced down at it then quickly looked away. "That's her."

"You're sure?"

"Positive."

"What did she say her name was when you met her?"

"Danielle."

"So when she first called you, that's what she said her name was?"

"Yup, then she said something like, 'I'm a woman who's going to pay you a lot of money for a good time.'"

"Those were her words."

"Well, pretty close."

Crawford shrugged. "So who'd you tell about what you and she did together?"

Nickie crossed his feet and looked down.

"Who'd you tell?" Crawford repeated.

"Just another guy who's a lifeguard at the pool," he mumbled.

"You're an assistant tennis pro there, right?"

"Was."

"What do you mean, 'was'?"

"Got fired."

"Why?"

"The manager said I was spreading rumors about club members."

"How could you if you didn't know her real name?"

"This lifeguard, when I described her said, 'Oh, yeah, that's that hottie, Ms. Hasleiter.' Something like that."

"So you did know her real name?"

"Eventually."

"You're confusing me, Nickie. You could've told me that a long time ago, man."

"Sorry, I forgot her name. I—"

Crawford held up his hand. "So I'm guessing you told the lifeguard what you had been doing with Ms. Hasleiter, and word got around."

"Yeah, I guess that was it. Plus, I don't think the manager was too crazy about my tattoos."

Crawford nodded. The Beach Club, by reputation, was a pretty conservative place—like most clubs in Palm Beach. He guessed the only tats you'd find there were hidden under the bathing suits of the sons and daughters of its straitlaced members.

"You got any leads on new jobs?" Crawford asked.

"No, and I gotta find one or I'm gonna have to move in with my parents."

Crawford reached into the breast pocket of his jacket and pulled out a pad and pen. "How are you at pounding nails... and painting?"

"Not bad. Why?"

"A friend of mine's a contractor. Told me he's looking to hire a few guys," Crawford said, writing a name and number.

"Hey, thanks man," Nickie said. "Appreciate it."

"Speaking of your tats, weren't you gonna look into getting them removed?"

Nickie nodded. "Yeah, costs a couple hundred bucks."

Crawford handed him the name and number of his contractor friend, put the pad and pen away, and reached into his pants pocket for his wallet. He pulled out a fifty, two twenties and a ten and handed them to Nickie.

"This'll get you started."

A big smile lit up Nickie's face. "Wow, dude, thanks."

"You're welcome. Now go call my friend. Maybe he can get you workin' by the end of the week."

*****

By noon, Crawford had put in three calls to Janny Hasleiter's cell number he got from Bettina and left three messages.

Then he called Rose Clarke, real estate agent extraordinaire.

"Hi, Charlie. What's new in the world of murder and mayhem?"

"Nothing new, I'm happy to say. So just a quick question: don't I remember you saying Janny Hasleiter lived in Palm Beach?"

"Yup, up on Jamaica Lane. If you give me a sec, I'll give you the street number."

"So. She and her husband have two places? The penthouse at the Bristol, too?"

"The penthouse at the Bristol is just hers, I think. John David's probably not even supposed to know about it, though I'm guessing he might."

"So the penthouse is her, ah—"

"*Fuck pad*," Rose blurted, and Crawford laughed. "Oops, sorry, I meant to say something more socially acceptable but I slipped."

"You're forgiven. Is the place general knowledge?"

"I doubt it, but any real estate agent and gal-about-town worth her salt knows about stuff like that."

"Gotcha. Do you have that address on Jamaica?"

"Yeah, here you go. It's 253. On the north side."

"Thanks, Rose, you're a doll."

"What do you expect from your third partner?"

*****

Screw it, he decided, he was going to go straight there. To 253 Jamaica Lane.

Ten minutes later he pulled into the paved driveway. There was a white Porsche parked there. Crawford got out of his Crown Vic, walked up to the brick front porch and hit the buzzer.

No one came to the door after a few minutes, so he decided to walk around to the side of the house.

He got to about two-thirds of the way back and heard classical music playing.

There was a hedge between him and the house's backyard.

"Hello, anyone back there?" he shouted.

"Who is it? Who's there?"

He came to a break in the hedge and walked in to the backyard.

An older man with a thatch of wild Albert Einstein hair and a computer in front of him was sitting at a table with an umbrella over it.

"My name's Detective Crawford, sir, Palm Beach Police. Are you Mr. Ranieri?"

"Yes. What is it you want?"

"I'm actually looking for your wife, Ms. Hasleiter," Crawford said, walking up to the table.

"Sorry, she's not here. What do you want her for?"

"Just a few questions about an investigation of mine."

"Well, I'm not sure where she is. She left without telling me. A good guess would be riding out in Wellington."

"Do you know the name of the place where she rides, Mr. Ranieri?"

"Ah, I think it's called the Wellington Equestrian Center. Never been there myself."

Probing time. "Do you have another residence in the area, by any chance?"

"Another residence? Why would I need another residence?"

"Just asking," Crawford said, sneaking a glance at Ranieri's screen. "You a bridge player?"

"Yes, I play. Just practicing now," Ranieri said, pointing at the screen.

Crawford nodded, remembering how Rose had said he was a renowned international competitor. "Can you think of anywhere else Ms. Hasleiter might be?"

Ranieri rubbed his chin. "Well, shopping maybe, but she's not much of a shopper. Or maybe visiting one of her friends."

"Okay. Well, thank you. When she comes back, would you ask her to call me, please?" Crawford slipped a card out of his wallet. "I've left her a few messages."

"Sure will," Ranieri said, taking the card. "Equestrian place is probably your best bet."

"Thanks," Crawford said and made his way back through the break in the hedge.

*****

Crawford walked into Ott's cubicle.

"Feel like going riding?"

"Bikes, trikes, motorcycles, what?"

"Horses. I need you to see if you can track down Janny Hasle-iter. I'm going to go to her place at the Bristol. She might also be at a place called the Wellington Equestrian Center. Want to take a ride out there?"

"Okay, sure. I'm dying to meet the woman."

"Watch out. Something tells me she plays rough."

"My kind of woman."

*****

Crawford stepped out of the elevator facing Jenny Hasleiter's penthouse suite at the Bristol. He pushed the buzzer to the right of the double doors. He thought about how many hours he had spent waiting for people to open their doors over the years. Hundreds. Then, the door opened and there was Lulu Shamburg, clad but just barely. This time it was a polka dot bikini and white-framed Jackie-O sunglasses.

"Well, *hello*, De-tec-tive."

"Well, *hello*, Ms. Shamburg."

She pointed her finger at him. "We've known each other long enough, you can call me Lulu."

"Okay, Lulu, I was hoping to see Ms. Hasleiter."

"And you've known her long enough, so you can call her Janny."

"Do you know where she is?"

"You just missed her."

"She just left, you mean?"

Lulu shook her head. "Nooo, she just went into her bedroom... nap time. 'Bout fifteen minutes ago."

The way Lulu said it, Crawford knew Janny had a nap-mate with her.

"Think she'd mind if I waited for her to finish up her... nap?"

"Nah, but in the meantime, how about a cocktail, a little chitchat out by the pool, maybe?"

"No thanks on the cocktail, but you're on for the chitchat."

"Oh, I forgot you're a teetotaler."

"Um, hardly, but I do wait 'til six."

"Oh my God, that's an eternity. By then I've had three or four."

Crawford smiled as he followed her out to the pool. "Do you happen to know a...man"—that was really stretching it—"named Nickie?"

Lulu turned around to him. "Nope. Can't say I do."

She sat down in one side of the double chaise lounge and patted the vacant side.

Once again, Crawford demonstrated his considerable restraint and sat down opposite her at a covered, glass-topped table. "Thanks. I'm trying to stay out of the sun."

All of a sudden there was a caterwauling scream from inside the penthouse.

Crawford jumped up. "What the hell?"

Lulu didn't move or react. "Don't worry, everything's fine. Janny just sometimes has, ah, dreams during her naps. Sit down. I promise you she's all right."

"You're sure?"

"Yes, of course. She's my friend. I know everything about her."

He wondered about that.

"Do you have a girlfriend, Charlie?"

Oh God, did he ever not want to go there. So he just nodded, hoping the subject would go away.

"Is she pretty?"

"I think so." So did everyone else who had ever laid eyes on Dominica McCarthy.

"I was married once," she said. "It didn't work out."

There was another ear-piercing shriek from inside.

"Jesus!" Crawford instinctively reached for his sidearm.

TOM TURNER

Lulu put up her hands. "Nothing to worry about, I promise you."

"If you say so," Crawford said, taking out his cell phone, then glancing up at her. "You mind if I make a quick call?"

"Not at all. Go right ahead."

He dialed and Ott picked up after the first ring.

"Don't bother going out to Wellington."

"You tracked down Janny, huh?"

"Yup."

"Okay. Well, I was on my way out there, maybe I'll just go up to Good Sam. I think DeeDee's getting out tomorrow or the next day."

"Oh, good. Give her my best."

"Will do."

"Later." Crawford clicked off.

Just as he did, he saw the door from the inside to the terrace open and Janny Hasleiter walk out. Over her shoulder he saw the outline of a male body opening the door from the penthouse out to the elevator.

"Well, hello, Detective," Janny said. "You decided to take us up on our offer after all."

"'Fraid not. I have some questions about Antonia von Habsburg that I'm hoping you can answer."

Janny glanced over at Lulu, who gave her a finger flutter wave and a smile.

"Why don't we go inside?" Janny said, then lowered her voice as Crawford joined her. "Lulu can be a little distracting."

Crawford followed her inside and sat down in a wing chair across from her.

"So, ask away," she said opening her hand to Crawford.

"Last night I had an eight-hour Janny Hasleiter Retrospective."

"Meaning?"

"Meaning I watched four of your movies beginning to end and skimmed a fifth one."

"Well, I'm flattered, but what in God's name for?"

"The idea was… the idea was actually to get a read on you."

"Wait a minute, you said you had some questions about Antonia, not about some old movies of mine."

"Well, what I should have said is I have some questions that *pertain* to Antonia von Habsburg."

210

Her expression turned hostile and cold as she almost physically withdrew from him.

"Well, get on with it then. What do you want to know?"

"So that one—*The Warlord*—had a pretty grisly scene where one of the main characters, a Chinese guy, is killed by his enemy. I think they call it death by a thousand cuts. *Lingchi* is the Chinese name for it."

"Yeah, what of it? That was a while back. In 2007 or so. I was one of the writers on it."

Crawford nodded. "Then there was that rom-com with the big wedding scene in the Hamptons—"

"Nantucket, actually. Yeah, *The In-Between Years*. We did a $175 million at the box office on that one. Bought me a few extra baubles."

"Nice. Then the last one I saw was called *The Marked Man*."

"Talk about downers."

"Yeah, it was. Especially that scene where the hostage gang member gets branded on his face and neck with the other gang's sign."

Janny cocked her head and narrowed her eyes. "We could probably sit here and talk about movies for the rest of the day, but what's your point?"

Crawford glanced up at the living room's coffered ceiling for a full ten seconds, then his eyes bored in on Janny's. "Do you know a woman named DeeDee Dunwoody and a young guy named Nickie."

"Never heard of either one of them," Janny said defiantly.

"Well, I know you know DeeDee Dunwoody cause she knows you. She knew Antonia; she was one of her 'girls.'"

"Okay, I think I know who you mean. Never said more than two words to her in my entire life. And Nickie, absolutely no clue."

Crawford pulled out his iPhone, clicked the button for photos, and held up the photo of Nickie. "Take a close look," he said pushing the phone close to her face. "He didn't have those tattoos on his face when you first... met him."

She shoved the iPhone in his hand away. "I don't know what it is you're trying to prove with all this, but you're starting to irritate the hell out of me."

"Let me make it clear: I think you got the idea to do what you did to DeeDee Dunwoody and Nickie from your movies. And I'll bet that if I had the time to go through the hundreds of hours of all the other movies you've done, I'd find one that uses the same rat torture that killed Antonia von Habsburg."

Janny remained ice cold, slowly shaking her head. "Wow. You have the most wildly creative imagination of just about anyone I know. And that's saying a lot since I know half of Hollywood. Next, you're going to accuse me of killing Antonia."

He was dead silent. He just stared at her.

Janny quickly pushed out of the club chair. "Let yourself out, will you, Detective? Take all your phantasmagoric delusions back to the police station and amuse your cop buddies with them."

FORTY-THREE

A theory consisting of postulation, speculation, and supposition doesn't really get you anywhere in law enforcement without specific facts, evidence, details and information—collectively known as proof—which show, beyond a shadow of a doubt, that someone committed a crime. Crawford was nowhere near that point.

But at this point he was absolutely sure that Janny Hasleiter, along with an accomplice, had killed Antonia von Habsburg, tortured DeeDee Dunwoody, and inked up Nickie's face. The problem remained his lack of hard evidence. Motive he had; proof, nothing solid.

Since Ott was not in his cubicle—still up at Good Samaritan Hospital visiting DeeDee Dunwoody—Crawford did something unusual and, one might argue, against his better judgment. He went into Norm Rutledge's office and laid the whole thing out for him.

Rutledge looked very thoughtful throughout, tapped his desk top at the end of Crawford's monologue, rested his chin on his fist like *The Thinker*, then farted.

"Sorry… that onion and egg sandwich I had at lunch," Rutledge said.

"Onion and egg? Why would you ever think that was a good combo?"

"Been eating 'em all my life. With a little mayo and seasoned salt."

"Disgusting," Crawford said.

Rutledge ignored his comment. "I think she did it, too."

"Problem is, conjecture doesn't cut it."

"I mean, DeeDee What's-her-name can't ID anybody 'cause she was blindfolded, and the kid with the tats was unconscious."

"You're good at recapping, Norm, but not so good at figuring out what to do next. And how to nail her."

"I'm not a homicide detective, Charlie."

No shit, Crawford started to say, but bit his tongue.

"What about alibis as far as the three timelines go?" Rutledge asked.

"I thought about that. Problem is, I'm sure she could get any number of people to alibi her. Her husband, that friend of hers I mentioned. I'm sure others."

"And you've got nothing on any possible accomplice."

"Not a damn thing," Crawford said, then as an afterthought. "Except that the guy who cut up DeeDee Dunwoody was a wheezer."

"A wheezer?"

"Made a lot of noise breathing."

Rutledge shook his head dismissively. "Fuck of a lot of help that is."

Crawford shrugged. "Didn't say it was."

FORTY-FOUR

John Croswell didn't waste any time swinging into action after he got the agitated call from Janny Hasleiter. Janny said she had another job for him, but a rush job that needed to be done right away. He told her, "Well, that'll cost you extra," and she had no problem with that. He Googled Charlie Crawford and within a half hour knew everything he needed to know about the man. Hero cop who solved just about every case that came his way. A seventy-percent homicide clearance rate back when he was up in New York. That was crazy good. He guessed the average must be half that. It seemed that since Crawford had been on the job in Palm Beach, he had solved every homicide he had gotten his hands on. Well, maybe with the exception of one. Even crazier.

Finding out where Crawford lived was a piece of cake, too. The Trianon, just south of the middle bridge to Palm Beach. So, Crawford's route to work was simple: from the Trianon, over the bridge to North County Road, then a block or two south to the Palm Beach Police station on the left. Nice commute. Probably took him less than five minutes. Unless, of course, he caught a bridge. He wondered what kind of car Crawford drove... or did he use a police car?

He had been set to call the desk at the Trianon, claim he was detailing Crawford's car tomorrow and just wanted to know what kind of car it was and where it would be parked. Sure, it would make more sense if he simply called Crawford himself, but the guy at the desk would never suspect anything. His job was just to be pleasant and helpful to everybody.

Croswell had learned that the apartment directly above Crawford's was on the market. He'd gotten the listing agent to show it to him earlier in the day. As the agent unlocked the front door, he took careful notice of the lock and key. The lock couldn't have been more basic—a standard-issue apartment building lock, easily pickable. Next, he checked out the balcony.

He leaned out over it and saw Charlie Crawford's balcony directly below. The detective seemed to believe in minimalist outdoor furniture: he had only two Adirondack chairs on his balcony.

Perfect. Pick a lock, lower himself down to the balcony below by rope, jimmy open the slider—quietly—and then, end the long, illustrious career of hero homicide detective Charlie Crawford. Maybe an hour's worth of work for two hundred grand. What did that work out to…? Jesus, more than three thousand dollars a minute. Hell yeah, he was down with that. He could live for three years on the take. It beat the hell out of what he was making as a mostly-out-of-work actor who had heard a lot of promises but garnered nothing but a few walk-on roles to show for it. Well, except for the real-life role of cutting up the girl. She'd paid him a 100K for that. After this new job, well, he could finally just say, *Fuck Hollywood!* and not have to fuck Janny Hasleiter anymore.

FORTY-FIVE

The biggest challenge for John Croswell was getting into the Trianon undetected that night. He had come back to case the building a few hours after he was shown the apartment on the tenth floor. As it turned out, getting to the elevator without being spotted by the man at the desk wasn't that difficult. He just had to come in the side entrance. To make sure that he wouldn't be remembered by someone who might have been on the elevator with him or who might pass him in the hallway, he wore a Covid mask, Ray-Bans and his Palm Beach Knights baseball cap.

To ensure nobody saw him, disguise or no, he parked and sneaked into the building at half past midnight. He saw no one as he came in and no one rode the elevator with him. His concern, of course, was that someone might arrive or come out of their apartment on the tenth-floor hallway while he was picking the lock. He figured he could pick the lock in five minutes, max, so that would be the extent of his exposure. But if he were noticed, there was potentially a lot of downside. He'd need to walk away quickly and disappear, and whoever spotted him would probably alert the late-night man at the front desk. Worst of all, Crawford could get wind of it and realize that there was a connection between a man picking the lock on 10C and him living one flight down in 9C.

But as it turned out, he surprised himself. The lockpicking only took three minutes and nobody saw a thing. Croswell walked through the vacated apartment, out onto the balcony, and glanced at the quarter moon off in the distance. There was a light breeze but nothing that would affect his one-story descent. He unzipped his light jacket and raised it up over his waist where he had wrapped the twenty-five-foot length of climbing rope, which he had purchased at Dick's Sporting Goods that afternoon. He unwrapped the rope and tied one end around three of the metal posts of the balcony railing. He gave it a quick tug but could see the posts were solid and would easily support his 160 pounds. Next, he measured a section of the rope that he guessed would extend twenty feet from the knot he'd tied. He then tied the rope around his waist, knotted it, then added a second loop around his waist and knotted it, too. About fourteen feet or so of the rope remained. He walked back inside 10C and, when the rope became taut, thrust his weight against it several times. The railing held firm, as did the knots.

Thank you, Scoutmaster Johnson, Boy Scout Troop 113, he thought.

He walked back outside and put one leg over the top of the railing, then the other, and, holding the railing tight, turned to face the building. Moments before he had pulled a pair of leather gloves out of his pants pocket and put them on. Making the rope as taut as possible, he slipped his way down to the balcony of 9C. He got inside its railing, sitting on the railing at first, then lowered himself a little further so his feet were on the balcony.

Then he shot a glance inside 9C to see if there were any lights on. There weren't and the blinds were all closed.

On the balcony, he undid the rope around his waist and just listened for a few moments. Nothing. Not a thing. Then he saw a seagull six feet away on the railing. It seemed to be eyeing him with a curious, *What the hell are you up to?* look. Like this was the bird's space and what right did Croswell have to be invading it?

He looked off into the distance to take in the detective's view. Funny enough, he could see the building where Crawford worked: a glint of moonlight reflecting from the barrel-tile roof of the two-story Palm Beach Police station, not more than two miles away.

He turned and looked at the apartment again. He hadn't even rehearsed a story about what he'd say if Crawford suddenly came out and said, "Uh, mind telling me what you're doing here?"

In that case, he'd just draw the knife sheathed around his waist and try to stick him as quick as possible. But if Crawford were pointing a pistol at him… well, that would be different. He wasn't all that concerned because, after all, what could they charge him with? Trespassing or attempted burglary was all he could think of. Not much more than a wrist slap. Didn't matter anyway because it wasn't going to happen.

He walked over to the slider and gave it a slight push to the right. It opened an inch. It wasn't locked. *Thank you, Detective, for making my job a little easier.* He drew his Maglite out of his pocket but didn't turn it on, then gave the slider another nudge so he could squeeze inside. Then he stopped again and listened and looked around the living room. All he could hear was his own breathing, which was louder than he would have liked, but there was nothing he could do about that. He slipped out the black-bladed combat knife and, careful to not bump into any furniture, walked toward the master bedroom, which he knew from the apartment above connected to the living room through a door to his right. The quarter moon made things easier since it illuminated just enough of the living room that he didn't need the Maglite.

He stood at the door to the master bedroom. He wanted to hold his breath, but couldn't. Damn breathing had always been louder than other people's. He turned the knob and pushed the door open. It was pitch black inside. He took two short steps, then stopped and listened again.

Again, nothing.

He took two more steps, figuring that the logical spot for the master bed would be against the far wall, as it had been in the apartment above. He listened for breathing. All he could hear was his own. It was now or never...

He clicked on the Maglite, ready to thrust the knife into the sleeping detective's body, but instead felt a sudden pain in his knees. He glanced over and realized that Crawford was standing next to the bed and had slashed his right leg into Croswell's knees. Croswell nearly fell over from the unexpected blow. It was like being tackled from the side, and he was wobbly. His mind registered that he must do something fast and forceful. He raised the knife and slashed at Crawford, but Crawford ducked it and grabbed a lamp. Wielding the lamp defensively, Crawford fended off another broad slash of Croswell's blade. Despite his throbbing knees, Croswell opted to charge the detective to deploy the killing stab, but Crawford swung the lamp two-handed, like a baseball bat, and again deflected the knife thrust. As Croswell turned to face him, Crawford, clad only in boxers, flung the lamp at him, hitting him squarely in the head. Then he bull-rushed Croswell, head-butting him in the center of the chest and laying him out in a heap on the bedroom floor.

*****

Crawford had been awakened by the sound of heavy breathing from inside his bedroom door. At first, he wondered whether it was left over from the vivid dream he was on the tail end of. But as he opened his eyes, a shaft of moonlight caught a figure approaching his bed. He slipped out of the bed as the loud breathing got closer. When the flashlight clicked on, Crawford instinctively reacted, slashing at the figure with his right leg as hard as he could. Instinct remained his guide as he fought off the intruder and finally brought him down on the bedroom carpet. The three-hundred-dollar lamp that Rose Clarke talked him into buying at Restoration Hardware… it was a goner, but… it was a life-saver.

He looked down at the man lying on the carpeted floor. He was unconscious. He was bleeding from his mouth and nose and pretty soon blood was going to be all over Crawford's carpet. He grabbed the man by the collar of his shirt with both hands and dragged him into his white-tiled bathroom. No way was he going to ruin the carpet. After a few minutes the man's eyes opened and he looked up and blinked. By now Crawford had him handcuffed.

"Who the hell are you, and what's this about?" Crawford said, though he had already hatched a theory.

The man was wheezing even louder than before. "You… you coulda killed me."

Crawford shook his head. "Yeah, coulda and probably shoulda."

Then he recognized the man. He had played a relatively small but memorable role in the wedding sequence in Janny Hasleiter's rom-com, *The In-Between Years*.

FORTY-SIX

Ott had arrived at the station cranky. Which was understandable since he had been rudely awakened by Crawford at 1:15 a.m.

Crawford had just given Ott a full rundown on what had happened at his condo.

"First time I ever head-butted a guy," Crawford said. "It did the job."

Ott patted him on the shoulder. "Atta boy," he said. "Nothin' wrong with a little violence every once in a while."

Brice Maldonado—for that was John Croswell's real name—sat across from Crawford and Ott in a metal folding chair, meant to be uncomfortable. Crawford and Ott had wooden chairs, a little less uncomfortable. In between them stood a metal table with numerous coffee cup and Coke can stains on it. Crawford had his MacBook Air open in front of him.

Crawford and Ott had done twenty minutes of pre-interrogation strategizing in Crawford's office while they let Maldonado cool his heels and maybe beat himself up for screwing up and getting caught.

"Okay," Crawford said, "we're charging you with attempted murder, breaking and entering, and more charges to follow. Probably first-degree murder."

"No, definitely first-degree murder," Ott said. "What's your name, pretty boy?"

"John Croswell."

Ott had Maldonado's wallet in front of him and was studying his license. "Okay, so why's it say your name is Brice Maldonado on your license," he said, holding it up.

Maldonado squirmed in his chair and coughed. "That's my real name. John Croswell's my stage name."

"That's the best you could come up with?" Ott said.

"Huh?"

"Nothing."

Crawford turned to Ott. "'Member I told you about seeing those Janny Hasleiter movies? Well, just so happens, Brice here was in one of 'em."

"Three actually," their suspect corrected.

"I'm impressed," Ott said. "Got any Oscars on your mantel?"

Maldonado smirked. "Fat chance. All she ever gave me were walk-ons."

"What I don't get is what's wrong with Maldonado as a name?" Ott said. "I mean, I get wanting to get rid of Brice but—"

"Okay, let's cut to it," Crawford said. "You tried to kill me tonight, Brice." He picked up his MacBook Air and turned it around so Maldonado could see the screen. "Can you read that?"

Maldonado nodded.

"Well, then, read it."

"'The punishment for attempted first-degree murder is either life in prison without the possibility of parole, or the worst scenario of all, the death penalty.'"

The wording came from the website of a criminal-defense lawyer in West Palm Beach.

"So, all clear so far?" Crawford asked.

Maldonado nodded.

"Okay, so as you can see, there's not a lot of difference in terms of punishment between trying to kill someone and actually killing them. Attempted versus murder. Know what I mean?"

Nothing from Maldonado.

Crawford leaned closer to Maldonado and repeated. "Know what I mean?"

"I guess so."

"Okay now, stay with me here, Brice... if you can," Crawford said. "We also know that you did a couple other jobs for Janny Hasleiter—"

"—killing Antonia von Habsburg, for one thing. Cutting up a friend of mine by the name of DeeDee Dunwoody for another, and inking the face of a helpless kid when he was unconscious."

Maldonado shook his head and gave them his best, Emmy-winning effort to project indignation and outrage. "I don't know *what* you're talking about."

Crawford thought his performance fell short, which explained why he only got walk-ons.

"Let's go down another road," Crawford said. "Janny Hasleiter, I can pretty much guarantee you, is gonna leave you high and dry when we charge her. Probably even claim she's never even heard of you before."

"Which would be a little hard to buy since you've been in three of her movies," said Ott.

"Yeah, but I've seen her in action," Crawford said, "and no offense, she's a better actor than Brice here. She could say something like, 'You think I know the name of every walk-on hack who's ever been in my movies?' That's what they call a hypothetical question, Brice."

"You're right," Ott said, then turned to Maldonado. "Just deny knowing you at all."

"So unless you say that Janny put you up to everything, she'll walk. Free as a bird. We've got nothing on her. So, while she goes on with her life like nothing ever happened, you either spend the rest of your life in prison or have a date with Old Sparky."

"Who?"

"Old Sparky—the electric chair."

Ott raised a finger. "Actually, Charlie, they retired Old Sparky. Remember? It's lethal injections these days."

"Oh, yeah, of course," Crawford said. "Well, that's no day at the beach either. Or there's another possibility… you could cooperate with us. Say that Janny put you up to Antonia von Habsburg's murder and the three assaults and we could put a good word in for you with the prosecutor. But I'm not going to lie to you: you're still going to have to do a lot of hard time. But I think we can make it so the death sentence goes away." Crawford turned to Ott. "Don't you think?"

"Yeah, I think you're right. You know what else we could do, Charlie?"

"What's that?"

"In exchange for Brice here pleading guilty to the murder and two of the assaults, you could maybe drop the charge for what happened tonight."

Crawford glanced up at the ceiling and was silent for a few moments. "I don't know, Mort. You saying I should forget that Brice here tried to stick a knife in me… in my own bed?"

"It's up to you, I'm just—"

"You know," Crawford said with a nod, "maybe I could forget that."

"But, at the very least, you should apologize to my partner," Ott said.

Maldonado turned to Crawford. "I'm sorry, I—"

"Apology accepted," said Crawford, "and just to sweeten the pot, we might even let you skate on what you did to DeeDee Dunwoody and that kid Nickie."

"Hey, by the way, Brice," Ott said leaning closer to Maldonado, "why did Janny, or Danielle as she called herself, want you to cut up DeeDee Dunwoody anyway?"

"I'm not sure," Maldonado said. "Something about her thinking DeeDee had heard about von Habsburg blackmailing her, and"— he shrugged—"I really don't know."

"Got it," Ott said, nodding. "Above your pay grade. You just take orders."

"Okay, Brice," Crawford said. "I want to be real clear about something. You gotta confess that Janny put you up to everything, and plead guilty to the murder of Antonia von Habsburg."

"You can't let me plead that down?" Maldonado asked.

"Oh, listen to *you*," Ott said with a smile. "You know all the lingo."

"Watched a lot of TV."

"So how'd you and Hasleiter cross paths in the first place?" Ott asked. "Out in Hollywood?"

"No, I worked as a valet at the Tennis & Beach Club. Parking members' cars for 'em."

Ott smiled. "So you got discovered by her there? Just like you hear about?"

"Yeah, I guess. She asked me for my name and number one night."

"Then called you?"

Maldonado nodded.

"And the rest is history, huh?" Ott said, then to Crawford. "Boy toy of the moment."

Crawford nodded.

"She promised me roles. Flew me out to Hollywood. Long story short, three roles in four movies. I couldn't live on that so I came back here."

"And rekindled the gig with Janny?"

Maldonado nodded again.

"In a totally different role, though," Crawford said.

"I'll say," said Ott. "The hitman."

"You ready to sign a confession, Brice?"

Maldonado sighed deeply. "I gotta think about it."

"Okay, we'll give you ten minutes."

"Maybe I should talk to a lawyer."

"You're more than welcome to do that," Crawford said. "But if you do, I'm not so sure I'd retract tonight's attempted murder."

Brice let out an even deeper sigh and drummed the metal desk a few times.

"I still want to think about it."

"Fine, you got nine and a half minutes."

FORTY-SEVEN

Crawford woke up the county prosecutor at two thirty and, after listening to him grouse for five minutes, read him every word in Brice Maldonado's detailed confession. The last thing Crawford and Ott wanted was for Janny Hasleiter's no doubt highly-paid defense attorney to poke holes in it and have grounds to throw the case out because of some bullshit technicality.

Speaking of Janny Hasleiter, they rousted her out of bed at 4:15 that morning at her Jamaica Road house after getting Maldonado to sign the one-and-a-half-page confession. They weren't surprised to find that Janny had a different bedroom from her husband, John David, but were taken aback to find a man—John David's Cuban chauffeur, in it. After the musclebound driver with a John Waters mustache scampered out of there, they read Janny her Miranda rights, although she refused to get out of bed.

"As I'm sure is obvious," Crawford said, "Brice Maldonado failed in his mission to stop me from breathing, but he was kind enough to sign a confession saying you and he both were present, and executed, the murder of Antonia von Habsburg and the torture of DeeDee Dunwoody. He said the tattooing of your friend and boy toy, Nickie, was your idea but he carried it out solo, as was the attempted murder of yours truly."

"This is all complete bullshit, you know," Janny said, mustering up a mountain of scorn.

"Nah, we got you cold," Ott said.

She shot him a deeply nasty look. "Who the hell are you, anyway? Never seen you before."

"I'm the guy taking you down to our station and putting you in a cell," Ott said in monotone. "That's who."

"Come on, Janny, time to get up and get dressed," Crawford said.

"I'm naked," she said.

"We'll look away, as long as you don't pull a gun out from under your pillow," he told her.

She didn't move.

"Come on—now!" Ott barked.

She pulled the comforter around her, slowly got out of bed, and shuffled into her walk-in closet.

"Better wear something warm," Ott said. "It gets kinda chilly in our cells."

FORTY-EIGHT

The four of them were sitting outside at a restaurant in the Northwood section of West Palm Beach. It had been a month since Janny Hasleiter was charged with murder, and she remained in prison awaiting trial. They were at a Thai restaurant called Malakor and it was a balmy night, but DeeDee Dunwoody wore pants and a long-sleeved shirt, contrasting conspicuously with Dominica, in her tight and short cream-colored skirt and sleeveless dark green blouse. Crawford and Ott, not that anyone was noticing, wore long pants and sports shirts.

"So, what about the son, Frank Lincoln, and the two wills?" Dominica asked.

"Unresolved," Crawford said. "My gut tells me that he planted the one that gave everything to his church, but we'll probably never know."

"Court'll have to sort that out," said Ott.

Crawford nodded. "Yeah, ain't our problem."

"What happened at Janny Hasleiter's arraignment?" asked Dominica. "She still denying everything?"

"Yeah, which was what we expected," Crawford said.

"Thank God for the judge, though," Ott said. "Denying any bail at all."

"Her defense lawyer said she could offer up three million," Crawford said. "But the judge decided she was a flight risk."

Dominica nodded. "I think he was probably right, don't you?"

"She," Crawford said.

"The kicker was me and Charlie found out she bought a place on the Mediterranean in Morocco right after she and Maldonado killed Antonia."

Dominica cocked her head. "How'd you find that out?"

"She kept all the paperwork in her penthouse at the Bristol. I don't think she wanted hubby to know about it."

"Morocco? Why there?" DeeDee asked.

"The main reason had to be that there's no reciprocity between Morocco and the U.S."

"So she couldn't be... what's the word?" DeeDee asked.

"Extradited," Dominica said.

"Exactly," Ott said. "Seems like she once filmed a movie there and knew her way around the country a little."

"Isn't that where Marrakech is?" Dominica asked.

"Yeah, that's inland a little," Crawford said. "Casablanca's there, too."

Ott raised his beer to DeeDee. "Here's looking at you, kid."

DeeDee raised her wine glass and they clinked. "Backatcha... you old romantic, you."

Ott put on his best Bogart voice. "Of all the gin joints in all the towns in all the world, she walks into mine..."

DeeDee blew Ott a kiss. "That's a really good, Mort. Sounds just like him... wait, I got one for you."

"Let's hear it," Ott said with a smile.

DeeDee leaned closer to him. "We'll always have Paris."

"Wow," Dominica said. "Nice Bogart. You guys are good."

"Yeah, oughta be in movies," Crawford said. "One of Janny Hasleiter's."

"Nah, too late," Ott said. "Ol' Janny's done her last one."

THE END

DYING FOR A COCKTAIL

Exclusive sample from Savannah Sleuth Sisters Murder Mysteries Book 3

CHAPTER ONE

Ryder Farrell, who could be very convincing when she wanted to be, was trying as hard as she could to talk her sister, Jackie, into opening a satellite office of Savannah Investigations in Charleston, South Carolina. She started working on Jackie after they'd both had had a couple of Texas Margarita's at Jalapenas in Sandfly outside of Savannah.

Ryder knew from experience that after a few stiff Marg's under her belt, Jackie was more apt to say yes to things that she might balk at if she was stone-cold sober. Case in point, Jackie had agreed to give her sister a raise after Happy Hour at Jalapenas. Then, a few months later, after the two knocked back a jeroboam of Whispering Angel celebrating Jackie's thirty-first, Ryder had talked her sister into buying new furniture for what they laughingly called their Savannah "world headquarters". It was long overdue because when Jackie had started out on a shoestring it was furnished with scratch 'n dent specials from Haverty's and a few homely gems from the Salvation Army.

"It' like... you know how doctors have a few different offices— like in Pooler, Richmond Hill, Garden City. Thunderbolt—"

"Thunderbolt? Where the hell's that?"

Ryder shrugged. "I don't really know. Around here somewhere. Anyway, you get the concept, right? A satellite office."

Jackie nodded. "Yeah. Where are you going with this?"

Ryder took a prodigious pull on her Texas Margarita.

"I told you, I think we should open a branch of Savannah Investigations in Charleston."

"Charleston? It's two hours away. Why?"

"For one thing, we'd have double the number of homicides."

Jackie smiled knowingly. "And for another, Beau is there."

"Well, yeah, but…"

"But what?"

Ryder shrugged. "Who knows whether that's gonna last or not."

"Why wouldn't it?"

"'Cause the guy's the biggest flirt I've ever met," Ryder said, putting up a hand. "Don't try to change the subject. See, the main reason would be so we could work on murder exclusively instead of taking on cheating husband cases, or missing persons, stuff that neither of us wants to do."

Jackie squinted and didn't say anything.

Ryder kept going, figuring the hook was at least half in. "Plus, I don't know about you, but I think they're more things to do up in Charleston. Better restaurants, museums, you know, *cult-chah*. We both could use a little culture."

"Has Beau been introducing you to this *cult-chah*?"

"The only culture Beau knows about is in the bedroom."

Jackie held up her hands. "Okay, okay, TMI."

"Sorry," Ryder said. "So, what do you think?"

"I think I'll think about it."

*****

And she had, and miraculously, she agreed to opening a Charleston office. Savannah would still be the main office, but one or both would go up to Charleston occasionally. Specifically, when they landed a homicide. They both agreed that they would turn down jobs that were not murder cases, which would eliminate a fair amount of the previous year's income. They figured if it didn't work out and there wasn't enough murder to pay the rent and allow them to eat, they could always go back to chasing cheating husbands to no-tell motels. Then, when they got no calls for a solid two weeks, they decided that in addition to homicides, they would at least consider the occasional missing person case.

The office they settled on in Charleston was dingy and had low ceilings, and with it, they inherited furniture from Habitat for Humanity and a Calhoun Street tag sale. So, they ordered a 30-yard dumpster, chucked everything, and spent half a day up in North Charleston outfitting their new space with furniture from two stores called Celadon and At Home. Fashion-forward it was not; functional it was.

Speaking of which, though the office had a King Street address, it was not the chic part of King Street, but a mile or two north of where the Charleston debs and fashionista's shop and strut their stuff.

Their three-room office was on the second floor of a loft building, and Jackie's office was almost double the size of her sister's, which got Ryder bellyaching from the git-go, but Jackie was, theoretically, the boss and, in fact, the one who paid the bills. The third room served as a waiting area, which had a telephone booth-sized reception space manned by a natty, two-hundred-fifty-pound black man by the name of Wendell (pronounced wen- DEL,) whose shoulders practically touched the walls on either side of him.

It was just past ten in the morning, a week after C.I. hung out its shingle, when the front door opened, and Wendell glanced up at a well-dressed woman. Things were slow, which was to say murder-free in Savannah at the moment, so both Jackie and Ryder were in the Charleston office, looking for something to do.

The woman, in her mid-forties, was wearing a stylish, cream-colored pencil skirt, a blue silk blouse, and Tory Burch flats.

"Mrs. Roberts?" Wendell asked.

The woman nodded. "Yes, here to see Jackie Farrell," she said.

"I'll let her know you're here," Wendell said.

The woman frowned. "*Her?*"

"Yes," Wendell said, "you'll be meeting with Jackie and her associate, Ryder."

The frown was still there. "I just assumed Jackie was a man."

"Nope."

Mrs. Roberts nodded, apparently satisfied that at least Ryder was a man.

Wendell got up and went and knocked on the door to Jackie's office.

"Yes, Wendell."

The big man opened the door. "Mrs. Roberts is here," he said, then lowering his voice. "You being of the female persuasion got what I'd call a negative reaction."

Jackie pinched off a smile and stood up.

"Tell Ryder, will you."

Wendell nodded.

"Thanks," Jackie said, going through her door into the waiting room. "Hello, Mrs. Roberts, I'm Jackie Farrell."

Jessica Roberts looked up from the waiting room's *Garden & Gun* magazine and rebooted her frown. Clearly, she didn't expect anybody so pretty and well-dressed to be a private investigator.

"Would you follow me back to my office, please?" Jackie asked.

"Sure," said Jessica.

"We're going to be joined by my associate," Jackie said, holding the door for Jessica.

"So I understand," Jessica said, taking in Jackie's office, which had three framed posters from old Gary Cooper movies on the walls that gave it some pizazz.

Ryder walked in wearing blue jeans with a tear in the right mid-thigh, electric lime Nikes, and a white T-shirt so snug it looked like it made breathing a challenge.

Jessica Roberts didn't look impressed with her wardrobe or her gender.

"Mrs. Roberts, this is my associate, Ryder," Jackie said.

"So, you're not only a female," Jessica said to Ryder, "but a teenager at that."

Ryder extended her hand and stifled a sigh. "That's flattering, Mrs. Roberts, but I'm twenty-six," she said, going for a world-weary tone she felt appropriate for a PI.

Jessica Roberts just nodded and eyeballed the rip in Ryder's blue jeans.

"When I called here and spoke to—I guess, that gentleman out front—I wasn't expecting, the Number 1 Ladies Detective Agency," Jessica said.

"The what?" Ryder asked.

Jackie smiled. "Mrs. Roberts is referring to a book about a woman who started a detective agency in Uganda," she said. "They made a movie of it, too."

"Oh, right," Ryder said, vaguely remembering it.

"It was Botswana, actually," Jessica said.

"My error," Jackie said. "So, Mrs. Roberts, clearly, we're both women...does that disqualify us from being of service to you."

Jessica shook her head, emphatically, like she didn't want to be accused of being a traitor to her sex. "Oh, no, not at all. I just didn't know, is all."

"I mean, there are other investigation companies which employ men," Jackie had the rap down. "In fact, most of them do... if that's what you want."

It came off as, 'if you want to stoop so low.'

"No, no," Jessica said, "let's just get past this and talk about why I came?"

"Oh course," Jackie said, "we're all ears."

"Okay," Jessica said, "are you familiar with the name Roland Roberts, my late husband?"

Ryder shook her head.

Jackie nodded. "Yes, I am, I didn't make the connection."

She had read about his murder when she was in Savannah. It was front-page news for close to a week.

"No reason why you would," Jessica said, turning to Ryder. "My husband was murdered six months ago. The police haven't found the killer. It's now a 'cold case,' though they don't officially call it that. They tell me it's still active, but, in reality, I'm convinced they're not really working on it."

"He was shot in his office, as I recall," Jackie said. "On Broad Street. Three shots from a semi-automatic, wasn't it?"

"Four, actually," Jessica said. "He was working late. It happened around eight at night."

Jackie remembered reading that a tipped-over bottle of bourbon with three glasses was found on Roberts' desk when the homicide detectives got there.

"I remember it pretty well," Jackie said. "Your husband was a very prominent real estate developer. As I recall, he had just been found innocent in a hit-and-run?"

Jessica frowned. "It wasn't a hit-and-run. Roland turned himself in right after it happened—" Jackie seemed to remember it was more like three or four hours later—"and the main suspect in Roland's murder was the father of the girl who was killed."

"Because he threatened to kill your husband. In court, right? After the innocent verdict was announced?" Jackie asked.

Jessica nodded. "And a week later Roland was dead. Come to your own conclusion."

"So, are you saying you think the father did it?"

"Actually, I don't really know," Mrs. Roberts said. "At first, I figured who else could it be? But the lead detective told me he was almost positive it wasn't him."

"The father's last name was something like Jennings, wasn't it?" Jackie asked.

"You have a good memory," Jessica said. "Jenner. Charles Jenner."

"So, what exactly would you like us to do that the police haven't?" Jackie asked, glancing over at Ryder whose foot was tapping restlessly.

"I'd like you to solve it," Jessica said. "Just like that case I read about on your website. That soap opera star who was killed up in New York."

They had gotten a lot of mileage out of the Philomena Soames murder.

"Well, of course, if we take it, our objective would be to solve it. We just need to be convinced that we can bring something to the table that the Charleston homicide detectives couldn't," Jackie said, suddenly conscious of the 'are you eff-ing kidding me?' look her sister was drilling into her. She knew Ryder was thinking, *come on, girl, lose the 'if we take it' BS. We need the damned work!'*

"The detectives just came up with the one suspect," Jessica said. "Then when they couldn't get anything on him, they just kind of ran out of steam."

"In fairness to the police department here, they're usually pretty dogged," Jackie said. It was a pure guess. "Tell us about your husband, will you?"

"Well, as you said, Roland was a prominent real estate developer," Jessica said, "Also, very active with a lot of charities, not to mention an alderman at our church."

Jackie nodded. Ryder yawned.

"But what was he *like*?" Ryder suddenly piped in.

The question jolted Jackie because she had told Ryder before the meeting to just listen and observe, since this was their first meeting with a prospective client in Charleston and her sister could sometimes—no, frequently— be a bit of a loose cannon. She knew, though, that Ryder couldn't stay quiet for long.

"Well, for starters, Roland was an extremely intelligent man," Jessica said. "Like number three in his class at Carolina. He worked hard and became very successful. Roland was also starting half back on the Gamecocks football team for three years and used to love to hunt and fish, too. I don't know what else you want to know?"

"What a Gamecock is?" Ryder blurted.

Jackie wanted to jam a tube sock in her sister's mouth.

Jessica looked at Ryder in disbelief but didn't say anything.

"Ryder moved down here just a little while back," Jackie explained. "Used to be with our New York affiliate—" then to Ryder— "a Gamecock is the mascot for the University of South Carolina football team."

Ryder was undeterred. "Mrs. Roberts, let me ask you a question, is it possible that your husband might have been involved in an extra marital affair?"

Jesus... where in God's name did that come from? Jackie had forgotten just *how much* of a loose cannon her sister could be.

But Jessica took the question in stride. Like she might have been asked it before.

"Possibly," she said. "We were married for twenty-one years. He was away a fair amount and clearly... women found him attractive."

"Did it occur to you that if your husband *was* having an affair, that the boyfriend or husband of the woman he was having the affair with... would be a logical suspect?" Ryder shrugged. "I mean, it happens quite often."

Like she had any firsthand knowledge whatsoever about what she was talking about, thought Jackie. She knew where it came from, though. When Ryder had first started out, less than a year ago, Jackie had recommended that Ryder read a few detective novels— instead of her usual chick-lit trash— as part of her on-the-job-training. Sure, it was just fiction, but at least it was a good intro to the vernacular. Turned out Ryder blew through everything by Michael Connelly, most of James Lee Burke and half of Elmore Leonard in a few weeks. It was safe to say, she had lots of plots dancing in her head. And a whole new vocabulary. Some of it a little dated, though.

"I guess that makes sense," Jessica said, nodding. "That it could be a boyfriend or a husband... if Roland actually was seeing someone."

"And if he *was* seeing someone, do you have any idea who it might be?" Ryder asked.

"No."

Jackie had her mouth open ready to speak but Ryder cut her off.

"Did you ever find any evidence at all that indicated your husband might, in fact, be having an affair?" Ryder asked. "You know, an email maybe? A whiff of perfume? A receipt from a hotel? Anything at all like that?"

"No," Jessica said.

Jackie wanted the floor back and opened her mouth again—

"That strikes me as a tentative 'no', Mrs. Roberts," Ryder said.

"A no is a no."

"You're sure?"

Jackie put up a hand to her sister and clawed her way back into the conversation. "Hang on a second. You understand, Mrs. Roberts, that my associate is simply pursuing one of the most common scenarios. A spouse being killed by the other spouse's—"

"I get that," Jessica said, turning to Jackie. "Now, let me ask you a question."

"Sure," Jackie said, "go right ahead."

"You keep referring to Ryder as your 'associate,'" Mrs Roberts said. "Isn't she actually... your sister?"

"How do you know that?" Jackie asked, feeling a sudden urge to deny it.

"Well, for starters, you both have the same eyes," Jessica said. "And also, you both seem a little..."

"What?"

"I don't know.... intense maybe."

CHAPTER TWO

Intense was not quite accurate but not way off the mark either. In Jackie's case, more like determined and persistent, but balanced by a distinct soft and feminine side. Ryder, unquestionably, was a woman with strong opinions, and never timid about voicing them. So, intense was pretty close. When it came to looks— except for the eyes— the two couldn't be more different. Ryder was a stunning five foot eight, though she looked taller, and had long mahogany brown hair, high cheekbones, and a laugh you could hear across the street. Not to mention a mouth on her that sometimes made her sister cringe. Jackie was a pretty five-two, with dirty blonde hair and an unblinking, watchful gaze.

Using her sister's middle name was actually Jackie's idea. They were born Jacqueline Nichols Farrell and Alexandra Ryder Farrell, but Jackie didn't think Savannah—and now Charleston— was ready for a private investigation firm whose PI's had names that sounded like they were interior decorators. Or ladies who lunched.

Jackie also pointed out to Ryder that "half the women in the south" had last names for first names anyway. Ryder said, oh, yeah, like who? Jackie had to think for a second, but—English major she was— came up with Harper Lee and Flannery O'Connor.

In any case, Jessica Roberts retained Charleston Investigations to find her husband's killer. What clinched it was when she asked Jackie a question about the Philomena Soames murder case that she had read about on the Charleston Investigations website. That was the reason why she had called CI in the first place and was apparently impressed by how Jackie had handled and, ultimately, solved the case.

"So, anyway, Mrs. Roberts," Jackie said, "I bill out at a hundred dollars an hour, my associate—" she flipped her hand at Ryder— "seventy-five. Plus fifty cents a mile in car fare. Just so you know, the competition charges seventy to eighty an hour and forty-five cents a mile. We will need a three-thousand-dollar retainer, none of which is refundable. I'm from the school of, 'you get what you pay for,' but, of course, you'll come to your own conclusion."

Jessica Roberts nodded. "I'm from the same school," she said. "And your terms are acceptable. But I'm still curious... why you came here from Charleston?"

Jackie chuckled. "Ask my sister."

"Well, I met a man... who turned out to be a douche," Ryder said.

Jackie wanted to bitch slap her. "I apologize for my associate's unprofessionalism, Mrs. Roberts. Now if you would write us a check we can get started right away."

Jessica wrote a check, shook their hands, and left.

Standing in the Charleston Investigations reception area, Ryder said. "I like this new office. I think it's gonna be fun here."

"Ryder," Jackie said, "let me point out a few things. First, it's just a job, not something that's supposed to be fun."

"Well, aren't some jobs fun?" Ryder asked. "Not that I'd know, since that ad agency job of mine was the most *un-fun* thing I've ever done in my short, boring life."

"There you go," Jackie said. "Second thing, let me ask most of the questions and make comments with the clients. You've still got a lot to learn about this business in general and, for that matter, the South Carolina football team."

Ryder exhaled dramatically.

"Gimme a break," she said. "The Gamecocks. Are you *fucking* kidding me? That's really their name?"

"Watch it, girl, they're the local religion down here," Jackie said. "And just for the record, most people call 'em the 'Cocks."

Ryder laughed. "Of course they do."

"And third of all, try reading something other than Elmore Leonard and Michael Connelly once in a while," Jackie said.

"What are you talking about?"

"Well, like that book she mentioned, *The Number 1 Ladies Detective Agency*," Jackie said. "It was a huge best seller."

"Hey, bro, if it ain't Elmore, Mike or chick lit… it ain't," Ryder said.

"You're scary, you know that," Farrell said. "And don't call me 'bro.' I'm your damn sister."

"You don't want me to call you 'sis' do you?"

"No, why not just call me my name?"

"Yes... Jackie. But, I still like 'bro,'" Ryder said. "It's got kind of a refreshing contrariness to it."

Jackie shook her head. "Whatever... and do you have to use words like 'douche' with prospective clients we've just met for the first time?"

"How 'bout 'dick?' Is that better?"

"Oh, for God sake, you're out of control."

"Mrs. Roberts said 'intense.'"

"Yeah, I didn't know whether she meant that as good or bad."

"I thought good."

"Why?"

"'Cause the opposite of intense is weak... namby-pamby maybe."

Jackie got up, figuring the conversation had run its course.

"Where you going?" Ryder asked.

"We still have to finish up that cheating spouse case," Jackie said. "'Member? The one we were working on before we decided to go all-homicide, all the time."

"I like that, *all-homicide, all the time*. Good motto," Ryder said, "Where we goin'?"

"A cozy little, no-tell motel out in West Ashley."

CHAPTER THREE

The no-tell-motel actually turned out to be a perfectly nice Comfort Inn.

"How do you know this is where our two love birds went?" Ryder asked as they pulled into the motel's parking lot in Farrell's Ford Escape.

"Because I stuck a GPS on the guy's bumper," Jackie said. "And in South Carolina a GPS is a legal means of tracking an adulterer or adulteress."

"I see," Ryder said, "but doesn't adulterer cover both sexes."

"Don't be a know-it-all. You were a college drop-out, remember?"

"Yeah, 'cause you remind me daily. So, you put a magnetized GPS on the bumper?"

Jackie nodded.

Ryder patted her on the shoulder. "Very good. Harry Bosch always does that."

Jackie looked blank.

"Come on, where you been?" said Ryder. "Michael Connelly's hero. You never saw the TV show? So, what exactly's the game plan here?"

"Okay, here's the deal. Our client, Francie Heyburn—the woman who suspects her husband of cheating—is worth a small fortune. Her husband, a charmer by the name of Tim Heyburn, is a serial cheater and Francie is *so* done with him. In South Carolina there are five grounds for divorce and the only one this guy is guilty of is infidelity, but he's very slippery, and she hasn't been able to get the goods on him yet."

"So, he's just hangin' in there 'cause of the money?"

"Yup, and she wants to cut him loose for once and for all. She's had it with the lowlife."

"Okay, so what are we gonna do?"

"Simple," Jackie said, turning off the car's engine. "We go see the desk clerk and flash some cash—" Jackie pulled her wallet out of her purse, reached in and lifted out five crisp hundred-dollar bills— "then I tell him or her I want to go say hello to the couple who just checked in—Mr. and Mrs. Smith, ninety per cent of the time—then he slides me a plastic card that opens the door."

"You don't think that just three of those Ben Franklin's would be enough?"

"Don't worry, it's in the budget."

"But can't the clerk get fired," Ryder asked, "if he or she gets caught giving you the plastic card?"

"Theoretically," Jackie said. "But what cheating guest's ever gonna go to the hotel manager and complain. They're in too big a hurry gettin' the hell out of Dodge."

Ryder hesitated, then nodded. "I still think that's too much to give the guy. I mean that's like a week's salary. I forget, how much do we get for a gig like this."

"We get a flat rate for a money shot," Farrell said. "Three thousand."

"Money shot?"

"Yeah, that's what it's known as in the trade."

"Well, come on then," Ryder said, "let's go get our money shot."

*****

The only problem was that when Farrell put the plastic card in the lock and opened it, the couple was having drinks. The man was sitting on the side of a built-in desk looking down at the woman who was sitting in the desk chair. Worse, they both had their clothes on.

Jackie snapped off four quick shots with her phone camera anyway.

By that time, the man was getting aggressive and hurling epithets chocked full of four-letter words.

Jackie and Ryder beat it out of there exactly twenty seconds after Jackie first opened the door.

"So, is that enough evidence for our client to get her divorce?" Ryder asked, out of breath, as they got back into the Escape.

"I don't really know, depends on the judge. It definitely would have been better if there was some boffing going on," Jackie said, turning the ignition key.

Ryder laughed. "'Boffing? Jesus Jack, what century are you from?"

Jackie ignored her. "I'd say it was pretty incriminating, though. I mean a guy in a motel with a woman. What's he gonna say, they went there to play chess?"

Ryder thought a moment. "Hmm, naked chess maybe… that actually might be a lot of fun."

TO KEEP READING VISIT:
https://amzn.to/3JAo9ag

Audio Books

Many of Tom's books are also available in Audio…

Listen to masterful narrator Phil Thron and feel like you're right there in Palm Beach with Charlie, Mort and Dominica!

Audio books available include:
Palm Beach Nasty
Palm Beach Poison
Palm Beach Deadly
Palm Beach Bones
Palm Beach Pretenders
Palm Beach Predator
Charlie Crawford Box Set (Books 1-3)
Killing Time in Charleston
Charleston Buzz Kill
Charleston Noir
The Savannah Madam
Savannah Road Kill

About the Author

A native New Englander, Tom Turner dropped out of college and ran a Vermont bar. Limping back a few years later to get his sheepskin, he went on to become an advertising copywriter, first in Boston, then New York. After 10 years of post-Mad Men life, he made both a career and geography change and ended up in Palm Beach, renovating houses and collecting raw materials for his novels. After stints in Charleston, then Skidaway Island, outside of Savannah, Tom recently moved to Delray Beach, where he's busy writing about passion and murder among his neighbors. To date Tom has written eighteen crime thrillers and mysteries and is probably best known for his Charlie Crawford series set in Palm Beach.

Learn more about Tom's books at:
www.tomturnerbooks.com

Made in United States
North Haven, CT
14 January 2023

31085909R00137